MW00533014

DEMONS & DNA

DEMONS AND DNA (Amplifier 1)
Copyright © 2019 Meghan Ciana Doidge
Published by Old Man in the CrossWalk Productions 2019
Salt Spring Island, BC, Canada
www.oldmaninthecrosswalk.com

All rights reserved under International and Pan-American
Copyright Conventions. No part of this book may be
produced in any form or by any electronic or mechanical
means, including information storage and retrieval systems,
without permission in writing from the author, except by
reviewer, who may quote brief passages in a review.

This is a work of fiction. All names, characters,
places, objects, and incidents herein are the products
of the author's imagination or are used fictitiously.
Any resemblance to actual things, events, locales, or
persons living or dead is entirely coincidental.

Library and Archives Canada
Doidge, Meghan Ciana, 1973—
Demons and DNA/Meghan Ciana Doidge—
PAPERBACK

Cover design by Gene Mollica
Models: Devon Ericksen & Jonathan Cannaux
Oracle Cards designed by Elizabeth Mackey

ISBN 978-1-927850-99-2

DEMONS & DNA

MEGHAN CIANA DOIDGE

Published by Old Man in the CrossWalk Productions
Salt Spring Island, BC, Canada

www.madebymeghan.ca

The Adept Universe is comprised of the Dowser, the Oracle, the Reconstructionist, and the Amplifier series. While it is not necessary to read all three series, **in order to avoid spoilers** the ideal reading order of the Adept Universe is as follows:

Cupcakes, Trinkets, and Other Deadly Magic (Dowser 1)
Trinkets, Treasures, and Other Bloody Magic (Dowser 2)
Treasures, Demons, and Other Black Magic (Dowser 3)
I See Me (Oracle 1)
Shadows, Maps, and Other Ancient Magic (Dowser 4)
Maps, Artifacts, and Other Arcane Magic (Dowser 5)
I See You (Oracle 2)
Artifacts, Dragons, and Other Lethal Magic (Dowser 6)
I See Us (Oracle 3)
Catching Echoes (Reconstructionist 1)
Tangled Echoes (Reconstructionist 2)
Unleashing Echoes (Reconstructionist 3)
Champagne, Misfits, and Other Shady Magic (Dowser 7)
Misfits, Gemstones, and Other Shattered Magic (Dowser 8)
Graveyards, Visions, and Other Things that Byte (Dowser 8.5)
Gemstones, Elves, and Other Insidious Magic (Dowser 9)
The Amplifier Protocol (Amplifier 0)
Demons and DNA (Amplifier 1)

Other books in the Amplifier series to follow.

More information can be found at
www.madebymeghan.ca/novels

For Michael
At first sight. And ever after.

Author's Note

Demons and DNA is the first book in the Amplifier series, which is set in the same universe as the Dowser, Oracle, and Reconstructionist series.

Rose

PARTNERSHIP

WE HAD RUN.

We had adapted.

And when our magic came back, we changed course again. Hiding instead of running, knowing that we needed to remain hidden from the Collective. Knowing that our lives, our freedom, depended on it.

Then the sorcerer showed up, drained and disoriented. And when my past came quickly following him, I had to make another choice.

Fight or flight.

Continue to deny the power that resided in my blood, in my DNA. Remain perpetually caught between being Amp5 and Emma Johnson.

Or face my demons.

ONE

SEPTEMBER 2018.

A sorcerer pushed open the door of the diner, both of his hands on the metal handle that bisected its glass. Holding himself upright. He raised his shockingly blue eyes, seeking out and pinning me into place in the red-vinyl booth situated at the far corner.

My heart fluttered oddly, even as my rational mind immediately snapped to assessing the situation.

Three exits.

The first required a vault over the stools and the laminate counter, then a quick dash through the kitchen beyond. This had the added advantage of putting me within reach of the shotgun gathering dust under the cash register. A shotgun I was fairly certain was illegal in Canada. I hadn't researched the country's gun laws, though, because guns rarely worked against the magically inclined. The Adept.

So even with his magic as drained as it felt, a gun might backfire if I tried to use it against the sorcerer currently blocking the second exit.

His hair was dark brown, his chiseled jaw shadowed with stubble. His black suit and rumpled white dress shirt were streaked with dirt. No tie. No objects of power on him. Not that I could feel, anyway. But I picked up magic in people more consistently than I did in artifacts.

The sorcerer looked as though someone had tortured him, drained his magic, then just tossed him from a vehicle and sped off—including a scrape on one of his cheekbones that was so sharply defined it might have cut glass.

Cheekbones? Cut glass?

That was an absurd thought.

The second exit was through the sorcerer himself. And by the way he stumbled as he stepped into the aisle between the booths along the windows and the red-vinyl-topped metal stools that lined the counter, he was slow. Likely so drained that I'd be on the sidewalk before he even reacted to my passing.

He placed his hand on the back of the nearest booth, earning a disconcerted glance from Harry Morris, co-owner of Cowichan Kayak and Tubing. Harry had just started eating his lunch—a burger with all the fixings, including bacon. He ordered the exact same thing every Friday.

The sorcerer straightened, visibly reining himself in, smoothing his demeanor. But he stood out among the small-town locals even more than I did, and I'd put a lot of time and energy into being accepted, even if I couldn't truly fit in. He was going to draw the attention of everyone in the packed diner. And then I'd be forced to make a choice instead of just sitting in the booth and gazing at him as if in awe. As if struck by ... something.

It was his magic, or lack of it, that intrigued me.

Yes. That had to be it.

Of course, that didn't explain the way I felt. Amped up, stomach churning, heart rate spiking. But at the same time, sedate, easy ... languid.

He flexed his hands. His fingers were long and unadorned, though distinct tan lines indicated that he'd recently worn rings on each finger, as well as spent significant time in a sunny climate. The rings had most likely been filled with his power. Practical adornments that had been stripped along with his magic.

I forced myself to focus on everything that was wrong about the situation and what my options were now that I'd allowed the sorcerer to close the space between us. I was down to my third possible exit. I could go through the window. A relatively easy move, which would in no uncertain terms let every Lake Cowichan local currently lunching in the diner know that I was more. More than human. More than I wanted them to know.

It would draw far too much attention, though it wasn't the mundanes—those without magic—that concerned me. Rather, such actions might allow the powers that enforced the secrecy of the Adept world—or the members of the Collective themselves—to become aware of my continued existence. Gaining the notice of either would mean a prison sentence. Just not necessarily one that came with a barred cell.

All three exits required me to run. Through the town, north along the lake, all the way home. Grabbing our go-bags, climbing into the Mustang, and leaving.

Leaving.

Leaving everything I'd spent the last ten months cementing, the previous five years making possible—risking exposure, and occasionally my life, to earn the money necessary to build ... a new life. An actual life.

The sorcerer took two more steps my way and his expression shifted, causing him to falter as if he'd just gotten a read on my magic. He had just figured out that I represented everything he'd lost, every iota of power that had been stripped from him. He stumbled, resting his hand on the back of another booth.

"Can I help you?" Mary Davis asked him, still chewing a bite of her chicken salad. Mary, along with her husband, Brett Davis, was a local real estate agent. They had held the listing on the property I'd purchased over eighteen months ago, even before the disastrous job in San Francisco that had nearly been my last.

The sorcerer ignored Mary. I was his sole focus. His sole desire.

In his obvious state of need, he might kill me to get the power running through my veins. And I realized with something like shock that I was fully capable of just stepping out of the booth and letting him have me. Letting him consume me.

At that ridiculous thought, my strange physical reaction to the sorcerer's appearance resolved into unmistakable, unbidden desire. That warmth curled through and settled in my lower stomach, informing me instantly that I'd only ever felt a shadow, the barest hint, of lust before.

I knew I should have been reacting. I should have been moving. Instead, I was just sitting there, staring at him as if he was the most beautiful thing I'd ever seen. As if his beauty had knocked every rational thought right out of my head, dampening every instinct.

Behind the long counter, Brian Martin, co-owner and operator of the Home Cafe, paused after placing a piping hot plate of tuna casserole in front of Lani Zachary. The ex-air force technician, now a mechanic, had cropped her dark hair short at the beginning of the summer, and her bangs were just long enough to brush her eyebrows now. She was perched on her habitual stool, eating at the counter. Brian, a barrel-chested and balding, soft-spoken man in his early fifties, frowned at the sorcerer, wiping his hands on his white cotton apron.

Lani swiveled on her stool, following Brian's gaze. Her hazel eyes narrowed as she traced the sorcerer's focused intent back to me in the corner booth.

I was going to have to act. I was going to have to make a choice. Otherwise, people were going to get hurt. Hurt in a way that would draw unwanted attention.

I wasn't ready.

I just wasn't ready. I'd wanted more than ten months. I'd been hoping... thinking that we might be able to stay. That Christopher, Paisley, and I might be able to put down roots in this small town, tucked away from all the powerful Adepts who'd want to use us, to control us if they knew we existed. If they knew what we were capable of doing.

The sorcerer was five steps away. He didn't seem quite so unsteady on his feet now.

Was this what looking into your future was like? A slow, torturous stroll punctuated by indecision, and yet... desire? A dreadful aching desire to reach forward and embrace what was coming, no matter where it took you.

"Can I help you?" Brian asked from behind the counter.

Lani plucked her napkin from her lap, placing it down beside her plate. Her own latent, untapped magic was coiling within her, but so quietly that the sorcerer wouldn't be able to feel it under everything emanating, beckoning from me.

I naturally and continually dampened my magic, of course. But a sorcerer of his power level would be able to trace any residual, even subconsciously. He could have followed the path I'd inadvertently laid along the roads I walked every few days in my almost obsessive need to create habitual routines.

Lani was going to reach out. She was going to touch the stranger's shoulder, holding him back from closing the space between us.

Then the violence that the sorcerer was barely keeping contained was going to explode all over the diner—taking those with whom I was building tentative relationships with it.

I set down my soup spoon, unaware that I'd still been holding it. I slid out from the booth.

The sorcerer hesitated, sweeping his hungry gaze down to my ankles and white sneakers, then up all the five foot ten inches of me—pale bare legs, sundress, wide shoulders. Long neck and green eyes, and red hair that fell in a straight sheet down to the middle of my back.

"Hello." I spoke as if I knew him. As if I'd been waiting for him.

And for the moment that the word hung between us, I thought it might just be true. I might have known him forever, though I was just meeting him for the first time.

Brian and Lani exchanged glances, their combined concern easing from protective to simply wary.

Oblivious to everything around him, the sorcerer closed the space between us far quicker than he'd been moving previously. He was taller than me, maybe six foot one. I had to tilt my head to maintain eye contact.

He reached out, wrapping his hand around the back of my neck, his thumb across my throat. His grip was harsh.

But though I was completely unaccustomed to being touched, even gently, I didn't break his hold. I didn't try to step away.

Frustration, restlessness, and a fierce need filtered through his touch, picked up through my latent empathic ability. I kept my gaze locked to his, slowly raising my hand and hovering my fingertips by the road rash on his cheek. "You're hurt."

His frustration turned to confusion. Then, as he felt the magic that hummed through my skin no matter how tight a rein I kept on my power, it shifted into amazement. Even awe. He gasped, his pupils expanding and his expression softening into a different sort of hunger.

A hunger much closer to the need, the desire, that was already brewing in my lower stomach.

"Hey!" Brian shouted.

"Are you here to kill me?" I asked in a whisper. "Or am I supposed to kill you?"

The sorcerer frowned. His grip loosened, hand falling away from my neck, severing our empathic connection. "I'm ... I don't know."

Lani stepped up behind the sorcerer, reaching to grab his arm, to pull him away from me.

Quickly, quickly, I brushed my already raised fingertips against the sorcerer's lips—a completely intimate gesture that I wasn't certain I'd ever made for anyone else. My touch carried a jolt of my magic, but not enough to do anything other than push the drained and magically starving sorcerer over the edge.

He gasped, his breath warm across my fingers.

His eyes rolled back in his head.

Then he collapsed. I helped him fall as surreptitiously as I could. It was enough that he wouldn't slam his head on the edge of the table or the tile floor, but not so much that anyone would notice the contact between us. Or that I was strong enough to hold his full weight aloft for any period of time.

Lani blinked down at the figure now pooled at my feet. Then she looked up at me. "Well, I guess we've all felt like doing that at first sight of you, Emma."

"Funny."

Brian hustled around the counter. "I've called the police."

I stepped back from the sorcerer, thinking about whether or not I should protest him being hauled away in handcuffs, or on a stretcher if he was still unconscious. But I had no claim to him, not even a name. And everyone had just seen him apparently trying to strangle me, if only for a brief moment.

I touched my neck, still feeling the warmth of his hand and the residual trickle of his hunger. His need for my magic. Not for me myself. Given my unusual reaction to his abrupt appearance, that was a rational, solid line to draw for myself. It took more than a slight squeeze to hurt me, but the locals wouldn't know that. So calling the RCMP was completely logical.

"Ex-boyfriend, eh?" Brian said, nudging the sorcerer with the toe of his kitchen clogs. He glanced over at Lani, then back at me. "Well, it wasn't like we didn't know you were running from something. I just assumed it was something in Christopher's past, since he keeps so much to himself."

Christopher barely left the property, but that had everything to do with his magic and nothing to do with the sorcerer unconscious on the floor of the diner. I opened my mouth to protest, to deny Brian's assumptions.

He and Lani gazed at me expectantly. And I could feel a steady regard from everyone else in the diner as well.

The first strains of a siren in the distance filled the silence.

I closed my mouth.

Lani smirked, exchanging a knowing look with Brian. Then they bent down and lifted the sorcerer between them.

They thought they'd figured out something about me, about why Christopher was practically a hermit on our two-hectare property, devoted to the gardens he was revitalizing. Lani and Brian thought we were running from something. Which meant all the locals thought we were on the run. And we were. It just wasn't from anything as mundane as an abusive ex-boyfriend.

They thought we were running. Yet they'd said nothing about it. They had welcomed us. Of course, rescuing Hannah Stewart from dying of exposure in the forest seven months before was what had cemented that acceptance.

Brian and Lani carried the sorcerer out of the diner. Harry Morris held the door open for them. An RCMP SUV cruiser pulled to a stop by the front curb.

Jenni Raymond hopped out of the driver's side, crossing around the vehicle to lay eyes on the burden Brian and Lani carried. Nostrils flaring, she stared at the unconscious sorcerer. Then she lifted her head, seeking and finding me through the diner window.

The shapeshifter smirked, as if sorcerers collapsing around me might be a daily, expected occurrence. Though she suppressed her shifter abilities with such willful intent that I was surprised she'd picked up the sorcerer's magic at all. Keeping her gaze on me, she opened the back door of the cruiser, directing Brian and Lani to dump the unconscious figure in the back seat.

I looked away, sliding back into the booth and applying my attention to my now-lukewarm lunch. Corn chowder with a side of thick garlic-crusted bread. I wanted to slip away out the back door. But Constable Jenni Raymond would just follow me home like a tenacious stray dog. She might be completely magically inept, but she was as annoyingly persistent as all her shapeshifter kin. Well, those of the canine persuasion. I'd never met any other species of shifter, not that I knew.

Arrayed on the sidewalk, Lani, Brian, and Jenni Raymond chatted. Brian was carrying the bulk of the conversation, including emphatic hand gestures.

They glanced back at me in turn. Lani's gaze lingered the longest.

I spooned cubes of potatoes out of the soup, savoring how they'd soaked up the creamy chicken stock and spices.

Outside, the conversation broke up. Officer Raymond turned toward the diner, but Lani and Brian lingered on the sidewalk, keeping a general eye on the sorcerer, who was still unconscious in the back seat of the locked cruiser.

Jenni Raymond could certainly swagger when she wanted to, though as far as I'd figured out, it was mostly false bravado. She milked the twenty paces it took to step inside and cross to my booth, greeting the locals, accepting a coffee and a pastry from Melissa Wilson, Brian's partner in the diner and in life. She must have stepped out of the kitchen at some point after I'd taken the sorcerer down.

The RCMP officer's dark-brown hair was slicked back in a severe bun. She was about five foot nine, slim and muscular—with an ease of movement and a coiled energy that came with the shifter magic she idiotically tried to ignore. She slid into the booth in front of me, blocking my view of the front door.

I shifted to the right, clearing my sight line.

She frowned, obviously not understanding.

I didn't enlighten her. It was a waste of my time. Experience told me she didn't want to learn anything more than she already knew. The shifter had actually thought Christopher and I were witches when she'd come to beg for help finding Hannah Stewart. A small town where little happened had probably been the perfect posting for her—until Christopher and I had relocated. Luckily for her, I'd avoided any conversations she'd attempted to start since we'd found Hannah.

Unfortunately for me, I couldn't avoid the current face-to-face.

I met her light-brown eyes steadily.

Officer Raymond dropped her gaze. Anger flitted across her face. She took a swig of her coffee, sucking in air to ease the burn that came with it.

A more observant person would have noticed the steam still coming off the white mug.

"So who is he?" she asked, covering not meeting my gaze by taking a bite of the icing-crusted danish Melissa had given her.

"No idea." I pushed my half-eaten soup aside, downing the rest of my water.

"Well, that's difficult to believe," she drawled, all bravado again. "Seeing as you obviously share an ancestry."

"I hope you mean magic, shifter. Since it's obvious I look nothing like the sorcerer, nor do I command the same power he does."

I kept my voice low enough that no one but her could have heard me, but she still hissed angrily. Since she apparently had no idea about the extent of her abilities, it seemed likely that she'd never fully tested her hearing, or compared it to that of a regular human.

I smiled. I enjoyed goading the shifter. Which was idiotic, really. It meant I was too invested, too engaged. Her lack of discipline mattered to me for some reason that I hadn't taken the time to figure out.

"I'm not playing games, Emma Johnson," she snarled. "If you won't talk here, I'll come to the farm."

"And when you get your head out of your ass and realize he's actually a stranger to me? Then what?"

She curled her lip.

I leaned toward her. "You do know you can smell a lie, right?"

"That's … that's just an urban myth."

I laughed, leaning back. "Maybe you should report the sorcerer. Bring the Vancouver coven into it. I don't think the League has a chapter in Canada, or on the west coast, so the Convocation would claim jurisdiction." I eyed her. She had no idea what I was talking about. "Or maybe you'd prefer to call the West Coast pack?"

Jenni Raymond took another sip of her coffee. Another bite of the pastry. Calming herself, ignoring my attempt to goad her. It was a good effort. Perhaps I'd been wrong about her ability to learn—managing me was an onerous task.

"If you don't know him, why is he here? Why try to strangle you?"

I lifted my chin, displaying what I was sure was unmarked pale skin. "He didn't put much effort into it."

She leveled a look at me, trying to be a hard-ass. "Why?"

I didn't laugh, but it was an effort.

"Why did you come to the farm and ask for our help to find Hannah?" I asked, being deliberately oblique because Lani and Brian were both in the process of crossing back through the diner.

Brian stepped behind the counter. Lani settled on her stool by the counter, within hearing range if she made an effort.

Officer Raymond nodded, acknowledging that she understood. I was intimating that the sorcerer had been attracted to my magic.

That was the simplest explanation.

Of course, it didn't even remotely answer a plethora of other questions. Such as what was a magically drained sorcerer doing wandering around in a tiny town barely on the map? A town literally on the edge of this part of the world? What were the chances he wasn't connected to me or Christopher, the only other newcomers with abundant magic?

Jenni Raymond narrowed her eyes at me thoughtfully. "I'll see what I can get from him when he wakes up."

I nodded, grabbing my plate and glass, then slipping out of the booth to hand them to Brian over the counter.

The balding man clucked his tongue. He hated it when I cleared my place. But he took the dirty dishes from me. "Wait here. Melissa has something for Christopher."

Officer Raymond stood behind me. I kept my back to her—an insult to most shapeshifters. But my disrespect of her fierceness, her position of superiority, didn't garner any magical reaction from her.

As expected.

"I'll call if I need you to come to the station," she said. "For an official statement."

I didn't bother acknowledging her. She was speaking for everyone else's benefit anyway. I wasn't under Officer Raymond's jurisdiction. I wasn't even under the RCMP's jurisdiction, though following the rules of the mundanes simply made sense when attempting to keep a low profile.

Yes, there was some higher Adept power governing all magic users. Beings whispered about in the dark, creatures of mythology. Few believed in fairy tales.

But I did.

Not because I'd ever met anyone of that ilk. But because I'd been bred in the first place. Bred to be powerful enough to stand between such creatures and those who had created me. The Collective. Unfortunately for the Collective, I'd rejected their control seven years ago when the organization's then-current overseer, a black witch, tried to kill me and the four others of my generation.

So if some higher power ever did swoop down on the Collective, I wouldn't be there to see it. And I was more than okay with that.

"You okay, Emma?" Lani asked quietly.

I'd been staring off into space.

That wasn't good, wasn't normal behavior.

I made a show of shaking my head. "Fine, thanks. Just a little … " I let the sentence trail off, not knowing how I was supposed to finish it anyway.

She nodded, lifting her hand as if she was going to touch my arm.

Melissa bustled out from the kitchen, holding a brown paper bag. I reached for it across the counter slightly too early, so that the gesture would put me naturally out of Lani's reach.

Her hand hovered in the air. Then she placed it back on the counter with a soft sigh.

"For you and Christopher," Melissa said commandingly, releasing the bag to my hold. "You call if you need me, Emma. Don't be brave. Unburdening the soul is underrated."

"Okay."

She smiled. Blond curls bounced around her face as she reached across the counter to pat my cheek in a motherly fashion, even though she was barely old enough to play the part.

"Thank you."

Melissa took Lani's plate, her meal only half eaten, and hustled away.

A shiver of magic slipped up my spine. I turned, meeting the sorcerer's inscrutable gaze through the window of the diner and the back window of the cruiser. He'd woken.

"You don't actually know him, do you?" Lani asked.

I didn't answer, though saying no would have been the simplest explanation. Easier. Except I was fairly certain that Lani's latent magic manifested as some sort of intuition. And a half-truth or an outright lie would draw her attention. Or at least draw it more tightly than it already was.

"But you let him touch you." This observation was delivered without heat or condemnation.

I looked at the dark-haired mechanic. "Do you know your parents, Lani?"

Her brow creased, but she answered readily enough. "Of course. Don't you?"

I hesitated. "No."

"Ah." She glanced back out the window. "That makes sense."

Officer Raymond pulled the cruiser away from the curb. The sorcerer kept his gaze on me until I lost sight of him.

"Why?" I whispered, oddly afraid of her answer. "Why does that make sense?"

Lani looked startled. "Because you and Chris, though both epically gorgeous, look nothing alike."

Relief flooded through me—a completely irrational reaction. But for a moment, I'd thought she'd been commenting on me... on my inability to interact like a normal person.

"Actually," she said, "if we're being completely specific, I'm adopted. So I don't know my birth parents. Don't want to know."

I nodded. Some sort of magical lineage was deeply embedded in Lani's DNA, carried by one of her birth parents. Witch magic, according to Christopher. But untriggered and unfostered, that power had never fully manifested for Lani.

So if I reached out and stoked that buried energy, could I bring it to the surface? Could I ignite it?

I stepped away from the counter, moving so swiftly that Lani flinched. Because I didn't want to entertain such thoughts. I didn't want to be beguiled into using my own magic to amplify. Especially not without permission. The encounter with the drained sorcerer had affected me strangely, and that unrequited desire was urging me to unleash.

But in that direction lay the ruin of everything I was trying to build.

"Text me, Emma," Lani called after me as I headed for the door. "I'll bring pizza and beer if you want someone around."

I had someone around. Always. I was never alone. But I smiled and waved over my shoulder because that was how I was supposed to act.

Actually, now that I had a moment to think about it, a regular person probably would have been shaken, been upset at almost being strangled by a stranger.

I pushed through the glass door, exiting the diner as I realized I'd reacted completely inappropriately.

Well … shit.

There was just too much to keep track of whenever I tried to interact with mundanes. I was supposed to smile when someone smiled at me, say please and thank you, praise the food or service, appear weaker than I was. Being a sociopath in a small town was difficult. It was easier to hide my social shortcomings in a city.

But Christopher did badly in cities. So I'd found Lake Cowichan and the property for him, and for Paisley and me.

And now the sorcerer.

Now the sorcerer.

I should have killed him. He was so close to the edge that I might have been able to give him a heart attack if I'd hit him with enough magic all at once. No one in the diner would have even suspected that I was responsible.

Except I didn't just go around murdering people.

Not anymore.

And there was something about the sorcerer.

Something had happened when I'd laid eyes on him, and then again when I'd felt the confusion and shift of his emotions. Something that the sociopath in me couldn't put together, couldn't resolve into a concise, detached mission report. Something that my years of training hadn't prepared me for in the least.

I could have blamed magic—claiming that he ensnared me, enchanted me somehow. Except that I would have felt it if he'd carried any object that held enough power to affect me—never mind that I was practically immune to such spells. It was an immunity that had been forced upon me, taken—stolen—from countless Adepts. 'Vessels,' the Collective had called them.

"Emma! Oh, Emma!"

Someone was calling my name. A name I had briefly forgotten belonged to me. It was only a momentary slip, but it felt longer. I glanced to my right. A young woman was waving at me as she held open the door to the thrift shop.

Light-brown hair. Blue eyes. Around five foot six, smiling tentatively.

Hannah Stewart.

"Emma! I … ah … I set aside a couple of shirts for Christopher."

Hannah no longer bore any of the bruises she'd had when I carried her out of the forest seven months before. But in the time it took for me to glance both ways along the main road, I recalled the weight of her in my arms, and the strange, fierce pride I'd felt in the knowledge that she'd saved herself. That she had said no to her abuser. That she had run.

Just as I had. Just as I should have been doing at that very moment.

Instead, I was forging human connections. Commitments, relationships, that I had no chance or ability to maintain.

I jogged across the road, slipping in behind a slow-moving pickup truck.

Hannah held the door open as I stepped inside the thrift shop. Under her curation, it was really more of a secondhand clothing store paired with a smattering of antiques. The shop always smelled of some essential oil or another, but I couldn't quite place its current citrusy scent.

Hannah hustled back through the shelving units and clothing racks, ducking around the short counter that held the cash register in the far corner and disappearing from sight.

I reached over and touched the handle of a china teacup I'd been secretly coveting for months. Grouped with a mix of other Royal Albert designs, the interior of the cup bore a black rose pattern on a white background. It had scalloped edges and a gold-trimmed handle, and the exterior and the saucer were a deep teal color. It was sixty-seven dollars, just for a single teacup. The pattern was called *Masquerade*.

Since the first time I'd laid eyes on the teacup, I had wanted to place it in the empty china cabinet in the dining room. Completely irrationally. Then I wanted to find more pieces of the pattern, one at a time, until I'd collected them all. Until I'd filled the cabinet the previous owners of the house had left behind. Until I'd made it my own.

But I didn't live the kind of life that came with rare, collectible china. And now that the sorcerer had appeared, there was no chance I'd ever have that life.

I dropped my hand, stepping toward the counter as Hannah popped out of the back room holding two folded, collared shirts.

"I thought the blue would compliment Christopher's … ah … eyes." She flushed.

"I agree. Thank you. How much do I owe you?"

"Oh … maybe he should try them on first?"

Payment had become a strangely strained issue since Christopher and I had rescued Hannah, and not just at her thrift store. I'd had to start leaving cash at the diner because I'd never see a bill there. And I was fairly certain that Lani was drastically under-charging me every time she worked on the Mustang.

I pulled a twenty-dollar bill out of the pocket in my dress, handing it to Hannah. She grimaced, then gave me the shirts and took the money without protest.

"I'm going down to Victoria this weekend," she said. "I was planning to poke around my mother's shop. It's end of season, so I think I might find you a great price on some dresses. And if the length isn't right, I can hem them. But really, you're so slim and … you … can pull off … "

Hannah dropped her gaze to the counter between us. She had thought Christopher and I were angels when we'd first found her in the forest, though I was fairly certain it was Christopher's magic that she'd picked up on in that moment. I'd had no chance to clarify that, however, because doing so would have meant having to admit to a mundane that magic existed.

But the embarrassment of thinking we appeared otherworldly to her had lingered for Hannah. And I had no idea how to ease it for her.

"Something blue, maybe?" I asked.

"Oh, yes. A royal blue. Or you would look fantastic in greens. Emerald or olive green, with a floral print."

"Sounds great."

She bobbed her head. "Everything okay then, Emma? I saw Jenni over at the diner."

I hesitated, not certain how to answer. I knew I should lie. Platitudes were expected in situations like these, weren't they? "I don't know."

"Okay. If you need anything, you let me know." She raised her chin, looking at me steadily.

And I believed her. I believed that Hannah Stewart would stand between me and any unknown that might occur. And that idea should have been hysterical to me. I was capable, when fully amplified, of wiping a small city from the face of the earth.

But it wasn't funny. It was real. I didn't have to touch Hannah, triggering my empathy, to understand that she was speaking with complete conviction.

I nodded, then smiled.

She laughed, quietly joyful. Then she gestured toward the brown paper bag I held in my other hand. "You'd better get whatever that is home to Christopher."

"I'll be lucky to get it past Paisley."

Hannah laughed again, opening the cash register and tucking my twenty into its depths.

I allowed my gaze to rest on the teacup just once more as I exited the store. I allowed myself to imagine it sitting in the empty china cabinet in the dining room.

Then I hit the sidewalk, rearranged my burdens so that my right arm was free, and headed home.

For the last time.

I had already lingered too long. Christopher and I should have been out of town by now, headed toward a ferry or an airport. I should have slipped out the back of the diner. I should have forced Officer Raymond to come to the house to talk to me—and to find us already gone.

Instead, I had chatted with the locals, and now I was wandering home, soaking up the late-summer sun and thinking about a completely impractical teacup.

Because it was just ... that I wanted. I wanted the teacup. I wanted it to be mine. To exist in my house.

And damn it if I didn't want the sorcerer and all the danger that came with him too.

But I wasn't just making decisions for me. I was responsible for Christopher and Paisley. They kept me anchored and focused, and I kept them safe. It was an even trade.

The sidewalk disappeared as I passed beyond the core of the town. I kept to the gravel edge of the road, picking up my pace.

ABOUT FIVE MINUTES AWAY FROM THE HOUSE, A truck roared up behind me. Its speed increased as it neared.

I glanced back. A rising wind caught my hair, spreading it like a great red sail.

An older-model blue Ford.

Peter Grant's vehicle.

He'd been waiting for me. I varied my schedule enough that he didn't manage to drive by every time I went into town, but he had shown up far too regularly over the previous three months for it to be a chance encounter.

Even though Hannah hadn't pressed charges in the end, Peter Grant wasn't pleased that I'd gone into the woods beside his property and come out with her, beaten and broken. The beating had been courtesy of his son, Tyler, who had fled town after getting hit on the head with a rock and losing track of Hannah. She'd broken her ankle during her flight into the forest.

As far as anyone but me and Jenni Raymond knew, Tyler had never returned to Lake Cowichan.

His father blamed me. And he was right, of course. Tyler would regret it if he ever came near Hannah again—a fact I'd made abundantly clear when I literally scared the piss out of him after he'd finally resurfaced, begging for Hannah's forgiveness. Hannah had thankfully been out of town at the time, and the perimeter spell Christopher and I had set up at her apartment and the thrift shop had done its job.

I had put the fear into Tyler, and then the shapeshifter had run him out of town.

It could have gone worse for him.

I had no idea whether Tyler had told his father what happened, though I suspected he wasn't keen to mention having been intimidated by two women to anyone. As such, it seemed most likely that Peter Grant was simply responding to my role in the initial events, and the fact that he wasn't similarly fixated on Christopher spoke volumes.

Peter Grant hated me because I was a woman. He'd instilled the same prejudice in his son. For three months, he'd been contemplating killing me, running me down in his old blue Ford pickup, because I needed to be shown my place.

I turned my back to the approaching vehicle, slowly angling my path to allow more of the gravel shoulder to lie between me and the road. I'd hear the crunch as soon as the truck dipped off the pavement.

This was Peter's fifth try at running me down.

But he didn't have the courage to actually go through with it.

I couldn't survive a direct hit from a large truck going sixty or more kilometers an hour. I could, however, dodge if I saw it coming.

And I wanted him to try.

I really, really wanted him to try.

I wanted to leap out of the path of the vehicle—or better still, fake being hit. I wanted him to stop, to see if I was dead. And then I'd chase him into the woods myself.

That was fair, wasn't it?

If he tried to kill me, I could kill him?

That seemed logical. Though it would draw far too much attention. And I couldn't really claim that I'd killed him without magic, because the only reason that I—a so-called amplifier—was strong enough that I could get sideswiped by a car, then beat a large man to death in the aftermath, was because of the magic I'd drained from others. Magic I had permanently taken for myself, for my own use. Under orders. But that still made me a murderer. Or—

The Ford blew by me, tires right at the edge of the road. My hair and dress were buffeted by the wind as it passed.

Coward.

The truck continued up the road.

I would have to deal with Peter Grant eventually.

Or at least I would if I was staying.

But I wasn't.

I couldn't.

The fence at the edge of our property came into view. The grass, long and brown from the hot, dry summer, stretched back toward the drive, the barn, and the house. The fence needed to be repaired. That was on my list. The house to-do list. But a fence wouldn't keep out whatever the appearance of the sorcerer heralded. If I ran, it wouldn't get fixed.

A sharp pain bloomed in my upper left chest. I gasped, pressing my hand against a nonexistent wound.

What was that?

Grief?

I exhaled in a harsh hiss, shoving my useless thoughts away, along with my irrational reaction.

I knew what I had to do. I always knew. There was no debate.

The shadows cast by the tree line to my right shifted. A large pit bull stepped out, slipping across the ditch to pad alongside me.

Well, she currently looked like a large pit bull.

"Paisley." I lightly brushed my fingers through the blue fur on the top of her broad, flat head, taking comfort in the contact. I allowed myself that comfort, let it shore up my resolve.

Paisley pressed her nose into the palm of my hand, then hinged her massive maw open in a deadly smile filled with double rows of sharp teeth. Even when maintaining her large pit bull form, Paisley could swap out aspects of her demon half at will—the double teeth, the blazing red eyes, the mane of tentacles.

Together, we approached the top of the gravel driveway, pausing at the white-painted, red-roofed farm stand. It was empty except for a single bouquet of red, pink, and orange dahlias. Christopher had put together over a dozen bouquets earlier that morning, setting them out alongside a dozen cartons of eggs and various containers of tomatoes and everbearing strawberries. The locals cleared out the stand daily, even though most of them had gardens and chickens themselves.

Unable to stop myself from continuing to act like an idiot, I reached up and touched the carving of an owl on the sign above the stand. I hadn't known it when the sign first appeared, but Hannah's aunt had carved and painted it, naming the property White Owl Farm. Some of the locals had banded together and fixed up the old stand after Hannah's rescue. Whatever Christopher set out in the mornings sold out before noon most days.

I took the bouquet of flowers. Dialing the combination into the lock on the slotted cashbox, I took the money within, stuffing it into the pocket of my dress. Water from the flowers dripped down my hand and wrist. I let it.

That ping of pain in my upper chest returned. I ignored it.

Leaving the gate open so I didn't have to get out once we had the car packed, I headed down the drive toward the house.

I'D HAD ALL THE REPAIRS THE HOUSE HAD NEEDED done before we moved in, communicating with the various trades through the real estate agents, Mary and Brett Davis. The property had been for sale for seven years previously, the gardens fallow for five years, and the house empty for two years after the previous owners died. The lone resident had been the caretaker, who maintained a suite in the converted hayloft of the barn.

The main residence and the suite had been re-painted white, inside and out, and I'd had the roof of the house replaced with red metal. The fir flooring had been sanded and varnished. Most of the furniture had been left by the previous owners after being picked over by various relatives. I still hadn't gotten around to filling all the rooms, except for new mattresses and bedding. Christopher had insisted on having all the bedrooms, including the suite, ready for guests. I had no intention of allowing anyone near the clairvoyant long enough to stay overnight, but it was easier to not fight over such things ahead of time. Especially if it made him happy.

The kitchen had been fully renovated. For Christopher, who loved to cook.

I'd never spent so much money so quickly, not since buying the 1967 light-blue Mustang convertible that was currently parked in the open barn.

Christopher's magic had returned about a year and a half after we'd destroyed the Collective's compound. Up to that point, it had been easier to stay off the radar and find low-paying jobs in cities. But when his magic came back, it became apparent that Christopher didn't do well surrounded by people. So I had risked raising my profile a bit to take on a number of magical contracts, quickly building a reputation as an amplifier who was willing to take any job as long as the pay was amenable.

I had earned more on my first contract than Christopher and I had earned combined in three years of cleaning houses and washing dishes. My third and fourth contract jobs bought the property, paid for the renovations, and left us some money for extras. And the fifth contract meant that with the right investments, I shouldn't have any need to work for at least another few years.

Which was good, because for that fifth contract, I had nearly sacrificed my freedom and exposed both of us.

The Mustang might have been a completely frivolous purchase. But I had seen it and I had wanted it, though I had no idea why. It simply looked like freedom to me. The property wasn't frivolous, though. It was completely and utterly practical.

The long gravel drive was lined with flowers—once-overgrown dahlias and roses, all brought back to health by Christopher. I paused three-quarters of the way down the drive, casting my gaze to the left, beyond the barn and beside the house.

I could see Christopher moving among the tall tomato plants, his pale-blond hair a beacon among all the green.

I felt rooted to the spot, when I should have been striding across the yard and into the gardens. I should have been telling Christopher that we needed to leave.

Paisley wandered ahead of me, skulking around the house in the hopes of startling the chickens because she wasn't allowed to eat them. Or perhaps she was simply intent on stealing eggs

I walked to the house instead of the garden, climbing the front stairs, crossing the patio, and stepping inside. I closed the wooden door behind me, feeling the cool of the house slide over me.

I crossed back through the long hall into the kitchen.

I emptied my pockets of the money, leaving it in a tidy pile on the corner of the gray-speckled white quartz counter of the kitchen island. I set the shirts from Hannah and the pastries from Melissa there as well.

I put the flowers in a clear mason jar from the batch that Christopher had slowly been filling with canned tomatoes, adding water. The pantry was full of his meticulously preserved bounty. The plums had started to ripen, and the apples would be next.

With the jar in hand and dripping water on the white tile floor, I crossed through the kitchen, past the eating area. I opened the French-paned doors onto the back patio. I stood there, still one step inside the house, and looked out. At the brown grass and the garden that Christopher had created from dirt and seeds.

I stepped forward, setting the flowers on the wide railing. Their color was a sharp contrast to the white of the house's exterior, made even sharper by the vibrant green of the garden behind. Photo worthy.

Except … I didn't collect photos of my life.

That wasn't because magic could sometimes adversely affect technology, because my magic didn't. I didn't have any photos because nothing...nothing until this point in my life had ever been a memory I wanted to collect. Because I'd spent the previous six years running. And before that, I hadn't been a real person, with wants and needs. I'd been a tool. Bred to follow orders, to lead a team of four other magically potent, genetically enhanced people to do the same. Together, we were simply known as the Five, an unrelentingly vicious arm of the Collective.

I hadn't even had a name. Just a designation.

Amp5.

Christopher had been Cla5.

The other three were Nul5, Tel5, and Tek5.

Paisley had just been a genetic experiment, a combination of demon and dog, bound to the Five by blood.

But that wasn't who or what we were anymore.

"It could just be a coincidence," I said, voicing the improbability out loud. "A conversation couldn't hurt."

It would eat into our head start. But if the sorcerer had intended to flush me out, he'd already found me. And he was no match for me, no match even for Paisley or Christopher alone. A single sorcerer was no match for the likes of any of us, especially not as drained as he was.

I spun back into the kitchen, jogging through the house.

The Mustang was parked by the front steps with its top down. Christopher, anticipating me, had already pulled it out from the barn. Paisley was seated in the passenger seat. The clairvoyant, feet bare, dressed in dirty jeans and T-shirt, leaned against the front bumper.

I slowed, gently clicking the door shut behind me.

Christopher raised his head. The white of his magic rimmed his eyes, simmering but not full-blown.

"I don't want to go," he said.

I traversed the steps slowly, giving him time to elaborate. To tell me what he'd seen of my immediate future.

He didn't.

"Go where?" I asked.

He shrugged. "Into one of the five contingency plans I'm certain you have ready. By land, sea, or air. Though we're running out of west coast."

I had picked west as a direction to flee in when the Five parted ways, knowing we'd draw more attention together than apart. But Christopher had needed to come with one of us. His clairvoyance was unpredictable, even debilitating. It would consume him one day. He and Paisley had chosen to come with me.

As they would if I ran now.

As they would if I dragged them away from everything we'd tried to build.

"Paisley agrees with me," Christopher said. "We want to stay."

"I know. I'll keep it in mind."

He snorted.

"I'm just going to have a conversation," I said.

Christopher tossed the car keys up in the air, catching and tossing them again. "Yes, you are."

"And why is Paisley in the car?"

A grin spread across Christopher's face, more devious than his outwardly angelic appearance. The appearance that had beguiled Hannah Stewart so. "You aren't that great with—"

"People?"

"Conversation."

"And Paisley is?"

He laughed. "You're going to need her, Socks." He dangled the keys from his fingertips.

I stepped forward, placing my open palm beneath them. He dropped the keys. They were warm.

"I'm not packing," he said. "I'm going to pick some zucchini and tomatoes, then I'm going to make us dinner."

"You should already be packed," I said caustically.

He shrugged again. "What would be the point of dragging any part of our lives with us? If we run now, after deciding to try to settle, we'll always be running."

"And if we don't run and the Collective is coming for us?"

The white of his magic flooded across his eyes. The power prickled across my face, neck, and shoulders, but I refused to step back, to give way.

He smiled. "Have your conversation, Socks. I'll be setting a fourth plate for dinner."

"No one will be joining the three of us for dinner."

He laughed, pushed off the car, and wandered toward the gardens.

I hissed, annoyed, but Christopher was choosy about what glimpses of the future he shared. Even after so many years, that was still a new thing for him—having a choice to speak rather than speaking at the expectation of his handlers.

The future was in constant motion. Christopher could steer it, but sometimes he saw only pieces. He'd told me more than once that sometimes I moved left instead of the step right he'd seen. And then everything reorganized and reset around me, rendering whatever he'd seen moot, so there was no point in mentioning it.

I climbed into the car, eyeing Paisley. "Don't eat anyone."

She blinked at me, feigning innocence.

"Christopher," I yelled after the clairvoyant's retreating back. "Text Jenni Raymond. Tell her I'm coming for the sorcerer."

He waved over his shoulder, not turning back to question me. So he'd already seen the sorcerer, had seen the coming conversation. He'd alluded to as much, even though I actually had no idea what I was about to say.

I looked at Paisley as I started the car. It came alive with a satisfying roar of power. I executed a three-point turn, heading up the drive to retrace my route back into town. Except I was going to the RCMP station this time.

"I hope the fourth plate isn't for Officer Raymond."

Paisley snorted her derision agreeably.

TWO

I PULLED INTO ONE OF THE THREE EMPTY VISITOR spaces adjacent to the single level, brown-metal-sided RCMP building, parking as far back from the front doors as I could. The six-space parking lot at the side of the building held two cruisers—the SUV Jenni Raymond drove and a pickup. The station was situated one block south of the main thoroughfare of Cowichan Lake Road, but I could still see the slow-moving traffic cutting through town and the bus stop at the corner.

I shut off the Mustang, then sat there for a while, running through all the questions I wanted to ask the sorcerer. All the questions I couldn't really ask without exposing large chunks of my own past. I wasn't clever enough. I wasn't skilled enough in the manipulation that appeared to be common practice among other people. Word games, wordplay, innuendo.

Even if the sorcerer hadn't been dropped in Lake Cowichan to draw me out, he had no reason to keep my secrets. In fact, even with no connection to the Collective, he could only benefit—monetarily and magically—by outing me to them.

And yes, I still believed the Collective existed. In some form. We might have destroyed the compound, along with all their research. We might have vanquished the black witch, Silver Pine, who had decided the Five were expendable for reasons that still weren't fully clear to me. But—

Officer Raymond pushed through the front door of the building, scanning the street and spotting the Mustang. She jogged down the short run of concrete stairs, then sauntered along the front path and across the grass toward me.

I opened the door, stepping out. "Stay here," I murmured to Paisley. Then just to remind her that she was supposed to be a dog, I added, "Good puppy."

She panted at me playfully, her blue tongue longer than it should have been when she was wearing her pit bull form. And forked. Such a brat.

Officer Raymond slowed to a stop on the sidewalk a few steps away from the nose of the car, crossing her arms. "So you know him now?" she asked mockingly.

I'd already answered that question. I just looked at her, since words hadn't worked the first two times.

She dropped her gaze, then snarled at her own reaction. "Stop doing that!"

"Stop repeating the same idiotic questions," I said mildly, surprising myself that I'd bother to offer the shifter any advice.

"You … put me off."

"It's not me. It's that you aren't used to being challenged, not used to not being able to bully someone."

She tilted her head. "Nah, it's just you. Not only don't you need my protection, I have a feeling I have to protect everyone else from you."

Ignoring the way her assessment rang completely true to me, I eyed her coolly. "Is that why you sent me after Hannah Stewart?"

"Well … I didn't know you then, did I?"

"You knew me from the moment you scented me, shifter. It isn't some vague foreboding you feel. It's instinct based on what your senses naturally pick up. It's the magic you've allowed to atrophy."

She curled her lip into a snarl.

I gave her a moment.

She did nothing.

As expected.

"Did you get a name from the sorcerer?" I asked.

She sighed, frustrated. "No. He hasn't spoken other than to ask for the washroom and a pen and paper. He's been doodling for over an hour in the holding cell. All he has to do is make one phone call and … and I can't really hold him without drawing attention, not even if you decide to press charges." She glanced over her shoulder toward the entrance. "He's on his way out. Didn't even have any personal belongings to collect. I asked Wilma to pick up donuts since she practically runs the rumor mill around town and

I didn't want to give her the chance to conduct her own interrogation. And Jake is on patrol."

The shifter had skipped over the part that would happen between the sorcerer making his phone call and drawing unwanted attention to Lake Cowichan. Specifically, that some faction of the Adept world would become involved—the witches Convocation, the shapeshifters Assembly, the sorcerers League. And despite my earlier goading, I didn't want that any more than she did. Not that I was on the wrong side of any of what was going on, but any Adept in a position to represent one of those governing organizations would know that I was an amplifier and that Christopher was a clairvoyant—possibly before even laying eyes on either of us.

A pack representative might not care in the least, though Jenni Raymond would definitely draw their attention. Closeted shifters were more than simply frowned upon, and the various packs were rumored to eliminate those who refused to offer their necks to an alpha. It was difficult for a shifter to maintain control of their beast without a pack's influence—though, as far as I knew, Jenni Raymond's biggest issue was acknowledging her magic and using it properly in general, rather than a lack of control. Still, Adepts carefully avoided any and all situations that might draw the attention of the mundanes.

But if the witches Convocation got involved, they would definitely want to keep tabs on Christopher and me. Maybe even try to draw us into the nearest coven.

Then there was Paisley, who wasn't even remotely a dog, and who would be a problem for anyone in a position of power in the Adept world. I'd have to prove I could control her, or they would demand her head. And proving any of my abilities would only paint a larger target on my back.

I had a more immediate problem, though. "I doubt a sorcerer was simply doodling, shifter," I said derisively.

She stiffened her back, but then hesitated. "That's … I thought sorcerers needed magical objects. He had nothing on him, not a ring, not even a penny."

Her ignorance was baffling. She could transform into an animal. How had that not made her seek out every bit of magical knowledge she could?

"Some sorcerers cast with magical artifacts, often handed down through generations. Some steal those objects. The magical black market is robust, and hazardous. Some commission objects, but alchemists are extremely rare." I paused, waiting to see if Jenni Raymond's head was going to explode from information overload.

She waved her hand, encouraging me to continue.

That was surprising. She had previously displayed what I'd taken as xenophobic tendencies, including not wanting to interact with her own kind. Perhaps I'd read her wrong. "But some sorcerers … particularly skilled magical workers … can call forth and harness magic with runes."

"Runes? Like … elf language?"

"Elves don't exist. But yes, on the surface, it's a language that is based in many ancient languages. Though a sorcerer of power might spend years creating their own alphabet, sometimes building off a system of symbols and sigils handed down through a family over centuries. And a tremendously skilled sorcerer no longer needs to write down their spells. They simply speak and magic … moves."

Officer Raymond had paled.

But I pushed forward, feeling a need for some reason to impart a hard-learned lesson. "There are some Adepts who can bind you with a single drop of your blood and only a few words."

"Like … like the power an alpha has over a pack?"

I glanced at the RCMP officer. Some of her hair had come loose from her slicked-back bun, feathering around her forehead and temples. I couldn't read the emotion simmering in her light-brown eyes, though. With a single touch, I could have bridged the divide between us, but I had enough of my own feelings roiling uncomfortably around inside me. I didn't need hers as well.

"Why do you do that?" she whispered. "Stare for so long? What are you looking for?"

I looked away, answering her first question. "No. Not like the way an alpha has power over a pack. That's a reciprocal binding. It can't be taken by force. And it binds the alpha as much as the pack member."

She was staring at me, completely in doubt.

I snorted. "You've heard differently?"

She shrugged.

"Sure there are rogue pack-like organizations," I said. Because I had encountered one, in fact, when they'd been working with a black witch. I had rescued the sorcerer Kader Azar from their clutches—and had somehow signed my own death warrant by doing so. "Most groups of that nature are short-lived. As soon as they call attention to themselves, the Assembly wipes them from the face of the earth."

Jenni Raymond shuddered and rubbed her arms. So there was a story there, buried under her brusque and brazen attitude.

But then, we all had pasts we kept locked away in the deep recesses of our minds. Things done in the dark—to us, by us. Especially me.

"You think the sorcerer is one of those ones who can bind someone just by speaking to them?" she asked.

The aforementioned sorcerer stepped from the front doors of the RCMP station. He scanned the parking lot, then the street, setting his gaze on me.

Jenni and I looked back at him.

"Well, look who finally decided to join us," the shifter drawled. "I guess he had to fix his pretty hair."

"No," I said, answering her last question while ignoring her unnecessarily rude commentary. "Not in the shape he's currently in."

"Hurt?"

"Drained. Magically."

Jenni sucked in a breath. "That...that's possible? To drain someone of their magic? There are spells that can do that?"

"Complicated spells. Witch magic. Normally...normally triggered and performed during sex. And such spells don't work on females."

And there was me, of course. I could drain an Adept to the brink of death. But I didn't mention that as an option.

Jenni Raymond threw back her head, laughing uproariously.

The sorcerer frowned.

"Seriously..." She struggled to speak through her amusement. "You're telling me it's possible that someone fucked the magic out of this sorcerer?"

I didn't answer. It wasn't her language that put me off, though. It was that I found myself loathing the idea that the sorcerer had been intimate with...anyone. And that was a completely irrational reaction.

He meant nothing to me. I owed him nothing. And vice versa.

The shifter stopped chuckling. She was eyeing the sorcerer again. "You know," she said conversationally. "I don't think he's coming over here, Emma." She snorted, sauntering away toward the sorcerer, who had indeed paused just beyond the glass front door. "I'll put him on a bus. You can thank me later."

She continued toward him, digging into her pocket and pulling something out. "Yo, pretty boy," she cackled. "I guess you need bus fare." She flicked something into the air that caught the light. A two-dollar coin.

The sorcerer stepped to the side, raising his hand defensively and spitting out a single word. A lick of magic shot out from his palm, so weak that I could feel it more than see it. He wavered on his feet as the energy to fuel the spell was torn from him.

The coin froze in the air, held there by the spell the sorcerer had unleashed. He'd thought the shifter was attacking him and had reacted instinctively, using magic he couldn't afford to expend.

Officer Raymond stumbled, then stared open-mouthed at the coin. She swore, fragrantly and viciously.

The sorcerer stepped past her, moving steadily toward me.

"You can't just do shit like that here," Jenni Raymond howled at his back.

He ignored her.

The sorcerer was still wearing the dark suit and white dress shirt, but he'd cleaned up as best he could in the bathroom sink of a police station. As when I'd seen him in the diner, everything about him spoke of particular grooming habits—shoes polished to a high sheen, expensive haircut, manicured nails. But the custom suit was loose where it shouldn't have been, and he sported a few days' growth of facial hair. And the scratch that was just starting to heal on his cheek still looked a lot like road rash.

Something compressed in my chest. It was a completely different sort of pain than the grief I thought I might have been experiencing earlier when I'd contemplated fleeing town. My heart started beating erratically. But as if I were panicking, not like I'd been running.

That didn't make any sense. And it somehow hurt.

I clenched my hands.

The sorcerer's steady stride hitched.

I forced myself to relax, calling forth a cool resolve. I just needed to ask him a few questions, then we'd part ways. I'd go back to the house and would somehow persuade Christopher to leave.

The sorcerer took another few steps.

The coin clattered to the concrete path behind him. Officer Raymond snarled, snatching it up, then retreating to lean against her cruiser on the other side of the parking lot. She was glowering at the sorcerer's back. But assuming she actually accessed her shifter abilities, consciously or not, she was still well within earshot.

I'd have to be careful how I worded any of the dozen questions I needed to ask.

The sorcerer paused about ten steps away, keeping his hands loose at his sides. A town bus pulled up to the corner. His eyes tracked it to its stop.

He was thinking of leaving.

I needed to encourage that. "I'm Emma."

He looked back at me, his blue eyes cuttingly sharp in the bright daylight. "Aiden."

Aiden.

I needed to ask him what he was doing in Lake Cowichan. Ask him who sent him. Ask him if he was looking for me and Christopher.

"There's a suite over the barn," I blurted. Then, utterly aghast at what I'd said, I flushed, heat flooding through me. A half-dozen words in, and the conversation was already a confusing mess of emotions and—

"Are you inviting me home?" His question was pitched low, and perhaps a little amused.

"To the barn. Yes."

He nodded.

The doors to the bus whooshed closed behind us.

He watched it drive away.

My chest started to ache. I wanted to climb into my car, race home, and eat ginger snaps right out of the freezer. I would eat the dough if I didn't have any baked. It was absurd—the conversation, the offer, and my reaction.

"I know what it's like," I said. "Not having any magic. You'll need to sleep, eat, exercise."

"Yes." He didn't step any closer.

Paisley hooked her paws over the top of the windshield of the Mustang, pulling herself up.

Aiden eyed her warily.

Placing her feet deliberately, Paisley prowled down the glass and over the hood of the car. Pausing perched just behind my shoulder, she snuffled and huffed in my right ear, liberally dousing me with spittle and snot.

I huffed out a sigh, wiping the side of my face and neck. Some of the tension I was carrying through my chest eased.

Catching every nuance of our interaction with his razor-sharp blue eyes, Aiden's gaze turned amused.

Paisley stepped down onto the bumper, then padded over toward the sorcerer, flopping down right in the middle of the grass halfway between us. She rolled over on her back, wiggling back and forth and batting her front paws at him.

That ... she ... was she flirting?

The sorcerer cracked a smile. Then he laughed.

The warm sound spread across me, mellowing the remainder of the absurd pain that had lodged itself in my chest.

Aiden hunkered down, reaching out his hand. Paisley rolled onto all fours, obligingly closing the space between them and allowing him to pet her.

A thoughtful look replaced his smile, and he glanced up at me questioningly. So, even drained as he was, he could feel that Paisley was more than simply a dog. So perhaps it had been just my magic that had drawn him to the diner, and not anything more nefarious.

"I apologize," he said, still petting Paisley and peering up at me. "For laying hands on you without permission. I am ... I was not myself, but it won't happen again."

"It wouldn't have happened the first time," I said archly. "Had I not allowed it."

A slow smile spread across his face. I had amused him somehow, but I wasn't certain what he was reading into what I'd said.

I crossed around to the driver's side of the Mustang, climbed in, and started its beast of an engine. The vibrations under my feet steadied me further. I could navigate this situation, despite my weird reactions to the sorcerer. And it would be better to get the answers I needed before deciding to abandon everything Christopher and I had built.

Paisley gathered herself. Then, leaping from about three meters away, she landed perfectly in the middle of the back seat of the convertible.

The sorcerer's jaw dropped.

"Paisley," I hissed.

Aiden straightened, smoothing his suit jacket. Then he sauntered over, opened the door, and slid into the passenger seat beside me.

I pressed my foot to the gas the second he got his seat belt clicked into place. Jenni sauntered back into the station, eyeing us as I pulled away.

WE DROVE WITHOUT SPEAKING. WITH THE TOP down, even with the windows up, the barrage of air rushing past the Mustang wasn't conducive to chatting. It was delightfully brain numbing, though, so I didn't have to listen to my inner voice telling me for the hundredth time that I was being absolutely, idiotically insane.

It also didn't help matters that that same awareness kept noticing things about the sorcerer sitting next to me, close enough to reach out to, close enough to touch. Such as the fact that his magic came and went in a dull, irregular pulse. Or the way the sleeve of his suit jacket and shirt shifted back to reveal his wrist. Or a glimpse of a rune he'd inked on his palm, along with a ring of runes within the tan lines around each of his fingers.

The red roof of the barn came into view around the time the sorcerer turned to regard me. I could feel the weight of his steady gaze, squinting against the sun just beginning to dip over the valley.

I glanced at him. The wind caught my hair, blowing it all around us. He smiled, teeth white against his tanned skin. He raised his hand slowly, as if he wanted to capture my hair but would give me time to pull away.

Paisley shoved her way between the seats, breaking into the moment. Deliberately, perhaps.

I looked back at the road, slowing to pull into the drive. Though even as I moved my foot from the gas to the brake, before I shifted gears, I had the thought, the feeling, that I could have driven past and kept on going forever, following the sun. If he was sitting beside me. Aiden.

The tires hit gravel. I loosened my hold on the wheel, allowing the car to find purchase without forcing it into a skid.

It was an attraction. That was all. I was simply attracted to the sorcerer. Just because I hadn't experienced any attraction this intensely before didn't mean it couldn't happen. It was chemical, somehow. It would ease.

I would gain an immunity to him, just as I did to any other magic, any other drug.

Still, letting him get on the bus would have been the smarter move.

Aiden shifted his gaze out the window, seemingly taking in every part of the property as we traversed the driveway. The red-roofed, white-painted farmhouse at the end of the drive. The dozens of fruit trees of all varieties in the orchard to our right. Dahlias and roses in full bloom, edging the drive all the way up to the house from the mailbox and the farmer's stand by the open gate.

I pulled through the open doors into the barn, parking the car. We'd painted the exterior siding white to match the house in the spring, but the interior was still all aged wood and thick posts and beams.

Paisley climbed over the trunk before I'd even turned the key in the ignition, slipping into the deepening shadows toward the back door and heading off in search of Christopher. Or the chickens. I never could tell.

The light in the barn was muted, though the day was still sunny behind us. The car engine murmured as it cooled. Aiden didn't move from his seat, and neither did I.

"So … " he said. "White Owl Farm?"

He'd seen the sign, though I'd spun onto the drive and through the gate pretty quickly. "Yes."

He craned his head back, sweeping his gaze overhead to take in the wooden stairs that led upward into the hayloft, which the former owners had converted into a caretaker suite. It was a deliberate move. I'd already seen the sorcerer take in every detail of the barn as we'd pulled in. As I would have, had it been my first time seeing it. "And this is the aforementioned barn? With the suite?"

"Yes."

Silence settled between us again. He placed his hands, fingers relaxed, on his knees, waiting for something.

I could have reached over and wrapped my fingers around his wrist. I could have felt the warmth of his skin, then amplified his magic. Filling him up, making him as powerful as he was obviously meant to be.

And that might have been the exact reason someone had set him on me. Because as drained as he was, he'd be irresistible to an amplifier.

I curled my fingers into my palm.

He noticed. "Why am I here, Emma?" he asked quietly.

My name, carefully and deliberately articulated by him, was a slow caress across my heart. I refused to acknowledge the feeling.

I reached for him, slowly, deliberately.

He rotated his hand, palm up, fingers still relaxed and inviting my touch. I hesitated, wanting to press my fingertips to his, lining each finger up so that they perfectly mirrored each other. But there was something desperately intimate in that thought, in that gesture, that desire.

He murmured something in a language that I didn't recognize. Arabic, maybe. Possibly even an arcane version, if there was such a thing. It sounded apologetic. Then he turned his hand so that his palm once again rested on his knee.

I placed my forefinger and middle finger on the back of his hand, gazing at the inked runes that were already smudging on his fingers.

"Why are you here?"

He shook his head sharply, just once. Tension ran through his jaw. "I was hoping you could tell me."

"Which is why you got in the car?"

"Among other reasons." His lips curled into a smile.

I kept my gaze on my fingers, lightly pressing on the back of his hand, and my focus on the feel of his magic, of his currently nebulous emotions. He was tired. That exhaustion was overriding everything else he was feeling. I was actually surprised he hadn't passed out again.

I could boost his magic, just enough to jar him, to get him talking. It would be invasive, though, and would reveal way too much about me. Too much that I was still hoping to keep hidden. If Bee were present, she could have plucked the answers out of his head without even asking the questions.

He cleared his throat. "As best I've figured out, I've lost three days, along with most of my magic." He waved his free hand. "And I'm apparently somewhere in an English-speaking country, surrounded by mountains. But not the United States. The road signs are in metric."

Temporary amnesia wasn't uncommon when paired with severe trauma, such as having one's magic swiftly drained. Though that didn't mean he hadn't been sent by the Collective to draw me out. "Do you know me?" I asked quietly.

He didn't answer.

I lifted my gaze to meet his, ignoring the way the light blue of his eyes made them seem piercing, soul penetrating. Such concepts didn't exist. It was simply my mind's interpretation of the way the light played with the color.

"Do you know me, Aiden?" I asked again, firmer this time.

A smile slipped across his face. "Telepath?"

"No."

"True seeker?"

"No."

His smile widened. "I don't know you, Emma. You would be impossible to forget. And apparently impossible to deny, even when I already know that the safest course of action has to be getting out of this town. Quickly."

My empathy immediately picked up his sincerity, backed by a lingering frustration—along with the ever-present overwhelming weariness. He needed to sleep, to heal. I broke contact with his skin before I could pick up anything else. The quicker he healed and regained the memory of his missing three days, the quicker I would get the answers I needed.

"So am I telling the truth?"

"So far."

"Then I ask again, why am I here?"

"So I can keep an eye on you, sorcerer."

"In case I do what? If you thought I could hurt you in any way, why bring me to your home?"

"Perhaps you're more of a threat if I let you go."

He laughed quietly. "Am I to be under house arrest?"

He didn't sound displeased at the notion, which was confusing enough that I opened my door and stepped out of the car instead of answering. I crossed out of the barn, not waiting for him. But he didn't hesitate to follow.

He was right, of course. Inviting him to the property was absurd, ridiculously ill-conceived. And now I knew why Christopher had said he would set a fourth plate for dinner.

CHRISTOPHER WANDERED AROUND THE SIDE OF THE barn, Paisley at his heels. Her presence was easily explained by the blue strainer and the five multicolored chicken eggs that Christopher was carrying.

"Christopher, this is—"

"Aiden Myers." He said it even before he'd settled his light-gray-eyed gaze on the sorcerer, who was a few steps behind me.

"Yes."

"Why is your magic all curled up and hiding, Aiden?"

The sorcerer hesitated, glancing between me and Christopher. "It will come back."

Christopher nodded. "As it always does, I suspect. But you do like to play." The white of his magic flitted across his eyes so quickly that I hoped Aiden hadn't seen it. Though hoping to hide what magic either of us wielded for long was an idiotic notion. "It wasn't a good game, I'll bet."

I frowned at Christopher, catching his slip. He was quoting from the books he'd learned to read from—that he'd named all the Five from—which was unusual. That hadn't been an issue since the blood tattoos had been inked on all our spines, grounding all of our magic and helping Christopher stay rooted in the present.

He smiled at me, sedate but pleased.

The moment passed.

"Nice to meet you, Christopher." Aiden glanced over at the gardens. "You have a wonderful property. I'm honored that—"

"Brother and sister," Christopher said, randomly answering some unasked question likely plucked from a glimpse of our immediate future. "But we're not genetically related." He laughed. "Funny that was your first concern. But then, Emma is compelling. We're not related to Paisley either, so don't let her tell you differently."

Aiden frowned.

"Nope. Not a telepath." Christopher spun away, striding toward the house.

The stress of having Aiden on the property, even magically drained, was obviously triggering him.

I turned to Aiden, ready to tell him that I could ask our neighbors to the west, the Wilsons, if they'd open their cottage for him. They ran a bed and breakfast in the summer season, and I didn't think they'd turn me away.

"No, Emma," Christopher said, pausing at the base of the front porch.

I didn't voice the thought.

Aiden was watching both of us intently, most likely reassessing his earlier choice to climb into the Mustang and accompany me home.

"At least let the sorcerer sleep for a bit," Christopher said. "Before you kick him out. I made up the suite." He jogged up the steps and into the house.

Aiden settled his sharp gaze on me.

I felt an overwhelming impulse to explain everything—every last detail of our magic, our pasts, what we were running from, my concerns over who

Aiden was and what he was doing in Lake Cowichan. I quashed it. "The loft is separated from the garage section of the barn. Though you can access it through there as well."

"Up the interior stairs?"

I nodded. The sorcerer was observant.

"And the other entrance?"

I crossed around the barn. He followed. A set of wooden stairs at the back postdated the construction of the barn, and had been freshly painted white along with the exterior.

I climbed the stairs, hyperaware of the sorcerer behind me. I paused at the top landing, which over-looked the fenced vegetable garden. Christopher had placed a long rough-hewn wooden box filled with strawberry plants on the railing, and something about that tugged at my memory. There was some significance to the plants that I couldn't immediately recall.

I reached for the door handle, glancing back at Aiden, who had paused on the top stair to give me space.

From this vantage point, the eastern window of my bedroom was directly behind the sorcerer's shoulder. Which meant I'd be able to see into the suite if Aiden didn't lower the blinds. I'd never stood at that window for long enough to notice.

"Emma?" Aiden asked.

I shook my head, not certain how to otherwise cover my hesitation. I opened the door, formally gesturing for Aiden to enter. He stepped in, scanning the large room. Like the house, it was painted white, floorboards and all. A cream-colored quilt I didn't recognize had been tucked over the double bed.

Christopher had retrieved an old brass bed frame from the attic, pairing it with one of the extra mattresses he'd insisted on ordering months before. The clairvoyant didn't usually get glimpses of the future that far ahead, but perhaps tying his magic to the witch's oracle cards that I commissioned for him had lengthened his view. Granted, we hadn't fully tested his sight since his magic had returned after being drained by me during our escape from the compound. But by its tenor, I knew it was more powerful than before, and I had worried that testing it, amplifying it, would be detrimental to Christopher's daily life.

Suddenly, I remembered the significance of the strawberries.

Seven months ago, Christopher had pulled three cards from his oracle deck—three separate shuffles that had yielded the same three cards. Ginger, strawberry, and rose. Manifestation. Movement. Partnership.

The clairvoyant had caught a glimpse of the future then. Our present now. But he'd kept quiet about it.

Aiden stepped through into the bathroom, glancing around. His movement recalled my attention to the room.

Clothing was neatly folded on one of the two chairs in the small seating area to the right. Jeans, a T-shirt, a thin henley sweater in charcoal, a pair of shorts, and black boxers still in the package. The closet was partially open. A fleece jacket and a Gore-Tex hung within, along with an extra blanket and pillow on the upper shelf.

Aiden stepped back into the main room, pinning me into place with his blue-eyed gaze. Not that I'd been in a hurry to leave. "I thank you, Emma, for your and Christopher's ... and Paisley's hospitality." A hum of magic whispered through his words. "I will bring no harm to you or yours as long as I rest my head here by your leave."

The magic he'd called forth effortlessly faded.

"That's very specific wording, sorcerer."

He smiled. "Well, if you try to kill me, I must have some leeway to react."

"If I try to kill you, Aiden, you will have deserved nothing less."

"That goes without saying. I always reap everything I've sown."

"Everything? Or only the murderous repercussions?"

He tilted his head, feigning thoughtfulness. "I find I'm suddenly open to other possibilities."

I didn't know what he meant. The moment stretched between us unresolved. "Dinner is at seven." I turned away.

"Clairvoyant."

I almost said no. Almost tried to pretend he meant me, not Christopher. But he was smiling, pleased with himself. As if he'd won some game we'd been playing.

Except I didn't play games. And I definitely didn't play with anything that impacted Christopher's safety.

The sorcerer's smile slipped from his face. "I apologize. That was rude. Uncouth. If I claim exhaustion, can we move beyond my transgression?"

I almost voiced the threat that I'd been formulating—but then I realized he'd already seen it in me. Seen that I'd do anything to protect what was mine to protect. I tried smiling instead. "Have you ever gone up against a clairvoyant?"

He raised his eyebrows, surprised. "I've never met one. But I can't imagine why I would ever jeopardize such a valuable relationship."

There it was.

As expected.

Apparently, sorcerers were all the same.

For some reason, I'd hoped Aiden was different, even though everything about him—or at least my sense of what had been stripped from him—had pointed to a predilection for collecting power.

"You were saying?" he prompted.

I turned away, heading toward the stairs.

He closed his eyes, swearing softly under his breath as if pained.

I kept moving.

I WANDERED AROUND THE BACK OF THE HOUSE, finding Christopher in the kitchen as expected. The scents of roasting tomatoes, garlic, basil, and oregano wafted through the open French-paned patio doors. The mason jar of dahlias that I'd left on the railing had been moved to the center of the kitchen table.

The kettle whistled. Christopher had already set the stoneware teapot and two of our four mugs on the island.

He removed the stainless steel kettle from the stove, clicking the gas burner off. Then he glanced over at me.

I hadn't moved from the door, as if stepping into the house would allow the future to continue moving forward. The future I'd somehow triggered by bringing Aiden home. It felt as though stepping onto the white tile would acknowledge that future, unraveling our shared life—assuming I wasn't reading too deeply into what Christopher had seen when he'd tied his magic to the oracle cards.

"The Collective?" I finally asked.

"Not that I see. And if they come, they come." Christopher poured water through the strainer set over the teapot. Usually I selected and steeped the tea. "We'll fight. We're stronger now, even just the two of us. Not even factoring in the sorcerer you've collected and Paisley. And the others are only ever a day away."

"You think they'd come?"

He set the timer on the oven. "Without question."

"Tell me you haven't seen it." I never asked for visions he didn't voluntarily share. I didn't want him to ever feel the need to lie to me.

"I'd always tell you, Socks."

"Even if I was going to die?" I asked, somehow finding it within me to tease.

He laughed. "Especially then. And you know it wouldn't be the first time. How many times have we avoided each other's death?"

I laughed, weary and keyed up at the same time. "I never counted."

I also didn't know how many Adepts I'd amplified or drained of magic, whether on command or in self-preservation. I didn't know how many beings I'd slaughtered either, on demand or when thwarting one of the many attempts on my life or the lives of one of the other four.

I only knew who I cared for, and who cared for me. All two of them. And I had put both Christopher and Paisley in jeopardy with my actions, with my infatuation with the sorcerer.

I wasn't sure how long I'd stood in silence before I noticed Christopher leaning against the white-speckled quartz counter, his gaze on me. No hint of his magic traced his eyes now. "I've never seen you like this."

"Like what?"

"Conflicted. What is it about the sorcerer that bothers you? He's no match for any of us."

I strode through the kitchen instead of answering, pulling the strainer out of the teapot a moment before the timer went off.

Christopher snorted.

I poured, relishing the scent of the tea. I enjoyed smelling tea even more than I liked the taste. "Darjeeling?"

"Mim. Your second flush."

I set the first mug in front of Christopher. He added a teaspoon of sugar, stirring. He took his tea differently every time, even the same brew.

I always drank mine the same way, with a splash of milk if hot brewed, or a teaspoon of sugar if it was cold brewed, unless it was fruit based.

"Is he going to stay?" I asked without looking at the clairvoyant.

"I don't know yet."

"He's that hard to read?"

"No. But apparently you are."

I frowned. Christopher didn't usually have a difficult time reading me.

"Shall I get out the cards?"

"No." I didn't like deliberately tuning Christopher's magic to me. Occasionally it got stuck, and then he would suffer through seeing five or ten minutes into my future for days. "I'll be in my sitting room, if you need me."

"As always."

AFTER TAKING OVER THE FRONT SITTING ROOM AND the TV with so many gaming units that I had no idea how he remembered what controller went with which, Christopher had dragged furniture down from the attic to set up a sitting room for me in the spare room across the hall from my bedroom. He'd painted an old armoire sky blue, distressing the edges and installing a flat-screen TV within. A cream love seat with a faded floral pattern and wooden arms, plus a low wooden coffee table, completed the decor.

Neither of us had gotten around to putting up pictures or even purchasing artwork, though I knew that was something people were supposed to do.

I curled up on the couch with my mug of tea and turned on *Downton Abbey*, scrolling back through and selecting episode one of the first season.

I contemplated peeking through the windows to see if I could catch sight of the sorcerer in the suite above the barn, even though the angle was wrong from the sitting room's corner of the house.

I didn't.

But it was a struggle.

I had gained immunity to magically boosted poisons quicker than I was developing any resistance to this torturous physical attraction.

I wrapped my fingers tighter around the mug, sipped my tea, and opened my email on my iPad. My inbox contained three unread messages, dating back to sometime the previous week, which was the last time I'd checked it.

All three were from Karolyn Dunn, a recruiter who operated within the Adept underworld—or at least the section of it that I had come into contact with. She arranged introductions and various jobs. Contracts, it was rumored, that she enforced with her reputation of casting impossible-to-thwart curses. All of our communication had been conducted by email. Christopher had set up some system that routed my email through different addresses, so I'd never needed to worry about my physical location being traced.

But, as I'd previously told Karolyn, I wasn't interested in taking on any more contract work after the final job she'd arranged in San Francisco in October 2017. I had told the recruiter so even before I'd agreed to the job that had nearly cost me my freedom. Her finder's fee for that assignment had been deposited the moment I signed my name to the contract. And unless she had placed spies in the warehouse, she had no way of knowing whether or not I'd actually even walked away from that job alive.

No one else on site had.

I was alive only because Christopher and Paisley had rescued me. We had fled the city that evening, worrying even as we made our way up the coast and across the border into Canada that any rumors or fallout of the bungled job, the dramatic rescue, and a clairvoyant working with an amplifier would draw the attention of the Collective.

It hadn't. Yet.

Unless that was why Aiden Myers was currently installed in the suite over the barn.

I wouldn't have put anything past the Collect-ive, including the patience it would take to wait until I'd settled, to wait until I'd made a home for myself. And then instead of attacking outright, to send the sorcerer, drained, vulnerable. To see what I would do. To test me.

If Aiden was a pawn in the Collective's long game, he might not even know it.

I shoved that line of thought out of my mind. Paranoia wasn't going to get me anywhere. Actively seeking what information I could while Aiden re-covered his recent memories would be a far more productive use of my time and energy.

Karolyn Dunn was persistent, though. Even though I hadn't answered a single one of her emails since San Francisco, the 15 percent commission she would make off an amplifier of my power level was clearly keeping her hopeful. I deleted the messages in my inbox unread.

Then I began to compose an email to one of the six people in the world who could connect the name on my passport to my magical abilities. Ember Pine.

Ember Pine was a witch, but her magic re-volved around contracts and estates for the Adept. She worked out of the Seattle location of Sherwood and Pine, but that law firm maintained offices all over the world. If you were magically inclined and needed a lawyer, you went to Sherwood and Pine—as I had quickly discovered when it became clear that I hadn't actually permanently drained all of my and Christopher's magic when we'd broken out of the compound. Though the name of the firm, and of Ember herself, was disconcerting, apparently the Sherwoods and the Pines were prolific, and not all branches of the family even knew each other.

How she might have been connected to Silver Pine was the first question I'd asked Ember. I hadn't mentioned my connection to the black witch, of course. Specifically, that Silver Pine was one of the members of the Collective, and that while she was overseer in 2011, she had tried to kill me—kill all the Five. As a result, she'd died by my hand instead.

It wasn't easy to murder me. Not when I saw it coming.

Using the umbrella of the oath that enforced her confidentiality in all the work she did for me, Ember had declared that she had no conflict of interest, and no connection to a Silver Pine or to the black witch's immediate family.

Of course, in a magical family as widespread as the Pines or the Sherwoods, I was certain there were many blackened, even diseased branches.

I typed *Information pertaining to an Aiden Myers* into the subject line of the email.

Then, trying to decide how nonspecific I could be and still give the witch lawyer something to go on, I wrote:

Ember, I have happened upon a sorcerer who calls himself Aiden Myers. In his early thirties, dark hair, blue eyes, with tanned skin that might indicate a different ancestry than his last name implies.

I paused, fingers hovering over the iPad keyboard. I wasn't certain how to phrase my core request, over email, to a lawyer.

Please reply with any information you deem pertinent to any continued contact with him.

Specifically, was he a threat who needed to be eliminated? But I didn't need to add that. Ember Pine had drawn up five magical contracts for me, skillfully hiding my identity while ensuring that those who hired me couldn't renege on payment if I completed the task the contract set forth.

Ember was also aware of some of what had happened when my last contract had been broken, when Christopher had to step in and rescue me. Because she'd sent an extraction team to the warehouse, which had arrived without engaging us just as we'd been leaving, the moment after the magic binding both parties was severed. As per our agreement. That was how skilled Ember was when it came to wielding her pen. The moment the sorcerer who'd contracted my services had tried to double-cross me, Ember had known.

I could have broken through the blood-fueled barrier that the sorcerers had held me with that night, but doing so would have killed the young witch they'd used to ignite and feed the containment spell. Harvesting her life force one drop at a time, in order to drain me of my magic.

I hadn't stuck around to figure out their long-term plan. Most likely my death or my imprisonment.

After Christopher had freed me and we'd slaughtered every last sorcerer on site, I'd carried the young witch from the warehouse, half dead despite the magic I pumped into her. I'd left her in the care of Ember's team. And then I hadn't asked after her since, not wanting to draw more attention to her, no matter how often she strayed into my dreams.

It was odd that not murdering the young witch to save myself haunted me more than any of the lives I'd taken out of necessity or on command.

Ember had also handled all the paperwork when I'd purchased the Lake Cowichan property. She had drafted and now held my will, overseeing the estate that needed to be in place to look after Christopher should I die before him.

Seven years ago, I hadn't known that I needed anything like a will, or magically binding contracts. The Five had been educated by the Collective, covering basic language and math skills, but everything else had been carefully curated as need to know. I had to be taught to drive, to read maps, understand directions, and deal with certain levels of technology, such as computers. I had been trained to mastery level in multiple weapons and martial arts disciplines, until I showed a skill and a preference for blades and mixed martial arts.

But other than children's books as we were learning to read, I wasn't given access to literature or history or anything the Collective considered the province of the mundanes.

I wasn't taught to cook. I couldn't do my laundry. I didn't really know how to exchange goods for money, though I understood the process. YouTube turned out to be a valuable source of information about many mundane activities.

I added a thank you and my name to the email, then hit send.

Feeling utterly moronic when I had first signed up for them, I took remedial classes at a number of community centers over the first two years when Christopher and I were figuring out how to function, how to hide among the mundanes. But when I'd shown up for the first class—Christopher had taken cooking, while I took a life skills class—I saw that everyone else was my age or older. So I didn't feel so stupid, so ignorant. Apparently, everyone had gaps in their education.

Stretching the forty thousand dollars that Bee had sourced for us let us plug what holes we could in our education, including basic Spanish, and had let us get by on entry-level jobs. For me, that was cleaning. Christopher took up dishwashing, then cooking. And yes, I hadn't had any idea how to actually clean a house. Those jobs allowed us to move regularly as we headed north along the west coast of South, Central, and North America, always trying to figure out if we still needed to run from the Collective.

I set the iPad to the side, sipping my tea and refocusing on my TV show. Yes, it had taken me seven years to get to the point of owning a home and trying to figure out who we were if we weren't running from the Collective. And attraction or no attraction, I wasn't going to let Aiden Myers disrupt everything I was building.

If his amnesia wouldn't let him tell me what I needed to know about how he came to be in Lake Cowichan and who sent him, maybe Ember Pine could dig up something.

And then some decisions would have to be made.

THREE

CHRISTOPHER WAS STIRRING FRESH LINGUINI IN A large pot of boiling water on the stove when I wandered back into the kitchen. I had changed into a dark floral sundress, pairing it with a light black cardigan because it was starting to cool off at night, and Christopher still wanted to eat with the patio doors open. I might have also brushed my hair. A lot. Until it fell in a thick gleaming sheaf down my back. I also heavily considered applying what little makeup I owned, but settled for clear gloss with just the hint of a glimmer.

"You look nice," Christopher murmured, though he hadn't actually looked up at me.

I stepped around him, pulling the glass pitcher I usually used for iced tea out from the cabinet over the dishwasher, then filling it with water. I carried it and three matching glasses to the table, which Christopher had already set with plates, napkins, and utensils. I set out the glasses, pouring the water.

With the sun in the process of setting in a deep wash of oranges, the yard and the far edges of the back patio were cast in shadow. I flicked on the patio light for what I realized was the very first time, and was surprised to find it worked. Then I allowed myself a glance at the clock on the stainless steel exhaust fan over the stove.

7:05 P.M.

He wasn't coming.

Paisley appeared out of the shadowed yard, skulking up the back steps and brushing past my legs with a grumble. She prowled around the kitchen, circling the island and continuing to voice her discontent in a series of snorts.

"She wanted chicken," Christopher said, tossing the pasta under running water in the sink, then dumping the contents of the dripping strainer into a large bowl. He carried the bowl and a smaller pot over to the table, placing both on the quilted potholders set in the center. Another bowl covered with a tea towel was already on the table, along with a green salad.

We sat down at our usual places across from each other. Christopher passed me tongs. I pinched a serving of steaming pasta, allowing it to pool on my plate. I passed the tongs back to Christopher, lifting the top off the pot.

The smell of creamy garlic-and-tomato sauce wafted out. I took a generous scoop of the sauce and poured it over the pasta on my plate.

Paisley paced around the table, knocking her shoulder against the chair nearest the open French-paned patio doors.

"That's enough," I admonished gently, reaching over to discover that the tea towel hid thick slices of garlic bread.

I smiled at Christopher. He bobbed his head, already twirling a bite of the pasta on his fork.

Paisley huffed out a long dramatic sigh, pacing out to the patio.

Aiden wasn't coming, wasn't joining us for dinner. I was oddly relieved.

I tore a hunk from the garlic bread, dipped it in the creamy tomato sauce that had slid over the pasta and onto my plate, then took a bite. "Very good. Thank you."

"Thank you for staying, for not making us run."

I nodded but didn't meet his gaze. I hadn't ruled out running as a possibility yet. But Christopher already knew that.

"There's apple crisp for dessert."

That got my attention. "Did you try making ice cream?"

"I did."

With the eggs from the chickens. Our chickens. "I'm looking forward to it."

Footsteps drew my attention to the back patio. The sorcerer's magic was so muted that I hadn't picked it up until he was only steps away.

Aiden paused in the doorway, narrowing his striking blue eyes until they grew accustomed to the light level.

My stomach squelched, then fluttered. But I ignored my reaction and kept my gaze on him, steady. Even if Christopher had caught a glimpse of him joining us for dinner, Aiden was a complete unknown.

"I'm sorry I'm late." The sorcerer's voice was full of gravel. He'd been sleeping, but had changed out of the suit into the jeans and the charcoal henley, leaving the top two buttons undone. I dragged my gaze away from the hint of dark chest hair this revealed.

Aiden stepped forward, hesitating at the chair that Paisley had knocked off kilter. It was obvious that he would have preferred to not have his back to the doors, open or closed.

Christopher gestured to his right, offering up the other chair. Aiden crossed around the table. I tried to not track his movement as he passed behind me. He didn't brush against my chair, but for a brief moment, I wished he had.

My emotions were getting idiotically out of hand. I was going to make a fool of myself, if I hadn't already. I didn't get to have crushes, and doing so with an unknown entity like the sorcerer was beyond idiotic. It put everything we were building in jeopardy.

Aiden settled to my left, immediately unfolding his cloth napkin and placing it across his lap. He scanned the food, his gaze settling on the fourth plate, but he didn't comment on it. He served himself.

Christopher and I continued to eat in silence.

Paisley, half-hidden in the shadows on the back patio, threw her head back and let out an undulating howl.

Aiden flinched.

"That's enough," I said, firmer this time. "Join us or don't eat."

Paisley stepped inside, skulking up to the table and standing so that just the top of her head, eyes, and ears were visible over the top. She stared at Aiden.

He froze with a piece of garlic bread halfway to his mouth.

Christopher reached over, dropping three-quarters of the remaining pasta and three scoops of sauce on the fourth plate. "Take it with you."

Paisley grumbled.

Christopher added two pieces of garlic bread to the plate.

Paisley, still glowering at Aiden, took the edge of the plate in her mouth and pulled it off the table.

The sorcerer suddenly looked far more alert than he had just a moment before. He ate the garlic bread, but didn't take his eyes off the demon dog.

Paisley skulked out onto the patio, perfectly balancing the plate. She stepped to the right, settling down just out of sight.

"I didn't know if you ate meat," Christopher said, speaking to Aiden. As if that would explain Paisley's undoglike behavior.

"I'm grateful to share your table and your meal," Aiden said, not answering Christopher's implicit question.

I tucked the tea towel back over the garlic bread, then rolled another bite of pasta in my fork.

Aiden tracked the movements of my hands.

I quashed the urge to ask if he could see magic. That wasn't a common trait. But I was already all but certain that Aiden's magic was uncommon, powerful. Why else would someone have taken the trouble to drain it?

"He didn't check the food for poison," Christopher said.

Aiden paused, glancing up at him, then over at me. He slowly resumed chewing the bite he'd just taken.

"Why would Aiden think you've poisoned him?" I asked patiently, just in case Christopher's clairvoyance was leaking.

"Well … you know, he's that type of sorcerer."

Aiden took a sip of water. "What type is that?"

Christopher tilted his head, plainly befuddled that he needed to clarify. "The type that someone would strip the magic from."

Ah. Apparently in some timeline, I'd actually asked the question I hadn't figured out how to articulate, since I had made it clear that I wasn't to be questioned about my or Christopher's magic. And Aiden had rather heroically managed to not interrogate us about Paisley. Yet.

Aiden raised an eyebrow. "Evil?"

Christopher frowned, looking at me.

"Dark," I said, clarifying. Good and evil weren't the sort of distinctions any of the Five made.

"Dastardly." Christopher grinned. "Devious."

I looked at my plate. "The kind you'd want at your side in a fight."

"But not at your back," Christopher said.

"Don't you mean front? Not facing in a fight?" Aiden asked, seemingly not at all thrown by the turn in the conversation.

Christopher laughed. "If you were facing Socks in a fight, you wouldn't be standing long. The only reliable way to drop her is to sneak up."

I glanced at Aiden. He had stopped eating again, watching me instead and clearly conflicted as he tried to reconcile Christopher's description of me with the woman who sat before him.

He looked down at his plate, taking another bite. "I don't plan on sneaking up on either of you."

"Oh," Christopher said brightly, "that wouldn't work with me anyway. I'm most dangerous up close." He eyed me. "Though I suppose you are too, Socks."

"The pasta is excellent," I said, deliberately trying to distract the clairvoyant. "Did you add any spices?"

Christopher chuckled, shaking his head. Then he took his empty plate to the sink, pausing to put a covered casserole dish in the oven and set the timer.

I had no idea if he'd been laughing at my question or something that was about to happen. I could feel the hum of his clairvoyance, simmering but not fully activated. But I wouldn't have been surprised if he was being triggered by my reactions to the sorcerer—or by the presence of the sorcerer himself.

Aiden took another bite, appearing completely unaffected by the oddness surrounding him. Though I had no idea of his background, so perhaps he'd grown up around magical pets and strange siblings.

"Shall we play twenty questions?" Aiden asked, glancing over at me with a curl of a smile. "You must have them?"

"And so must you."

"Indeed I do. But an exchange would be less … intrusive."

"Oh, yes. Let's play." Christopher hustled back to the table before I could formulate my first question for the sorcerer. He cleared a space at his end, then tugged his oracle cards out of his back pocket. "My deck."

I had commissioned a set of twenty-two botanical cards from a witch skilled in herbology months before. I'd intended them to be a birthday gift for Christopher, but had given them to him in the aftermath of finding Hannah Stewart in the woods. I had hoped at the time that they might help to settle his magic after he'd keyed into me so we could locate her. He had suffered through an onslaught of glimpses of my future for days after we'd brought Hannah out. It was just a starter set, but the clairvoyant hadn't felt the need to expand it yet.

The witch had used her knowledge of herbology to shape the discussion of what I hoped to achieve with the oracle cards, pairing certain plants with simplified tarot card intentions as a result. Christopher read the cards as his magic willed, but used the herbs and flowers alongside the cards' intentions to direct that reading. Pulling them out in front of the sorcerer was a provocative move—a deliberate flaunting and use of Christopher's power. And my stomach curdled uncomfortably at the gesture, at the direction the conversation was likely to take.

Aiden's suggestion of playing twenty questions had been meant to ease the tension, to make the sharing of information reciprocal. But there was nothing easy or playful about Christopher's cards, except for the clairvoyant himself.

Aiden's focus snagged on the deck, but his tone was casual when he spoke. "Your deck, your rules?"

"One draw per question." Christopher shuffled the deck, infusing the cards with his magic.

Aiden's shoulders stiffened. Then he relaxed, deliberately, tearing another chunk from his garlic bread and eating it.

"Seven questions, two passes per player." Christopher placed the cards in a neat stack on the table, then he sat down.

"No," I said.

Christopher lifted his gaze, meeting mine across the table. "I made you apple crisp."

I didn't answer.

Aiden glanced back and forth between us. Still chewing the last bite of his pasta, he stood, reaching over to take my empty plate. He carried it along with his own to the sink, rinsing both along with Christopher's. Then, displaying a level of domesticity I wouldn't have expected for a sorcerer who so obviously came from money, he loaded the dishes into the dishwasher.

Christopher placed his fingertips on the deck, still holding my gaze.

"No," I whispered, trying to communicate my concern without exposing Christopher in front of the sorcerer. "I … I need you here. Present."

"Let it be as it will be?" Christopher smirked. "How out of character for you, Emma."

Aiden leaned back against the end of the kitchen island, arms crossed, gaze on the table. Listening, but removing himself from the conversation, the equation.

"I never thought you'd be scared of the future." Christopher fanned the cards, their identical backs facing up. Then he ran his fingers back and forth, lifting and ruffling them prettily. A trick born more out of magic than skill.

Paisley appeared in the open doorway of the patio, eyeing the clairvoyant.

"You know I'm not. Being concerned … being protective is not the same as being scared."

Christopher shrugged his shoulders.

I gripped the edge of the table.

Paisley prowled forward, eyeing the cards as if she was thinking of eating them—her default response to tension.

Christopher dropped his gaze from mine, gathering the cards into a stack in his hand, then fanning them again, backs up. He repeated the pass, flipping the cards to display the botanical drawings, then once more with the backs facing up.

"I have no issue with being read," Aiden said, breaking the silence. "I have nothing to hide. Nothing relevant to our current situation, anyway. At least not that I remember."

Christopher's magic had suffused each of the cards. If I had been more sight sensitive, I would have seen them glowing with his white-tinted power. He gathered them together, holding them and all the magic he'd generated, captured in his right hand. "How mad are you going to be, Socks?"

"Mad."

"Mad enough to leave?"

"The room. Yes."

He laughed quietly, his power coiling around him.

I wanted to snap at him, to slap him, to say something nasty to stop him from playing around. But I couldn't bring myself to hurt him. Using his magic always had repercussions for Christopher. In the middle of a crisis or an unavoidable situation, that fallout was an acceptable cost. But deliberately casting cards, treating it like a game? That was just stupid.

There was a lot of idiocy going around today, starting with me.

Christopher held the cards toward the sorcerer. "Draw three."

Aiden stepped forward.

Swiftly standing, I shoved my chair back from the table, then had to grab it so it didn't crash into the far wall.

Aiden paused, leaning over with his hand extended and staring at me. His expression was inscrutable.

I'd moved too quickly. Too quickly for whatever type of Adept he'd assumed I was. Some sort of witch, most likely.

I set the chair down gently. Carefully and deliberately, I folded my napkin and set it to the side.

Aiden pulled a card, placing it face up on the table to expose the black-inked botanical drawing and intention.

Ginger. Manifestation.

Fear coiled in my belly.

The sorcerer regarded the ginger card for a moment. Then he looked up and locked his gaze to me as he pulled a second card from the stack in Christopher's hand. He flipped and set the second card next to the first.

I broke Aiden's gaze to glance down at the drawing and intention he'd revealed.

Rose. Partnership.

Christopher laughed quietly. Delightedly.

I pivoted, crossing out of the room, wanting to take myself out of the equation before the sorcerer could pull the third card. But avoiding Christopher's magic was impossible with his blood tattooed next to my spine.

Behind me, Aiden flipped the third card, murmuring, "Strawberry? Movement?"

"You, I believe."

"Is that why there's a box of strawberry plants outside on the railing of the loft?"

"You're quick, sorcerer."

I practically jogged the length of the hall, taking the stairs two at a time, trying to get out of earshot before—

"And ginger? Emma?"

Christopher laughed, loudly enough that I could hear it from upstairs.

I made it to my bedroom, shutting the door and leaning against it.

Ginger. Rose. Strawberry.

Christopher had pulled those three cards, three times in a row, the day I'd presented him with the oracle deck.

Something was coming.

Something had already arrived.

Christopher's sight of the future usually only manifested in glimpses of a few minutes ahead. Sometimes as far as thirty minutes out. But occasionally he saw further. He'd been working with the oracle deck for only seven months, but it was possible that it focused and magnified his power—on top of the fact that his magic had come back stronger after being so thoroughly drained by me.

In the aftermath of that draining, we had thought that we might be free of the responsibility that came with wielding such power. Well, I'd thought it. I had hoped I might be free. But Christopher believed in fate, in destiny, and he wielded his magic accordingly. Perhaps that was an easier attitude to adopt when you didn't have as many stolen lives on your tally as I did.

It was also possible that sleeping one room over from me, unshielded—that sharing space with me for the last seven years—had amplified the clairvoyant's magic.

He had obviously seen Aiden coming. At a minimum, he'd caught a glimpse of the sorcerer in the oracle cards seven months before. And he hadn't mentioned it.

I crossed to the window, gazing out into the now-dark night, exceedingly aware that I was standing over the clairvoyant and the sorcerer. Only fir flooring, timbers, and plaster stood between us.

He had thought that I would run. That was why Christopher hadn't shared the details of that first reading seven months before. But he was forcing it on me now. That realization eased the trepidation that had taken up residence in my stomach. The cards, and the future they hinted at, were about me. Not about the sorcerer then. About my choices.

Seven months ago, I would have run.

And now I was only thinking about it.

Christopher wanted to stay.

It was possible he was using the cards, and Aiden, to influence me.

I had approved the list of plants the witch had chosen to tie to the basic tarot deck when I'd commissioned the oracle cards. And each card had a wide range of interpretations, of course. In Christopher's hands, in his castings, they became tied to his magic more than anything.

But I knew what the rose card traditionally represented. What lay behind the Partnership intention carefully handprinted underneath the black-inked drawing of the flower.

Love.

Relationships.

Marriage.

I could handle lusting after the sorcerer, even if that feeling was unlike any desire I'd ever experienced before. Finding him interesting, intriguing, being drawn to him—all that I could blame on chemicals or magic.

But love? At first sight?

The idea was absurd.

Ridiculous.

Unbelievable.

I LAY AWAKE, TRACKING CHRISTOPHER'S MAGIC AS he wandered out to the garden in the moonlight, then finally came upstairs to his bedroom at the front of the house. I couldn't feel Aiden at all.

Around 2:00 A.M., I finally admitted to myself I wasn't going to fall asleep. I rolled out of bed, crossing over to the east-facing window and peering out through the curtains.

A single lamp set on the side table in the seating area illuminated the suite over the barn. The curtains were open but I couldn't see the sorcerer. He might have been on the bed, but I could see only the bottom right-hand corner, and the quilt appeared to be neatly tucked in.

Movement drew my attention down and to the right. Illuminated by only a sliver of moonlight, Aiden appeared at the base of the exterior barn stairs, jogging up. He was barefoot, wearing shorts but no T-shirt. He paused on the landing, breathing heavily and looking out across the garden. Over the strawberry plants on the railing.

He'd been running.

His lower rib cage and stomach were bandaged. The dressings were white against his darker skin, catching the soft light filtering out of the loft through the window in the door behind him.

He pivoted, sweeping his gaze over the main house, scanning the windows of the lower floor, then those above. It was too dark to clearly see his face, so I wasn't certain of his expression, but his body language appeared relaxed. Even weary.

I remained still, holding the curtains open. If the sorcerer picked up magical auras, I couldn't do anything about him spotting me gazing at him from my bedroom window, but I was otherwise standing in the dark. My heart thumped painfully. I recalled his long fingers flipping the rose card from Christopher's oracle deck. The runes he'd inked within his tan lines had been almost completely faded, likely washed off.

Aiden lifted his face to the sky, settling his feet deliberately on the painted wood deck.

The moon was just a sliver overhead. A waxing crescent.

The sorcerer swept his arms forward in what I assumed was a tai chi move. The motion was slow, labored. He was still hurt. He'd hidden it well at dinner. But then, I would have been careful to not act like prey in a greater predator's den as well.

It wasn't tai chi. Not any sequences that I recognized from my martial arts training, at least.

He took a half-step turn, executing the moves again.

Another turn.

As if he was facing the individual points on a pentagram.

If I had been closer, I would have felt the magic he stirred with each move. It would be muted, dull. Unfocused without an actual pentagram. But the sorcerer wouldn't want to waste energy on sealing or filling a barrier. He was simply gently coaxing his magic to heal, to grow.

A witch would have chosen the middle of the garden or the yard to call forth such magic, as did Christopher, because witches naturally drew energy from the earth. Some sorcerers sneered at magic that could be called forth without proper artifacts or written spells. But seeing as he was currently barefoot and choosing to stand in the filtered moonlight instead of stepping back into the suite, it was obvious Aiden wasn't one of them.

I could have crossed out of my room, slipped down the stairs, then through the kitchen. Moving silently through the dark, I could slowly climb the exterior barn stairs to the loft. Meeting his piercing, intense gaze, I could slip off my cotton nightie, then press myself against him. Running my fingers over every inch of his warm skin, slick with sweat. His muscles would flex, moving under my touch. I would match him movement for movement as he gathered his magic, ghosting each of his steps around the pentagram that existed only in his mind, my lips pressed to his neck, his shoulder, behind his ear.

I could open myself to him, fully and without hesitation, without worry. Meeting his magic with my own, filling him, giving him back everything he'd lost and more. I could make him powerful, even more than he already was. Stronger, faster. I could make him my match.

He would lift me, carry me into the loft and over to the bed with all of my limbs and magic wrapped around him. Energy would roll and spike between us as he in turn filled me, entangling our power and joining our bodies. Tasting each other, breathing the same breath, pleasure building ... cresting and —

I pushed myself away from the window, away from the sight of Aiden in the moonlight. The curtains fell into place, shuttering my view. The desire I'd allowed free rein was almost debilitating. My heart was racing, my limbs loosened, weak.

I stumbled to the bathroom, leaving the lights off so I didn't catch sight of myself in the mirror. I didn't need to see the flush I could feel on my face, neck, and chest. My nipples were almost uncomfortably hard against the soft cotton of my nightie. A heavy warmth had pooled between my legs.

I ran the cold water, wetting and pressing a hand towel to my face, neck, and upper chest. Heating the towel with my skin, then cooling it off again. Again and again. On repeat until my desire faded to a slow simmer.

I wasn't going to force myself on the sorcerer. He'd be a fool to actually say no to me, of course. As drained as he was, as possibly addicted to magic as he was.

But I didn't want to be desired for my magic. Even for a night of pleasure, I didn't want to be sought solely for my body and my power. And I most certainly didn't want to be falling for someone who would take what I had to give that way, offering nothing in return.

And what could Aiden offer me? Even if he wasn't a threat, he was unnecessary to the life I was building. He wasn't an asset in any way. He was the opposite, in fact, because he distracted me. And Christopher. He was a liability in every way.

Steadier, I returned to my room.

Paisley was stretched across my bed.

She was currently the size of a mastiff, and more than capable of getting through any door in the house, whether manually or magically locked. She glanced at me lazily over her shoulder with red-slitted eyes, daring me to kick her out.

I climbed into what little space she'd left for me, and finally fell asleep to the sound of her breathing.

FOUR

THE SPOTLESS KITCHEN SMELLED LIKE COFFEE. A quick investigation unearthed used grounds wrapped in brown paper towel in the compost bin in the fridge, but Aiden must have cleaned and put away whatever items he'd cobbled together in order to brew it.

Which didn't explain where he got the coffee in the first place. Presumably, Christopher had ordered it from our regular grocery delivery service without telling me. Another part of whatever events he'd seen around the sorcerer's arrival.

Needing to do something with my hands, I pulled butter and eggs from the fridge and set them on the kitchen island.

The sorcerer in question was out on the back patio, leaning against the post at the top of the stairs, gazing out at the grounds, and sipping from one of my stoneware mugs. The French-paned double doors were closed, and Aiden's magic was still so muted that I couldn't feel it through the glass and wood that separated us.

He looked like he belonged there—hair mussed, scruff further darkening his jawline, mug in hand.

I liked the smell of coffee in my kitchen. Far more than I would have thought, since I couldn't stand the taste of it.

Christopher appeared in the doorway to the hall, hesitating for a moment at the edge of my vision before striding in. "Breakfast?"

Ignoring him, I removed two eggs from the container, setting them in a bowl to come to room temperature, then returning the carton to the fridge.

"I'll make anything you want," he cajoled.

I pulled a chef's knife from the drawer to cut the butter.

Christopher flinched.

Ignoring his reaction—though it bothered me—I placed the butter on the cutting board, slicing it in half, rewrapping one side and returning it to the fridge.

"Emma," Christopher whispered. "The cards focus my sight, as you hoped they would. I feel no ... residual effects this morning. I was just pleased to have someone new to play with."

It was a deliberately childish statement from a twenty-eight-year-old man, meant to remind me that he lived like a hermit and hadn't had anyone—any friends but the four of us—growing up.

If the past seven years in the great wide world had taught me anything, it was that some people didn't even get that much of a childhood. And suggesting that Paisley and I weren't good enough companions was simply nasty.

Christopher sighed, rubbing his eyes. "Aiden wants to work on the fence. The new posts were delivered two days ago. I'll be in the garden."

He crossed toward the French-paned doors, yanking one open so quickly that he startled Aiden on the patio, who spun to take us both in behind him.

Apparently, the sorcerer wasn't accustomed to people sneaking up on him. So sensing magical signatures was likely an innate ability for him—an ability that was currently compromised.

But then Christopher spun back, pinning his gaze on me, angry. "You're acting like a spoiled child. Pitching a fit that she was forced to share a shiny new toy."

I looked at him. Then kept looking.

He faltered, anger draining away. "I'm ... I'm sorry. That was projection, I suppose. I'm ... you know it's me who doesn't want anything to change."

It was both of us. But change was upon us whether we wanted to accept it or not.

"And how are you going to justify your attempt to manipulate me?" I asked coolly.

Behind Christopher, Aiden frowned.

"I'm not trying to manipulate you."

"What did the cards tell you seven months ago?"

He didn't answer.

"What did they tell you last night?"

"What is the point of telling you? Outside of a battle, when did you take any direction from me?"

"From magic, you mean? Because certainly you don't think you should be able to control me."

"Don't twist my words into something they aren't."

"Then use them properly."

He clenched his fists. His magic rose, then settled. "You are impossible to talk to when you're angry."

"Stop trying to slot me into your version of the future like a card from your deck."

He laughed harshly. "If only you could be moved so easily. Maybe I'm just trying to get you to not simply tear it all down, like you destroy everything."

His words, his accusation, ripped through the calm facade I'd been holding on to fiercely. The small pottery bowl snapped in my hands, and I almost dropped the eggs it had been holding on the ground.

Christopher looked aghast, taking a step back into the house.

"Socks ... you know I didn't mean ... " He swallowed, fighting through another flush of his magic. His clairvoyance was likely giving him some hint of where this conversation was going. He stopped talking.

I carefully set the eggs on the counter, gazing down at the broken bowl in my hand and fighting back the need to throw it at him. He'd made me break something I cherished, no matter that it was silly to place any value on mere things. But the bowls, the set of pottery, was something I'd chosen for myself. Something that couldn't be replaced.

I set the two pieces of the bowl on the island. Then I stepped back and returned the eggs and butter to the fridge. Baking would have made me feel like I was at home, but I wrapped my anger around me instead.

"Oh, Emma," Christopher whispered. "Don't … "

Aiden stepped around Christopher, crossing back through the kitchen, rinsing his mug, and putting it in the dishwasher. He glanced over at Christopher, then at me. "Good morning, Emma."

A tiny soft spot opened up somewhere in the vicinity of my heart at his use of my name. I ignored it. "Good morning, Aiden."

"I noticed the fence was in need of repair last night."

"Yes."

"I'd like to focus on that for the morning."

Being physically active would be a good way to help his magic recuperate. It also put him as far away from me as possible while still remaining on the property. Which, if my magic was a lure, was also a smart choice. "Have you remembered anything about your missing three days?"

His lips twisted into a tight smile. He offered his hand to me.

I didn't take it. After the previous night, I wasn't certain it was a smart idea to touch him, unless I really needed to do so.

"Flashes," he said thoughtfully. "Black magic wielded by a witch, as you likely already expected." He paused, giving me space to comment.

I inclined my head for him to continue.

He did so, still holding his hand out for me. "Possibly the beginnings of a memory charm? Though what I was spelled to not remember, I haven't figured out. Yet. It's unlikely that such a spell will hold against the full return of my magic, though. But I've remembered nothing that tells me why I'm here." He took a step closer. "Care to verify my sincerity?"

I eyed his hand, still hanging between us, warring with my need to touch him for all the wrong reasons. "No. If you feel that fixing the fence will be helpful, then thank you."

"Call it room and board." His smile lost its edge.

I didn't reciprocate.

He cleared his throat. "But you'll have other questions."

"You'll have other questions."

He laughed quietly. "Yes. Many."

I nodded. "I'm here."

"I'll find you." Then inexplicably, Aiden reached over to collect the two pieces of broken pottery. I didn't ask him why. I didn't try to stop him. He crossed back out of the kitchen, wordlessly stepping around Christopher and down the patio steps.

Paisley appeared—she must have been sunning herself on the far side of the patio—padding after the sorcerer silently.

"I'm sorry," Christopher said.

"I'm not going to run away from whatever the cards are telling you. I'm not going to destroy everything we've built." I pinned him with a hard look. "I don't only destroy."

"I know … that was a shitty thing to say, to even suggest. It isn't even remotely true."

"It was uncalled for, and needlessly nasty."

"I'm saying sorry."

"You shouldn't need to say sorry. You shouldn't have said anything you need to feel sorry about."

"You are the only person on the face of the planet that only fights with the truth. Not all of us are capable of rising to your exacting standards."

"You were apologizing?"

He sighed harshly. "Yes, I was."

I waited.

His magic shifted, pulling his focus elsewhere for a moment. He shook it off. "It's not what the cards are telling me, but what I'm reading into them that … that … "

"I'm not going to leave you," I said, taking a guess at what was bothering him, at what his magic was whispering to him. "But if you want to go to one of the others, we can arrange that. I would never keep you here if you needed to go."

"It's not that. It's never that. If I have to pick only one of the Five, I pick you. Always and forever." He stepped forward, then faltered again. His magic rose and fell.

He was definitely struggling with something his power was showing him. Glimpses of the future, which he was trying to absorb while still continuing to converse with me in the present.

Giving both of us a moment, I pulled apple juice out of the fridge and poured myself a glass.

Christopher laughed, smiling sunnily as if we'd moved through making peace.

And maybe we had, in his head.

"Paisley would never leave you," he said. "And I'd miss her."

"Paisley is free to go with you," I said stiffly, not allowing myself to be dragged forward into his foreseen future with everything still unresolved between us in the present. "She's more attached to you, anyway."

He snorted. "Because you're so unlovable. A murderer. A force of destruction, annihilation."

I glared at him.

"Sorry," he said. Again. "I think I might be having a few different conversations at once."

I shook my head. "Go. Garden."

"Are you banishing me?"

"If that's how you want to see it, then yes."

"Such a hard-ass."

"The garden will ground your magic. Then we'll talk about your manipulations. I won't have you playing with me."

His face blanked. His magic quieted. "I would never play with you, Socks."

"You can't say you'd never do something when you've already been doing it."

He opened his mouth to protest, but I cut him off.

"Don't blame your magic. You're more than capable of channeling it properly. But you're bored with the restrictions you think I impose upon you."

"You do impose them."

"You want to use your magic wildly? You want to let it consume your mind and soul? Go to Samantha. Run wild with her." Both of us knew that the telekinetic would never say no to anything Christopher wanted. She would encourage him, use him up, in her vendetta against the Collective. And yes, I still assumed she was pursuing that vendetta even after all the years that had passed.

Christopher smiled. He had finally gotten a rise out of me.

"This is a ridiculous conversation," I said.

"It is."

"Go. Garden."

"Do I get cookies later or not?"

"I'll think about it."

He turned away.

"Does he stay?" I asked. "You read his cards last night, yes? What did they tell you?"

He paused at the doorway, not looking at me. "I don't know. The ginger card represents you, of course... a power boost, energy. An increase in potential."

"But it also represents manifestation. Action, awareness, success... "

"Love."

"Change."

"Yes. Change." He looked back at me over his shoulder. "But we're accustomed to that, Socks. Nothing is going to sneak up on us."

"But it might knock us over the heads."

He laughed as if I'd been joking.

I hadn't been.

"The sorcerer isn't here to cause you harm."

"And you?"

"Not me, either. Or Paisley. You know I would have seen it."

"In the short term."

He laughed again. "Well, no one can give you guarantees about the long term, Socks. And you've never needed it before."

He was right. I had never fretted so much about the future as I had since laying eyes on Aiden.

A KNOCK ON THE FRONT DOOR ABRUPTLY CALLED MY attention away from the grimoire I'd been working on deciphering since even before Hannah Stewart disappeared. The sorcerer-crafted spellbook was written in a customized rune-based language. But even with three additional reference texts, I'd only been able to compile a key of two dozen characters so far. And honestly, half of those were guesses based on similarities rather than perfect matches.

Ember Pine had sent me the leather-bound, magically potent grimoire when I requested information about magical transference. Then, upon realizing I couldn't read a word of it, I'd had to request her to source and send the reference texts. Which weren't particularly readable themselves, as Adepts weren't big on sharing magic outside of their covens or familial units.

Runes were not my area of expertise. Not in the least. I excelled with a sword in my hand, not a pen. And I had spent the previous two hours refusing to take the grimoire and as much of the translation as I had already cobbled together to Aiden, who was obviously well versed in rune-based spells. But asking the sorcerer to look over my work and help fill in the blanks would open up an entirely new set of questions—such as why I was interested in magical transference in the first place—and we hadn't even gotten the first set of questions answered yet. Specifically, why Aiden was in Lake Cowichan and if anyone was going to be coming to collect him.

I wasn't going to put him in a position of knowing more about me than I did about him. Adepts might be naturally secretive, but they traded in power. Especially sorcerers, since they wielded their magic through artifacts and written spells. And I wasn't going to put myself in the position of being collected or contained ever again.

Even more so because Aiden made me feel ... things.

Brushing a remembrance of the sorcerer bathed in moonlight and mostly naked aside as swiftly as it surfaced, I set the books on the coffee table. Then I was off the couch and peering out the front window quickly enough that Lani Zachary actually squeaked and jumped back from the door when she saw me.

Then she threw her head back and laughed.

Because I'd startled her? That was an odd reaction. Wasn't it?

Still chuckling, Lani held up her red toolbox and called through the window. "Will you flip her, Emma? Nose out?"

I had completely forgotten that Lani was dropping by to continue cataloging various parts for the Mustang. The first time she'd tuned the car up, she insisted it was my duty to make sure it was fully restored, with only original parts. And I hadn't been able to figure out how to demur. I had bought a vintage collectible, after all. But I had done so on a whim, because it was flashy and looked like freedom. Not because I thought it came with any responsibility. But Lani had quickly disabused me of the notion of driving the Mustang simply because I liked the way it felt, or how it handled the curves of a road.

"I'll be right out."

Still chuckling slightly to herself, Lani turned to lean against the front post, facing the front yard, the orchard, and the barn. The ex-air force tech did that often, as if she didn't like open spaces at her back.

Yet the most dangerous being in Lake Cowichan who could possibly attack Lani was currently in the house behind her. Me.

I grabbed my cardigan and the car keys. Normally I would have backed the car into the barn knowing that Lani was coming, because she preferred natural lighting if she could get it. But bringing the sorcerer home had made me forgetful. That was annoying.

I joined Lani on the patio. Her hazel-eyed gaze dropped to my bare feet with a grin, but she pushed off the post and sauntered across the yard toward the barn without a word.

The wide front doors were already open, which was typical when Christopher was gardening, so he could come and go easily.

As we drew near, a blue nose poked up from the back seat of the Mustang, sniffing the air. The nose was followed by pointed ears and sardonic black eyes.

Paisley had been sleeping in the back of the car. Exactly where she wasn't supposed to be.

"Out," I said, crossing around to hold open the driver's side door.

Paisley rose, taking her time to stretch. Then she made a production of yawning, flashing single rows of teeth for Lani's benefit.

"Don't make me repeat myself," I said.

Paisley grumbled, her look telling me she was considering walking over the trunk.

I shook my head at her. Paisley was entirely capable of keeping her claws from damaging the paint, but Lani would have a fit.

Grumbling some more, Paisley exited through the driver's side door, slinking around the side and back of the car. Then she circled around, past Lani, climbing the stairs up to the loft. Heading for Aiden's bed.

No. The bed in the suite.

It didn't belong to the sorcerer.

"Jesus," Lani said, watching Paisley. "I know I say this every time, but it bears repeating. She must have some mastiff in her bloodline."

I slid into the driver's seat and started the car, then carefully pulled it out of the barn, turned, and reversed back in. Lani propped her toolbox on the narrow workbench, heaving open the hood before I even got the car turned off. I made certain that the parking brake was fully engaged, then climbed out.

She opened the hood all the way, securing it as she propped her phone off to one side of the engine, already peeking delightedly at the mechanics arrayed before her. "I think I have a pretty comprehensive list of internals. I just wanted to double-check a few things, part numbers and such. Whoever you bought this beauty off of kept pretty good care of her."

"Okay."

"We'll also have to discuss the tires. You've been driving her for a while?"

That last part was an actual question. Lani most often spoke to herself while she was mesmerized with the Mustang's engine. I hesitated long enough in answering that she actually looked at me.

"Emma?"

"I drive … occasionally. Around the lake … and …"

Lani snorted. "I wasn't asking for an accounting of your whereabouts, Emma. You bought the car about three years ago, right?"

I nodded, feeling stupid for not understanding her initial question. I'd purchased the car on a whim, literally after cashing the cheque from my third contract job, in the fall of 2015.

"And you drove it into town?" Lani grinned. According to her, Christopher's and my arrival in Lake Cowichan had caused a bit of a stir. More so because we then hadn't left the property for three months afterward. "From?"

"From?"

"Did you get the car shipped into Vancouver?"

"No." I cleared my throat. This was regular conversation. I was acting like an idiot, but I couldn't shake the feeling, could never shake the feeling, that anything I said, anything I admitted to, would be used against me. That all of it would somehow be transmitted to the Collective. "I bought it in Southern California. We drove up and down the coast for ... a while."

"Yeah, the paint job is still practically pristine," Lani said, taking a moment to admire the Mustang. "No salt damage, so I figured you'd been in a hot climate."

"Salt?"

"You know, from the roads."

Roads weren't made out of salt.

Lani glanced at me. "Though I guess it's more chemicals than salt now, isn't it? And it didn't snow much last year."

"No." Right. They salted the roads to melt the ice and snow in the winter, to keep them clear.

"So ... " Lani typed something into her phone with her thumb. "That Aiden is hot as hell."

Completely thrown by the segue, I didn't answer. Actually, even with forewarning, I wouldn't have known how to answer. I also didn't know where Lani had picked up Aiden's name.

She flicked her gaze up to look at me, grinning. Then she returned to glancing back and forth between the engine and adding to her list on her phone. "I saw him as I drove in. Might have stopped to interrogate him. Apparently he's fixing your fence." She laughed in a way that presumably meant she was at least partly joking about the interrogation part. "He's as closemouthed as you. Though he didn't have any issue declaring his peaceful intentions." She eyed me again, tilting her head. "I figure everything must be okay. If Christopher is cool with Aiden being here."

I nodded, again not certain what parts I needed to elaborate on or lie about in order to move beyond the subject.

"Going cold turkey is tough," she said, looking at me expectantly.

I had no idea what she meant by 'going cold turkey.'

"He's gorgeous, of course. In that 'tear out your heart, hollow out your soul' sort of way. But anyone with eyes can see he's missing about twenty pounds of muscle. Possibly due to rapid weight loss. And pairing that with his appearance in the diner and your reaction, I figured... smack?"

She paused again as if I was supposed to fill in the blanks, but I had no idea what she meant by 'smack.'

"So... you're helping him detox? That's a big responsibility." She eyed me again. "I've been there, on your side and his, if either of you need to talk about it."

Right. Lani thought Aiden was a drug addict. Oddly, I was pretty certain she was right about the addict part, except the sorcerer craved magic. Power. I was also pretty certain the offer of support she'd just made was a very big deal.

"Thank you," I said.

She grinned, returning her attention to the engine and her phone in equal measure. Triple-checking her list.

"He's hot?" The question came out more tentatively than I'd planned.

Lani laughed. "Yeah. If you like that sort of thing."

"What sort of thing? The soul hollowing?"

She shook her head. "Men."

"You … don't?"

"Oh, I do. I mean, enough to appreciate it when it's all sweaty, swinging tools, and carrying around lumber right in front of me. But if we're being serious, I was holding out hope that you'd at least consider batting for the other team."

"I'm … not sure … "

She waved her hand. "No matter, I was fairly certain you were straight. And the way you looked at Aiden in the diner made that pretty obvious."

"Oh, you're gay."

"Yeah." She laughed. "Is that a news flash? Though I guess 'fluid' is a better description. And I tend to flow toward girls."

I frowned.

She barked out a laugh. "Your literal streak is a mile wide, Emma. Women. I tend to date women."

"I thought that was called … I thought that made you a lesbian."

"Right. Except I switch around."

"That's … bisexual."

"It is if it's at the same time. I tend to be attracted to one or the other in different parts of my life. Some people refer to that as phases, but 'going through a phase' is so … derogatory." She glanced at me, laughing again. "Let's just say that it depends on the person for me."

"Okay. I can understand that."

"So I can appreciate the pretty boy…man… swinging a hammer on the northeast corner of your property, or I can acknowledge that your brother looks like a Greek god, but not want to wrap my legs around either."

"I always assumed a god would be taller," I said.

Lani lost it then, actually leaning against the car as she laughed. "Jesus … he's tall enough. You're just an amazon yourself." She wiped tears from her face. "Anyway, I knew what I was getting into when I bought the mechanic shop. Small towns aren't fantastic for the sexually fluid."

"Why not?"

She shook her head at me. "You don't watch the news often, do you?"

"I watch *Downton Abbey* mostly."

"Well, there you go. There's a gay character on that show, isn't there?"

I frowned, putting together where she was trying to lead me. "Homosexuality isn't illegal in Canada."

"No, of course not. Canada is very progressive, but in a small town … it's hard to be different." She eyed me for a moment. "You already know that. But you chose to come here, settle here. Because you think this is the best place for Christopher, right? We all thought maybe you were running from someone, then Aiden shows up and everyone is ready to go mob scene on him. But before the torches and pitchforks can come out, you motor down to the station, pick him up and bring him home."

"I did do that."

"So …" Lani shrugged. "We'll be outsiders here, together. How about that?"

Not quite certain what I was being asked to agree to, I didn't answer.

She closed the hood. "You got any of that amazing fruit iced tea?"

"It might not be ready. I just started cold brewing it this morning. But I could bake some ginger snaps."

"Yeah, you could."

I gave her a look, not quite understanding her phrasing.

She dropped the grin, then nodded. "Ginger snaps and iced tea sound lovely, thank you. But I've got an engine that needs an overhaul in the shop. Another time?"

"Okay. Yes. That would be nice."

"We'll sit out back and you can dish on your Aiden. He looks like he went through hell to get to you."

I didn't nod in agreement. But I did wander back to the house to pour Lani a glass of water while she went over her list of Mustang parts and the order in which she wanted to replace them.

DEMONS AND DNA

AN EMAIL WAS SITTING IN MY INBOX FROM EMBER
Pine. The subject line read *Aiden Myers*. The lawyer
hadn't replied to my original request, but had sent a
separate email. I didn't know what that indicated, if
anything. But it made me pause for a moment, fingers hovering over the screen, before I opened it.

It contained a simple biography, with details
suggesting it had been pulled from Aiden's passport.

Aiden Myers.

DOB: June 23, 1987.

Height: 185 cm

Hair: Brown.

Eyes: Blue.

Citizenship and address on record: French; Paris,
France.

That was interesting, I hadn't picked up anything particularly 'French' about the sorcerer. I kept
reading.

The sorcerer's surname and the address on record
are likely used for mundane purposes, as I find noth-
ing to corroborate either in my quick search. This, of
course, is not unusual among the Adept, as I'm sure
you are well aware.

Yes. Even before coming into possession of my
own falsified documents, I had known that Adepts
often had an official persona with which they moved
through the mundane world, rather than using the
name they were born with.

The Myers surname does have roots in the magical
community. They are witches by blood, focusing on

delicate, precise magic, which doesn't make them particularly valued—for lack of a better way to explain it—among the more powerful witch families, such as the Camerons, Fairchilds, or Godfreys. But they do hold a seat on the witches Convocation.

It would not be completely unusual for a sorcerer to rise from a witch bloodline, but it certainly wouldn't be typical.

Well, I knew all about atypical magic, didn't I?

There is an Aiden Myers represented by the law firm of Sherwood and Pine, out of the Paris branch. Which seems to line up. But of course, his dealings with the firm would be confidential. If you need any contracts drawn up, I'd be happy to discuss the parameters with you and take them to my Paris partners. I have a few more 'feelers' out—requests for information in less easily accessible databases. But on the surface and using the name Aiden Myers, the sorcerer hasn't been involved in anything that could give me cause for concern if you wish to continue your association with him.

I laughed quietly, wondering what contracts Ember expected to draw up with a sorcerer I was thinking of 'associating with.' But the lawyer's next sentence wiped the smile from my face.

If you wish to provide me a DNA sample, I can have an analysis done, with full confidentiality, of course. If both parties agree, the Sherwood and Pine database could provide a detailed family tree, including anything of note. As well as a magical compatibility report.

Anything of note?

And... Ember could build a family tree with a DNA sample? Not only did that feel utterly intrusive, it also triggered too many unanswered questions. Including questions I'd never bothered articulating, not even to myself. Because I truly didn't care where my genetic material had been scraped together from. I was the sum of those parts, yes. But I had no desire to meet or interact with any Adept who would have willingly aided the Collective in creating me.

And a magical compatibility report? Why would... she meant...

I laughed, the sound harsh even to my own ears. Ember thought...

I was trying to figure out if I needed to kill the sorcerer, and the lawyer thought I was thinking of breeding with him. That was ridiculous on so many levels.

Yet my chest inexplicably ached as I typed my reply to Ember, thanking her and asking her to let me know if her contacts uncovered any other information she deemed pertinent. I didn't address the option of obtaining and analyzing a DNA sample, knowing that she wouldn't mention it a second time. Ember prided herself on being professional, offering her clients a wide range of services but following their directives explicitly.

I SLICED THE CHILLED GINGER SNAP COOKIE DOUGH into half-inch rounds, then pressed one side of each round in brown sugar. I carefully arranged each slice on a parchment-covered cookie sheet, sugar side up and as evenly spaced as possible.

The oven pinged behind me, alerting me that it was up to temperature.

Aiden appeared at the base of the patio stairs, glancing in through the open doors and spotting me working at the island. He slowly climbed the stairs and removed his shoes, setting them off to the side of the mat. Then he crossed through the eating area.

"Hello." I turned, sliding the tray into the oven and setting the timer.

"Hello."

The sorcerer had showered, but hadn't bothered shaving. His loose jeans were slightly short, showing off his bare ankles and feet. Given his broad shoulders, it wasn't a stretch to guess he'd recently lost weight, as Lani had indicated. I remembered the sight of him shirtless on the exterior stairs of the barn, illuminated only by a sliver of moonlight. He probably wouldn't bulk up much. His musculature would be lean, taut and—

Shutting down that line of thought harder than I'd ever had to shut anything down in my own head before, I started evenly slicing the second roll of dough, dipping and placing the rounds on the second parchment-lined cookie sheet.

Aiden placed a wooden baseball bat and a length of copper piping on the island across from me. Both appeared to have been scrubbed clean. Then he crossed around and poured himself a glass of water.

He stepped back into my view, tipping his head back as he downed it.

I wanted to wrap my hand around the back of his neck. I wanted to thread my fingers through his hair, feeling his muscles flex in response to my touch. I wanted to coax the slow simmer of his recovering magic into a full boil.

I focused instead on slicing perfectly uniform rounds of cookie dough, half an inch thick, careful to not crush the roll with my knife as the dough warmed and softened.

Aiden set the glass down, nodding toward the unbaked cookies. "I'd surmised that Christopher was the cook."

"He is."

"But you bake."

"I bake ginger snaps."

"I see. Because you want to bake ginger snaps. And how does something make it onto your list of wants, Emma?" One side of Aiden's mouth curled into a smile as he waited for me to answer.

I didn't. There was nothing more to say on the subject.

"Am I interrupting you?"

"No."

Aiden settled down on a stool at the far corner of the island, giving me as much space as he could without actually leaving the room. Though perhaps that distance was for his own benefit.

"The baseball bat?" I prompted.

"May I have it? Christopher thought it might have come with the house. I found it when I was sorting through the toolshed."

"And the copper pipe?"

"Must have been replaced when you renovated the kitchen. I'm surprised the contractor didn't salvage it. Though..." He eyed me. "I doubt you get ripped off very often, Emma."

"He never met me."

"An honest person. Excellent find."

"It's a small town."

"Yes. On the west coast of Canada."

"You're remembering more?"

"It was news to me." He smiled tightly. "My first visit."

"And you still don't remember the trip?"

"No." His tone was stiff, almost angry. But at the situation, not my questions. He raised his hand palm up and flexed his fingers. "The magic is seeping back. Slowly."

"It must be frustrating."

"It wasn't to you?"

I didn't answer.

He softened his tone, his gaze on the bat before him. "You said you knew what it was like. Outside the police precinct."

"The RCMP. The Royal Canadian Mounted Police have mundane jurisdiction here."

He nodded.

"I do know what losing your magic is like. But … " I hesitated, feeling as if I was exposing myself along with the confession. Though how it might possibly have been used against me, I didn't know. "It wasn't a burden. For me."

Aiden hummed thoughtfully. The noise did strange, gooey things to my insides. I ignored the feeling as he placed his fingertips on the bat, looking up at me questioningly.

"It's yours. And as much of the piping as you need."

"Thank you."

We stood there in silence for what seemed a long while before the oven timer went off. I checked and rotated the cookie sheet, then set the timer for another seven minutes. I leaned back against the counter, just looking at Aiden, taking him in. Trying to look beyond the fierce attraction that had permeated my every sense, trying to weigh him as he truly was. Not as some part of me apparently hoped he could be.

He sat still and silent, looking at me in turn.

"You said you aren't here to harm us. Or to bring harm to us."

"As best I know."

"That's a different way of putting it."

He looked away, gazing out at the yard. "Swift magical depletion can cause memory lapses, but … it never has for me before."

I already knew that draining someone's magic could result in temporary amnesia. Or, in my experience and under my not-so-tender touch, permanent amnesia. But it was telling that he had personal experience. "But you must know the witch who drained you?" My question was more pointed than I'd intended. It wasn't any of my business what he did, or with whom. I only needed to know if any fallout was heading our way.

His shoulders stiffened. "Yes. Of course. I don't remember the actual … final casting, but I know who was at least in the position of spelling me. What I apparently didn't know was that she wouldn't take too well to being refused."

"Most of those seeking power by any means don't."

"Are you placing me in that category? At first sight?"

I wasn't. And no, I had felt something quite different at first sight of him. The thought made me feel exposed, concerned that he could read my mind, my intentions. "I should be."

He nodded stiffly.

I looked away, checking the timer on the oven. Only two minutes had passed.

"Aiden. Did this witch send you after me, or after Christopher?"

"Not that I know of. And … " He spread his arms to the sides. "Well, I'm a little useless, aren't I? It would be a hell of a sneak attack."

Right. Except if the witch knew who I was. Unless she'd set Aiden on me intentionally, so that I'd amplify him and expose myself.

But to what end?

Setting aside all the weird reactions I was having to the sorcerer, I knew that an attack from the Collective would be more overt. If they were going to grab us, they would do so with resounding force. Because that was the only way to contain us. If we got a chance to fight, they'd have to kill us to keep us. And even after everything we'd done to them, the Collective wouldn't throw us away.

No. They would keep us, harvest our DNA, and use it to build their next generation—because we had destroyed all their research when we'd broken out of the compound. Maybe they wouldn't even kill us when they were done. Maybe they'd keep us comatose or otherwise incapacitated. Forever.

The thought made me feel utterly ill.

"Are you running from someone?" Aiden asked quietly, even gently. "Hiding? You don't seem … suited to this environment."

"No." We were, in fact, running from several someones—assuming they were still looking for us.

He narrowed his eyes. "Care to elaborate?"

"No. Do you?"

He chuckled quietly. His teeth were white against his tanned skin, just like any part of me would have been paler when held up against him, pressed against him.

His sharp gaze remained but the smile slipped from his face. "Your magic..." He hesitated. "It seethes from you when you're angry. I find myself both dreading and anticipating it exploding."

I shrugged belligerently. "I'm not angry," I said. Though it was a relief that the sorcerer read anger into what was most likely a magical reaction to my lusting after him.

He frowned, then nodded. "The cookies smell amazing."

I snorted. "Myers is a witch name, not a sorcerer."

"Yes. My mother's family. And Johnson? That surname is common among the mundanes, but not the Adept."

I didn't respond.

He tilted his head. "So I'm to answer, but you won't reciprocate?"

"What question have you actually answered?"

"Any that I'm able to."

"Is your witch going to come after you, Aiden?"

Tension ran through his jaw, but his tone was steady, dispassionate. "She's not my witch."

I curled my fingers into my palm, so that I didn't reach out to try to access his emotions, to feel what he was feeling so that I could better understand the words building up between us. I wasn't certain that I'd ever wanted to touch someone so badly before. How could someone so opaque be so compelling? Touching him would make me vulnerable on so many different levels, including opening myself up to being attacked, physically and emotionally. And then I'd have to retaliate.

So why would I crave that connection?

Aiden's gaze dropped to my hands.

I forced myself to relax them.

He shifted his eyes to the baseball bat on the counter before him. "What value do I hold to her now?"

"The magic will come back."

He ran his fingers along the length of the bat.

Something fluttered in my stomach, reacting as if he were caressing me across my most vulnerable skin. It might have been purely desire, simply lust, but I was starting to worry that it was more. And that emotion—assuming I was even capable of it—had no place in my life.

I knew nothing about Aiden. He didn't know me either. And when he did, when he knew what I was capable of doing, of being, he wouldn't want me anywhere near him. Unless he had a death wish. And given how drained he was, and the process by which that magic had been taken, maybe he did. Maybe coming home with me was just another step farther down whatever spiral of darkness he was riding.

Maybe he did see death stalking him when he looked at me. He wouldn't be wrong if he did.

But I didn't want to be that person anymore. I was fleeing that person as much as I was fleeing the Collective.

"Where did you go?" he whispered.

"What do you mean? When?"

"Just now. You went somewhere. In your head. Somewhere dark, somewhere that shutters all your light."

All my … light. Light? He saw some sort of light when he looked at me?

My heart cracked. Just a sliver, but it felt as though I were dying. I stopped myself from pressing my hand against my chest, but only barely. I managed to exhale, and the pain eased. "What do you mean?" I whispered. "My magic?"

He frowned thoughtfully. "Do you … shut it down deliberately?"

"All the time."

"So … no, not your magic. Or not the magic you intentionally wield."

The question he hadn't actually asked—specifically what kind of magic I wielded—wedged itself uncomfortably between us, adding to the pile of words building a barrier of tension in the kitchen. Words had power when they were uttered with intention by a truly powerful person. And even though no magic had passed between us, I felt the wall nonetheless.

He shook his head, glancing down at the bat again. "You don't need me here. But I'll try to be useful."

He glanced at me.

I didn't respond.

He nodded curtly. "I should be healed enough to move on in three days, maybe sooner. I can make some calls. I remember the name of my lawyer, at least. From a cellphone, of course. Christopher indicated he had one I could use that wouldn't be traced back to you. I'll have a credit card and a passport sent to me."

"Through a third party. I'll need the number and the name of your lawyer."

"Sherwood and Pine. Paris branch. They represent the Myers family."

So he was the Aiden Myers that Emma Pine had tracked down.

He straightened, collecting the bat and copper pipe. Then he paused as if expecting me to speak.

But there was nothing more to say. I would confirm with Ember that he was related to the Myers witches, then let him leave. It was best that he leave, and soon.

He nodded stiffly, then crossed toward the open patio doors.

"Will you have tea with me … us?" I had voiced the question before I'd thought it through. But the closer he'd gotten to the door, the more worried I'd become that he would leave before I could see him again, lay eyes on him again. As ridiculous as that was.

Maybe I was the one with the death wish. Or at least a desire for chaos.

He glanced back at me, smiling thinly. "I'd be delighted. What time should I return?"

"Four."

He nodded, then exited to the patio, down the stairs, and out of sight.

Watching him leave, tracking his every move, cataloging his expressions—it was all ridiculous behavior. But when he'd talked of leaving and passports, I'd felt ... faint, weak.

I didn't know what to do with that feeling, but tea and cookies always made me feel settled. So I would start with that. And another conversation. Eventually, the sorcerer would remember what had brought him to Lake Cowichan, and I'd know what action I needed to take as a result.

The timer went off. I pulled the cookies out of the oven, making sure they were perfectly brown at the edges before placing the cookie sheet on the cooling rack.

EARLY THE NEXT MORNING—STICKING TO ROUTINE as much as possible, which meant a training session—I climbed out of bed, dressed, retrieved my wooden batons, and made my way to the backyard. Once there, I stretched, then began moving, focusing on deliberately placing my bare feet in the dry grass as I shifted seamlessly from one kata to another. The forms were so ingrained, studied since childhood, that I didn't need to consciously recall them. I held a wooden baton in each hand for balance, shifting from one form to another and allowing muscle memory to propel me while I tried to not obsess about all

the unanswered questions and uncomfortable obser-
vations the sorcerer had brought with him.

Afternoon tea the previous day, and then dinner, hadn't provided any further insight into Aiden's
abrupt appearance at the diner, even though the
sorcerer's magic was slowly reasserting itself. Christopher had been polite but subdued, conversing about
his garden and plans for the property. But thankfully,
the oracle cards hadn't made a reappearance.

Ember Pine hadn't followed up on her first
email, which meant I had to assume for the moment
that Aiden was exactly who he said he was. A sorcerer who'd gotten on the wrong side of a witch.

That was an experience we shared.

I graduated into spins and kicks, picking up
speed. The long tail of my hair whipped around me
as if it were a weapon itself.

Christopher appeared before me, moving to
strike even before I'd seen him. I flung myself sideways. His practice sword brushed against my left
cheekbone.

I followed through with a right-handed strike
even while controlling my fall. But predictably, the
clairvoyant danced out of my reach. I hit the ground,
rolling back over my right shoulder, making it to
my knees, and parrying three rapid overhead strikes
from Christopher.

The key to beating a clairvoyant in a sword fight
was to not think at all. To simply react, to trust in
your training and instincts. But even knowing that,
I'd never beaten Christopher one-on-one—not once

in over twenty years of sparring with him. Simply reacting, and trusting that I wouldn't accidentally kill him, wasn't an achievable state for me. Especially not now, not outside the structured confines of the Collective, where a healer had always been on hand.

Christopher landed a hit on my left shoulder with the flat of his sword. My arm went numb, but I kept hold of the baton. I pushed forward with a flurry of strikes, slamming a kick toward his knee that actually glanced off his calf.

He laughed, skipping back, light on his feet. "There you are, Socks. I was worried you'd get stuck in your head and be boring all day."

My gaze shifted over the clairvoyant's shoulder. Aiden was seated on the patio steps with the bat across his knees and with what appeared to be a small chisel in his hand. His gaze was on me. With his magic so dim, and caught up within the tangle of my thoughts, I hadn't known the sorcerer was in the yard at all.

Christopher lunged, slipping under my belated attempt to block him and walloping me in the ribs. I took the bruising blow, absorbing it instead of spinning away. Then, still gripping the baton, I hammered a fist into the side of Christopher's head.

He dodged at the last second, but I still clipped him enough that he stumbled.

I stepped away, putting a few feet of space between us, smirking. "I thought you wanted to play?"

The white of his magic rimmed his eyes. He lunged forward.

I brought both batons up, spiraling them in a series of easy circles, countering his sequences of strikes effortlessly. Though my left arm was lagging. And as I grew more tired, Christopher would gain the advantage.

So I stepped forward instead of continuing to gradually cede ground to him, throwing him off balance. I knocked his sword away, dropping my right baton. I thrust my open palm toward his chest.

He froze in place. Shocked.

I didn't touch him, but I could have. And that would have been the end. The end of the fight, and possibly the end of Christopher if I'd so desired.

"Against the rules, Socks," he murmured.

"So is attacking when I was assessing potential threats." He'd hit me when I'd paused to look at Aiden.

He frowned, then glanced toward the sorcerer on the patio. Aiden was bent over his bat, carving and seemingly ignoring us.

"That isn't ... I knew the area was secure."

"But I didn't." I picked up my baton and walked away.

"Socks," Christopher called after me quietly.

I shook my head, jogging up the patio stairs past Aiden and into the house. I wasn't interested in playing games with the clairvoyant, or the sorcerer for that matter. And the easiest way to avoid such games was to remove myself from the field.

I TOOK A SHOWER, GLANCING OUT MY BEDROOM window while towel-drying my hair to see Jenni Raymond, out of uniform, leaning against the fence that edged the garden and chatting with Christopher.

The shapeshifter's presence was annoying but not unexpected. I'd known she'd want to check up on the sorcerer. And I could only imagine how pleased she must have been to be talking to Christopher rather than me. So I combed out my hair, slipped on a cap-sleeved blue-and-white cotton dress, and headed out to kick the shifter off my property.

She was doggedly persistent.

At the base of the stairs, I glanced through the window of the front door, spotting a red Jeep parked by the barn, rather than the RCMP cruiser Officer Raymond usually drove. I cut back through the house, feeling Aiden's simmering magic as I did so. I had missed it earlier because Christopher's magic—tied to me through the blood tattoo on my spine—overrode the muted hum of the sorcerer's slowly recharging power.

I stepped into the kitchen, finding it sorcerer-free. Aiden was on the patio now, the doors closed behind him as he crossed the yard toward the gardens.

A small stoneware bowl was sitting on the corner of the kitchen island. I slowed, staring at it. Then I crossed to the cupboards, counting two matching bowls through the glass door.

Perhaps Christopher had left a bowl on the counter for some reason?

I opened the dishwasher. The third bowl was tucked into the upper rack.

I stepped back and hovered my fingers over the bowl on the counter, wishing I was sensitive enough to magic to feel if any was emanating from the pottery.

The repaired pottery.

Drained as he was, Aiden had fixed the bowl I'd broken yesterday.

That was oddly overwhelming. Firstly, that sort of thing was witch magic, as far as I knew. Delicate, precise spell work that I wasn't even certain I completely understood. Because it definitely wasn't as simple as just magically gluing the two pieces back together.

And secondly... why? Why would a sorcerer expend magic he needed to be fortifying on something like that? Was this just part of his effort to make himself useful? Or was it a ... gift? A gift for me?

I picked up the bowl, examining it more closely. I couldn't spot even a hint of the break.

I crossed toward the door, holding the bowl. Then I remembered that Jenni Raymond was in the garden. I didn't want to be thanking the sorcerer or asking questions of him in front of the shifter.

I stepped back and nested the repaired bowl within the other two on the shelf. I closed the cupboard and gazed at my stoneware set through the glass of the door. I could have bought a set of three, since there were only three of us and the pieces had been sold individually. But I hadn't.

That was just a coincidence, of course. I didn't believe in fate or destiny. I didn't believe that some part of me, some part of my energy or soul, had anticipated Aiden's arrival.

You couldn't deal as much death as I had and believe in fate. Or love. Or fated love.

I stepped away from the cabinet and went to deal with the shapeshifter in the garden.

JENNI RAYMOND TOOK ONE LOOK AT ME STRIDING over the dried lawn toward her, blanched, and stepped away from Christopher.

"Whoa," she muttered under her breath. "Here comes big sis."

I closed the space between us. "I'm the younger one, actually."

The shifter looked startled.

Yes, my hearing was that good.

Christopher laughed quietly. "By two months."

I shrugged, keeping my gaze on the out-of-uniform RCMP officer. "What can we do for you?"

She glanced over at Aiden, who was leaning casually beside the closed garden gate. Interestingly, he had placed himself between the shifter and the clairvoyant. But whether that had been on purpose or contained a separate hidden meaning, I didn't know. Even with our short acquaintance, I did, however, understand that the sorcerer never did anything without deliberation.

Which made me feel easier about the repaired bowl. 'Call it room and board,' the sorcerer had said about mending the fence. The same likely went for the bowl. That completely rational assessment didn't feel quite right, but I went with it anyway.

"Checking to see if the sorcerer had slaughtered us all in our sleep?" I asked. "How disappointed you must be to find us all still alive."

Jenni Raymond frowned. "I wouldn't..." She glanced over at Christopher, then back at me, not quite meeting my gaze. "I wouldn't wish harm on any of you. On anyone."

I nodded, knowing I'd stepped out of line with the nasty comment—nasty even for me—but not quite certain what to do about it.

"If you need anything, just let me know," she said stiffly, glancing between the three of us.

We remained silent.

The shifter rolled her shoulders uncomfortably, then nodded. "I'll check in again."

"This is our land," I said as politely as I could. "We aren't breaking any mundane laws."

"Your existence breaks mundane laws," she snapped. Then she closed her eyes briefly, perhaps regretting the statement.

But the barb was too on the mark for me, even if she had no idea of how we'd been bred by the Collective and why. I stepped forward, already reaching for her, intending to haul her off the property myself.

"Socks," Christopher whispered.

I glanced over at the clairvoyant. His magic was shining in his eyes. The fingers of his left hand were stretched out, stiffly.

Jenni Raymond's jaw dropped. She took a step back, then another. She actually lifted her nose to the air, smelling the clairvoyant's magic before she remembered herself. She grimaced and looked over at me.

I took a breath, aware that Aiden was watching me too closely as well. Then I actively decided to leave the shifter alone.

The magic seeped out of Christopher's eyes.

"Happy?" I asked him.

"I'm trying to be," he said. "You are making it rather difficult."

"Well," I said archly. "You always know how to fix that."

He laughed quietly. "Always trying to get rid of me. Think of how boring your life would be if you succeeded."

"Yes," I said, suddenly weary of the conversation, the continual conflict. Before the sorcerer had walked into our shared life, things had been easy, peaceful between us. For months. Seven months, to be specific. "And lonely."

Surprise flitted over the clairvoyant's face, then he spoke gruffly. "Well, I'm not going anywhere." He glanced over at Jenni Raymond. "Thank you for stopping by." Then he bent down, picked up a blue harvest bin from beside his bare feet, and disappeared into the garden, completely dismissing her.

I glanced at the shifter.

She looked confused. Then, catching my gaze, she curled her lip in a snarl. "I don't get you two at all." She stomped off toward the barn and her vehicle, calling back over her shoulder, "If I were you, I'd run far and fast, sorcerer."

Aiden chuckled quietly, then he looked over at me.

"Thank you for fixing the bowl," I blurted before he could say whatever he was going to say.

"You're welcome."

"I didn't know sorcerer magic worked that way, similar to a witch's."

His lips curled into a shallow smile. "I might have picked up a few spells and adapted them."

"From your mother?"

He nodded.

I wanted to ask him more questions, about his life, his childhood. But I couldn't reciprocate like a regular person could, couldn't build relationships based on shared experiences, so I didn't.

Instead, I turned away, crossing toward the front of the house and tracking Jenni Raymond as she drove down the driveway.

As I passed him, Aiden opened his mouth, lifting one of his hands as if he was going to call me back, continue the conversation. But he didn't.

"OH," CHRISTOPHER SAID AROUND A MOUTHFUL OF stuffed peppers. "A package came for you."

Aiden glanced at me, then back at his plate. We were about halfway through eating dinner. The evening had turned chilly enough after the sun set that I'd closed one of the French doors and gone back upstairs for a heavier sweater.

"A package?" I asked. "When? From a courier? Where did you leave it?"

"About an hour ago. It was on the front mat. Paisley has it. She refused to give it to me."

The aforementioned demon dog was sitting half in the house, half on the patio, her back side facing us. She was the reason I couldn't close both doors. The sorcerer's continued presence at dinner was the reason she was sulking.

She glanced over her shoulder at Christopher, eyes glowing softly red as she pinned him with a withering look.

Aiden paused his chewing.

"It's not addressed to you," Christopher said mildly.

Paisley huffed. Then she rose to prowl around the table until she was standing between Aiden and me. The sorcerer swallowed, spearing another mouthful of ground-turkey-and-tomato-laden orange pepper while keeping an eye on the demon dog.

A tentacle uncurled from Paisley's currently invisible mane, swooping up and depositing a small brown-paper-wrapped parcel on the table next to Aiden's right forearm. Occasionally, she hid small items in her mane that way, usually cookies or the odd chicken egg she managed to steal. I wasn't sure why she didn't just eat the cookies, but I had an inkling she was trying to hatch the eggs.

The sorcerer's eyes widened, but he heroically stifled any other reaction.

I leaned over, reading the name on the package. It was addressed to Aiden Myers.

He noticed at the same time I did.

"Thank you," he murmured to Paisley, his eyes glued to the package as he set down his knife and fork.

She grumbled, then knocked against his chair with another grumble as she prowled back to the patio.

"No address," Aiden murmured.

"No postage," I said, glancing over at Christopher. "Magic?"

"No," the sorcerer said.

"Stripped." The clairvoyant took another stuffed pepper from the platter in the center of the table.

Aiden looked at him sharply.

"Stripped?" I echoed, then glanced at Aiden questioningly.

The sorcerer shook his head, hovering his fingers over the package. "Even not drained, I'm not certain I could pick up the difference between it being simply not magical in nature and having been actively stripped of magic."

I glanced over at Christopher.

He nodded.

Sensing magic wasn't an aspect of clairvoyance, but neither was Christopher's masterful touch with plants and gardening. The Five all had mixed DNA. It had been obvious for some time that Christopher's magical genetics contained DNA from at least one witch. Enough that he could even cast basic spells, and could handle more complicated magic if he was accompanied by other witches. It was highly likely that my DNA contained witch genetics as well, though I could only wield stolen magic as the original wielder had intended. I couldn't cast it myself.

Being able to tell that magic had been deliberately stripped from the package was beyond basic witch skills, though. That was something Christopher could sense only because he'd spent the first twenty-one years of his life with a nullifier.

Nul5. Fish. Now known as Daniel Jones.

Aiden frowned.

"Stripping something of magic ... " I trailed off.

"To make it untraceable." Aiden opened the brown-paper packaging with quick flicks of his dexterous fingers, revealing a plain white box. He opened the box, reached inside, and plucked out a silver band etched with runes. No, not silver. Platinum by its look.

His expression became stony as he turned the heavy ring, its runes catching the overhead light.

"Yours?" I asked, already knowing the answer.

The sorcerer slipped the ring onto his left forefinger, growling darkly. "Mine."

I glanced over at Christopher. "And you didn't pick up anything from the package?"

He shook his head.

"So the question is … was it stripped of magic so Aiden couldn't trace it? Or … " I didn't finish the thought, which was meant for Christopher anyway.

The sorcerer glanced back and forth between us. "You think someone is targeting you through me? That's—"

"Don't say impossible," Christopher said, chewing thoughtfully. "Emma doesn't like that word."

Aiden shook his head. "No. The witch is playing with me." He pushed back his chair, tugged the ring off his finger, and shoved it in his pocket. Then, though he'd eaten only half his dinner, he collected his plate, utensils, and glass, crossing into the kitchen.

Paisley appeared beside him, relieving him of the plate before he could scrape it off into the compost.

Aiden flinched, but then stifled his reaction by turning back to the table, collecting the wrapping and the box. "I'll go," he said, speaking to the table rather than Christopher or me. "I'll take care of the witch."

"Drained?" Christopher asked archly.

Aiden pushed his chair up to the table. "I won't bring trouble here."

Christopher reached out his hand, palm up. Then he wagged his fingers toward Paisley. She grumbled. But while she continued to clean up Aiden's plate, a long tentacle snaked out from her neck and deposited the clairvoyant's oracle card deck in his hand.

"And why is Paisley holding those for you?" I asked.

Christopher chuckled lightly. "I tried to trade them for Aiden's package."

"And she kept both."

"Yes." He pulled the cards from their box, shuffling them. "Trouble was here before you came, sorcerer. Magic draws magic."

"Not this magic," Aiden said stiffly, watching Christopher shuffle the cards a second time.

I returned my attention to the food growing cold on my plate. "The witch is either toying with you, or us. If it is you, then you're better off staying, recovering, than going after her."

"That is only logical," Christopher said. Then he smiled at me smugly. "And if she's coming for us?"

I met his gaze. "What do you think will happen?"

He chuckled, pulling three cards in rapid succession.

Ginger.

Rose.

Strawberry.

The same three cards.

Aiden swore softly under his breath.

I was either being dogged by destiny or Christopher was playing with me. Though I doubted whether he could move quickly enough to fool me.

And why would he deliberately pull the same three cards over and over again? To what end?

"You, Socks," Christopher said, touching the ginger Manifestation card. "I think you'll happen. And the witch won't know what hit her."

Aiden frowned, looking over at me.

But I just nodded. No witch stupid enough to toy with a sorcerer of Aiden's caliber was going to run me off my property, not even if her intended target was actually me. Not even if she brought a Collective strike team with her.

The time for running, or even contemplating running, was over.

"Socks doesn't like being played with," Christopher said, speaking to Aiden. He scooped up the three cards, twirling them before him in a brief, showy magical display.

"All right." The sorcerer straightened, staring out at the dark yard beyond the patio doors. "Okay, then." It sounded as if he was making a statement rather than agreeing to anything.

Christopher flipped a fourth card.

Lavender.

Fulfillment.

The clairvoyant tilted his head thoughtfully. Magic was glowing from his eyes. Barely discernible, to me at least, the cards were glowing as well. He reached over and spun the lavender card, watching as it slowed, then stopped, now facing me. "Unfinished business," he murmured.

"Yes," Aiden said. "I'll take care of it. I apologize for bringing this to your doorstep." He glanced at both of us.

Christopher hadn't taken his gaze off me.

The sorcerer opened his mouth, then shook his head, changing whatever he'd planned to say. "Good night."

"Good night," I said.

Aiden released his grip on the back of his chair, then wandered out into the night beyond the back patio. I tracked his magic as best I could, making a guess at when he would be out of earshot. Then I spoke to Christopher.

"The Collective?"

He shook his head. "Still no. Not that I see."

"Okay." I returned to my meal, which had cooled.

"And … " Christopher swept the four cards back into the deck and reshuffled. "If the Collective is on its way in some form, it doesn't hurt to have a sorcerer with us."

I didn't answer.

"Though of course, it would be better for him and us if he were at full power."

Again, I just continued to eat, clearing the last of the stuffed peppers from my plate. They were still tasty lukewarm.

Christopher lowered his voice. "What are the chances that he doesn't already know what you are, Emma?"

"Even if he's met other amplifiers, even if his magic has strengthened enough to pick up the tenor of my magic and match it to those in his memory—"

"He fixed the bowl, didn't he?"

Ignoring the interruption, I picked up my plate and carried it to the sink, rinsing it. Then I said quietly. "He has no idea of who I can be."

Christopher settled back in his chair, nodding thoughtfully. "And you think that would scare him off."

"If he's even interested in staying at all."

"He's interested. And not in the farm. Or me. Or Paisley."

The demon dog huffed. Christopher stood up, crossing to pet her broad, flat head. Then he leaned against the counter next to me. "Why else fix the bowl?"

"Same as the fence," I said, placing my plate in the dishwasher, then drying my hands with a tea towel. "Exercising the body and mind helps recover magic."

"The point is—"

"I get the point. You think I should offer to amplify the sorcerer. Got it."

"You could just sleep with him. That works as well, doesn't it? Or so I hear."

I pinned him with a look. "And who would you have possibly heard that from?"

Christopher sighed. "I was joking, trying to lighten the mood. The only person I know who you've slept with is Fish. And it … that doesn't happen … " He waved his hand. "When you're with him. Not involuntarily. I just assumed—"

"Stop."

"Emma … "

"Just stop talking about it. I'm not going to have sex with the sorcerer because you'd like to see him all powered up, see what he can do, what visions he would trigger."

The clairvoyant scrubbed his hand across his forehead. "Why must we always be at odds about these things?"

"One thing. We only ever fight about using our magic indiscriminately."

"That's your characterization, not mine."

"Exactly."

Christopher huffed out a laugh. "The sorcerer isn't going to get scared off. He let that witch drain him, whoever she is, didn't he? Why would it scare him that you can do the same?"

"She … " I bit off the words one at a time. "She can't kill him with a mere spell. I can. Plus … he didn't let her have his magic voluntarily."

"Ah. I see."

"And while we're on the subject … " I raised my hand, hovering it before Christopher's chest. "I scare you. I scared the other four. For good reason."

"Yes. Yet any of us would hold your hand given the chance."

I met his earnest gaze. "Only because I've been forced on you, embedded underneath your skin. Given an actual choice, any of you would walk away. Just like the sorcerer will."

"Socks…"

I shook my head, replacing the tea towel on the handle of the oven door, then turning away and leaving the rest of the cleanup for Christopher and Paisley.

"Socks," Christopher called after me.

The magic in the tattoo that bound me to him, and him to me, shifted on my spine. But I ignored that magic and the plaintive note in his voice as I moved away, down the hall, up the stairs, and into my bedroom.

Not retreating.

Not hiding.

Just resolute.

I would meet whatever 'unfinished business' was headed our way—because I had no doubt it was coming for me, not Aiden. But I would meet it on my own terms. And those terms didn't include powering up the sorcerer, whether directly, or indirectly by having sex with him. No matter how much I wanted to be in his bed.

Or even better, to invite him to mine.

FIVE

I PAUSED THREE-QUARTERS OF THE WAY UP THE IN-
terior wooden steps into what had once been the
hayloft of the barn, the light of late afternoon filtering
in through the open doors below me. A pentagram
had been painted in straight, smooth black lines over
the white-painted, slatted floorboards, about a meter
in front of the open door to the suite.

Aiden sat cross-legged in the middle of the
pentagram, hands on his knees. Eyes closed.

Meditating?

I thought at first that he was naked. He wasn't,
but the combination of the low light and his black
boxer briefs had sent my heart racing.

The baseball bat, now half covered in carved
runes, sat on the floor in front of Aiden, spanning
the base of one of the five points of the pentagram.
The sorcerer wore two copper rings on each hand,
on his forefinger and ring finger—presumably cut
and carved from the copper piping he'd found. The

polished bands were also carved with runes. He wasn't wearing the platinum ring that had been delivered in the package the night before.

I hadn't seen the sorcerer since dinner. He had already been working on the outer fences when I woke up that morning, and hadn't joined us for lunch. I checked my email three times, finding nothing further from Ember, even while working on the translation of the runed grimoire. But I couldn't focus on it enough to absorb what I was reading.

About thirty minutes previously, our regular DHL courier had driven up to the house, giving me some temporary relief from my restlessness. Though she most often dropped packages that didn't need signatures in the mailbox, she'd had two this time. One for Christopher—some rare type of garlic bulb—and one for Aiden.

I had opened the sorcerer's package, of course. Revealing a passport and a credit card, then confirming that the information on the passport matched what Ember had emailed. I'd also made note of the return address—a PO box in California—and the credit card number. I immediately emailed both pieces of information and a picture of the passport to the witch lawyer as well.

The meditating sorcerer inhaled deeply. A lazy lick of magic curled around the inner edges of the pentagram. The runes on the bat and rings glowed briefly. And every inch of Aiden's tanned skin glistened as if the light sheen of sweat coating him carried his magic as well.

It was some sort of fueling spell, for himself and for the artifacts he'd created out of wood and copper.

He exhaled. The magic contained in the pentagram ebbed.

I was staring.

I shouldn't have been staring.

I turned away as silently as possible, grimacing when the wood under my feet creaked.

"Emma?" Aiden whispered behind me, his voice deeply edged with power.

A sliver of desire ran through me—triggered just by his utterance of my name. That had to be some sort of magic, didn't it? To affect me so viscerally? I paused to absorb the feeling. I might have been caught on the stairs, staring at Aiden, but I wasn't cowardly enough to run.

Behind me, the magic sealing the pentagram died with a sharp snap. Aiden had broken the spell.

"I'm sorry," I murmured, not looking back. "I should have called up before climbing the stairs. There's a package for you." I held up the thick envelope that had been dropped off by the courier. "I opened it."

"Of course. Thank you."

As Ember had also indicated, Aiden's French passport listed Paris as his main residence. But as far as I had seen or heard, there was nothing French about the sorcerer. Most Adepts had lawyers that facilitated things for them in the mundane world, just as I did. Of course, the sorcerer could have had other reasons to be tied to Paris specifically. Relatives living there. His mother, perhaps. Even a spouse...

I tamped down on that line of thought, glancing back over my shoulder. Aiden had stepped out of the pentagram and was in the process of tugging on his jeans with his back to me. His T-shirt was still slung over a chair he'd moved from the suite into the far corner of the open loft. The baseball bat was propped against the doorframe leading to the bedroom.

I climbed the last few stairs, again aware that I was staring at him, watching the muscles shift across his back, but not wanting to look away.

"I'll paint over the pentagram before I go." He spoke without looking back at me, buttoning his jeans.

"Of course."

"I went through three parties with the courier, as you requested. The delivery shouldn't tie me to the property or the town. Other than at your end." He smiled tightly. "And the locals already know I'm here."

"They are annoyingly observant."

He laughed quietly, grabbing his T-shirt and stepping forward into the low light filtering in through the upper windows. He had removed his bandages, revealing three ragged claw marks across his abdomen. The wound was still an angry deep red.

My mind blanked, all desire washed away as a hit of adrenaline numbed me through and through.

I had seen wounds like that before.

I saw the reminder of those claw strikes every time I happened to catch sight of myself in the bathroom mirror, stepping into or out of the shower.

My scars—currently hidden underneath my cotton sundress—were little more than a twist of flesh now. Three ridges slightly darker than my skin, running from my lower left ribs, across my belly, and ending near my right pelvis.

Aiden's scars, once healed, would match mine.

Matching scars.

The sorcerer had gone still, wary. The T-shirt was still bunched in one of his hands, his other hand slightly raised toward me. "Emma?"

He thought I was going to attack him.

I dropped the manila envelope, and it tumbled down the stairs behind me. But with my gaze still riveted to Aiden's wound, I stepped forward, unbuttoning my dress from just below my bra to the top of my lace-edged underwear.

Thinking that maybe I was misremembering, maybe I was projecting, I glanced down at the seven-year-old wound on my own stomach. A wound that had never wholly disappeared, even though my skin was smooth, unmarked by any other magical assault I'd endured. My healing abilities had been stolen from so many different Adepts over so many years, I couldn't remember the exact number anymore. And I'd never known their names.

I glanced back and forth from the wounds on Aiden to my scars. The angular form of the three slashes was definitely the same—thicker where the initial strike had penetrated the skin, then thinning to narrow points.

Aiden took a step toward me, drawing my attention to his face. His blue eyes were brilliant even in the low light, but I couldn't read his expression.

Another wave of adrenaline washed down my spine as I realized that I'd exposed myself to him without preamble, without saying a word or asking permission. I found my voice. "You were attacked by a greater demon?"

Shaking his head, Aiden took another step toward me without otherwise answering, his gaze flicking between my scars and my face. Then three more slow, measured steps, as if he was afraid I'd move against him. Then, inexplicably, he kneeled before me.

I swayed back, instinctively releasing my hold on the fabric of my dress to free my hands. The buttons clacked softly together, once.

"I asked you a question. You were attacked by a demon?"

"I … I must have been," he whispered. "I thought it was a shapeshifter when I first saw the marks, but … the shape of the wounds was wrong. Only three strikes. And once I could feel it again, the residual magic felt wrong, off. Even drained, I should be healing quicker. A demon … a demon would make more sense. And that gives some credence to the memory charm."

"If the witch summoned a demon, she wouldn't want you to know? Why? Trade secrets?"

He shook his head once, attempting but failing to smile. He glanced up to meet my gaze, then stilled.

I didn't step away.

Silence stretched between us, filled with all the filtered noises of the old barn, the chickens in the yard, the breeze, and the whisper of our combined breath.

Moving deliberately slowly, Aiden raised one hand, then the other. Snagging the edges of my dress, he widened the opening again. He didn't touch me, but I could feel the heat of his skin, the light shimmer of his magic within reach.

"It can't be," he murmured. His breath brushed my belly.

Inhaling, I contracted the muscles of my abdomen, but then forced myself to remain still. I desperately wanted to touch him, to run my hands through his hair.

"How old is this wound?" he asked.

"Seven years."

"Seven years," he repeated. "Yet the width of the strike is almost identical. So your wound was ... deeper. No one could walk away from a wound like this."

It wasn't a question, but I answered anyway. "I didn't."

He chuckled quietly. The noise somehow curled in my belly, beyond the scar that his attention was riveted on, blooming in a flush of warmth, urging me to invite the sorcerer to run his fingers where his eyes already rested.

Aiden looked up at me, blue eyes locking to mine, a question in his piercing gaze. But he didn't vocalize it, so I didn't answer.

We hovered there, eyes locked and with him holding open my dress. Not touching, but close enough to feel his magic. And even as tightly as I held onto my own power, I didn't doubt he could feel it as well.

I forced my attention away from the desire pooling heavily in my lower stomach. "Did you see the demon?"

"Not that I remember."

"And the witch?"

"Magenta." He laughed harshly. "Her I remember all too well."

"No last name?"

He twisted his lips. "You know how witches are. Go black, and they disown you."

"What are the chances that the ability to summon certain demons is passed down through families?"

He frowned. "Might be."

"Anything else you remember of the attack that left you with that wound?"

"No … not yet. I woke up on the side of the road. Then I instinctively followed your magical signature to the diner. I didn't even notice the bandages until I showered here."

"No pain."

"Mundane drugs, I assume. Given my depleted magic, a spell wouldn't have held as well. They wore off."

Heavy painkillers certainly would have added to his disorientation upon finding me in the diner. More questions flitted through my mind, but none of them were anchored strongly enough to actually be articulated. Not with him less than an inch away from me.

I toed off my sneakers, suddenly wanting to be barefoot.

A smile softened his intense expression. Again, I stopped myself from touching him, skin to skin, in order to solve the mystery of what he was feeling, if not thinking. I had never thought that using my empathy would be, could be intrusive. That it could rush, maybe even crush, the moment that was building between us. Ruin the anticipation, force the … climax.

I answered his smile with a curl of my lips.

Aiden's grin sharpened, becoming slightly edged. Holding my gaze, he ran the folded edge of my dress between the fingers of both hands. Then, painstakingly slowly, he began unbuttoning the rest of the dress until it hung all the way open from just below my breasts.

He gathered the fabric behind me in one hand, so that my entire midriff and legs were exposed. I was idiotically pleased that I was wearing pretty, light-pink lace panties.

Aiden shifted his attention back to my scars, his whisper warm across my skin. "Did you vanquish your demon, Emma?"

"No."

"And the witch who summoned it?"

"Her I crushed."

"I don't doubt it."

He hovered the fingertips of his free hand over the scars, tracing over them as close as he could without actually touching me, high to low.

"Aiden," I murmured, aching with my need to grab him, to shove him back on the floor and have my way with him. Instead, I gently brushed my fingers through the hair at his temples. It was thick and silky.

"Emma."

Magic, energy, heat shifted between us, slipping up and across from where we were barely touching each other, riding the licks of desire spreading through me.

Aiden loosened his hold on my dress, so that it fell around me again. Then he settled a hand on my right hip, with only the fabric of the dress between us. He ghosted his fingers over my scars again, achingly slowly, leaving a hum of his magic in his wake.

"Aiden ... " I breathed his name, swaying toward him, twisting his hair in my fingers, then immediately loosening my hold.

"Emma." He wasn't smiling now, yet there was laughter in his voice. No, not laughter. Anticipation. A hunger. But there was nothing dark about it.

In a moment, I was going to tug him to his feet and plaster myself against him. In a moment, he was going to slip his hands up my thighs, hook his long, dexterous fingers around the sides of my underwear, and tug it off me.

But sex with me wasn't—couldn't be—that easy. Sex with me was complicated. For multiple reasons. He'd already been assaulted and drained of his magic without consent. I couldn't move forward while he was ignorant of my own magic.

"Aiden." I touched his shoulder lightly, drawing his focus up to me.

"Emma," he said, grinning, thinking we were still just murmuring each other's names back and forth. Claiming each other.

I laughed. "No. I am … I'm an amplifier."

He grunted in acknowledgment, as if the revelation didn't change anything that was about to happen between us. "I know. Hence the no touching until invited."

I laughed. Unbuttoning my dress had been a pretty wide-open invitation, even if I hadn't intended it that way at the time. "How long have you known?"

"Since Christopher flipped the ginger card."

I sighed. Three days had passed since then. The sorcerer was not stupid.

"Admittedly, my understanding of herbology is rusty. But paired with your … demeanor, the connection to you was fairly obvious."

"Demeanor?"

"You don't touch. Anyone. Not even Paisley."

"I pet Paisley!"

He gazed up at me, deliberately and gently pressing his entire hand over my stomach. Three of his fingers aligned with the scars, the warmth of his hand making the rest of my skin feel cold. "I don't want your magic, Emma."

A hint of his lust, his anticipation, flowed through my latent empathy, filtered through skin-to-skin contact.

My heart rate ratcheted up. I took a breath, just watching him, feeling his skin on mine, his magic dancing underneath his fingers. He was maybe at quarter strength. "It's not only that. I don't just amplify … "

He waited, not moving his hand. Just kneeling before me, patient and steady.

I struggled with the next part. The further explanation of what amplification meant when wielded by me. Then I decided to set that issue aside for the moment. I wasn't going to accidentally drain his magic while having sex, which was where I assumed we were going despite all the conversational interruptions. The amplification continually seeped, especially if I was touching someone skin-to-skin or while I was sleeping. But draining someone's magic was deliberate and intentional.

"The truth seeking?" he asked teasingly.

"Empathy."

He frowned. "Paired with the … " He smoothed his expression and didn't finish the question. Boosting someone's magic and reading their emotions were completely different abilities. It was true that touch- or mind-based magic—amplification, telepathy, empathy—could appear in the same bloodlines, and witches often wielded similar power with the help of spells and charms. But a typical amplifier could amplify other magic and nothing else. A typical empath could only read emotions, though the more powerful ones didn't need to touch their subjects, as I did.

I understood there was occasionally some minor magical crossover, such as Aiden being able to cast spells learned from his mother to fix the bowl. Or a witch being able to wield an object of power, or to cast using runes as a sorcerer did.

Aiden cleared his throat as if carefully considering his next question. Then he grinned up at me as if something had just occurred to him. "Does it go both ways?"

He couldn't mean the amplification. There was no way he could have figured that out. "Does what go both ways?"

"The empathy." He slid his hand over my hip, pressing into the small of my back. "Can you project as well as pick up emotions?"

He pressed a kiss to the tip of the scar nearest my lower ribs, instantly stoking a hot flood of desire that had seemingly been simmering while it waited for his touch. I swayed forward, threading both my hands through his thick hair.

"No projecting," I said.

"Well, that is terribly disappointing."

"You are not remotely disappointed."

He laughed, delighting in being read. "You've got me figured out, oh empath."

I laughed. Then I stepped away.

He instantly let me go, swaying forward.

I took a step to the side, turning around as I undid the final few buttons on my dress, exposing my bra.

Aiden remained on his knees, a lusty grin lighting up his eyes as he watched me slowly prowl backward toward the suite, toward the bed situated within.

Then a distressed male voice ripped through the playful magic that had been building between the sorcerer and me. "Socks…"

I went still.

"Socks!"

Christopher. His voice was full of the thunder of his magic—a thunder I hadn't heard so intensely in years.

Christopher. In pain. In the grip of a vision.

I ran for the stairs, brushing past Aiden as he stood.

I jumped off the top landing without even thinking of the display I was putting on for the sorcerer. A feat of strength that revealed in an instant that I was more than just an amplifier with latent empathy.

I landed hard on the cement floor of the garage section of the barn, running past the Mustang and out into the yard. Momentarily blinded by the setting sun, I blinked my eyes.

Christopher stood about three meters beyond the open doors. He was unsteady on his feet, white magic ringing his light-gray eyes.

He took me in, sweeping his gaze upward from my bare feet to my face. Taking in my open dress, and all my bare skin underneath. He looked over my shoulder, his expression distraught, likely spotting Aiden as he scrambled down the stairs behind me.

"Oh, God. Oh, God. I'm so, so sorry, Socks. I—" He choked on whatever he was trying to say, straining his head back. Magic flooded from him, blazing from his eyes.

He reached out for me, fingers splayed, falling to his knees in the gravel.

I lunged forward, not thinking. My fingers brushed his before I remembered I shouldn't, couldn't touch him.

I froze, my outstretched arms mimicking his. Aiden, still shirtless, slipped by me, kneeling and wrapping his hands around Christopher's forearms. The naturally tanned skin of both of them, deepened from time spent in the sun, was closer in tone than I would have thought, though the clairvoyant's complexion was darker.

"No!" I cried.

Ignoring me, Christopher gripped Aiden back.

I stood, simply shocked that the sorcerer would touch a clairvoyant in the middle of an intense vision.

"It's okay, Emma," Aiden murmured. "My magic is too dim to change what he's seeing, not once he's in a full-blown episode."

Christopher pinned the sorcerer with his intense white gaze. "Aiden Myers. The last son of Azar."

Azar.

Azar …

Christopher's words ran through me like an ice-cold knife, washing away all my lingering desire.

I'd been all kinds of a fool. The feeling of having always known the sorcerer, the matching scars …

He was somehow related to Kader Azar. The sorcerer Azar. Who the Five had rescued in Los Angeles over seven years before. Azar of the Collective.

"I hear you, oh clairvoyant," Aiden said, his smooth, cultured tone underlaid with stress.

Azar. Azar. Azar. This was all about the Collective. Even if there'd been no way to have known for certain, even if Christopher hadn't seen the Collective coming, I was such an idiot. I wanted to shriek, to scream, to demand all the answers I hadn't even known I needed a moment before. But now wasn't the time, not with whatever was manifesting for the clairvoyant.

Now was the time to be rational and ready.

Christopher shook his head almost harshly, as if shaking off the vision. His magic receded to a simmer.

He loosened his grip on the sorcerer's forearms, then clapped him on the shoulder. "Have no fear, sorcerer. You've got Socks between you and disembowelment. For now."

Aiden frowned, opening his mouth to protest.

Christopher turned his gaze on me. "You're going to need your blades."

"Are the blades magic?" Aiden asked, clearly confused and trying to piece clues together.

Christopher snorted. "Socks is magic. But the blades help her decapitate things."

I hadn't needed to wield my blades in seven years. "And when will I be needing to decapitate things?"

"Now."

I ran. Leaving Christopher and Aiden behind me and swiftly buttoning my dress as I did so. I leaped onto the front patio and burst through the front door without closing it behind me.

I shoved away my questions about Aiden's connections to the sorcerer Azar, focusing on the immediate. I always functioned better in the present. Cooler, connected.

I could interrogate the sorcerer after I faced whatever future Christopher had seen.

THE BLADES WERE IN A BOX UNDER MY BED. HASTILY braiding my hair, I grabbed a T-shirt out of the pile of laundry on top of the bed, still warm where

Christopher must have dumped it just before the vision hit. I pulled the T-shirt on over my sundress, leaving my hair tucked within so it hopefully wouldn't hinder me in whatever was coming. Whatever demanded the reappearance of my blades in the glimpse of the future Christopher had just seen.

I kneeled, pulling the long wooden box out, then placing it on top of the bed, next to the laundry. I flipped back the lid, revealing the black, nonreflective, double-edged eighteen-inch blades within. The three raw gemstones embedded in each hilt were dull—drained of the spells that had once enhanced the weapons. But the blades were still perfectly suited to me, the right balance, size, and weight for simultaneous wielding.

Catching the murmur of voices from out back, I grabbed the hilts without further preamble. The weight of the blades was slightly heavier than I recalled. I made a note to start working with heftier practice dowels.

Instead of crossing through the house and doubling back through the kitchen or around the outside, I slipped out onto the narrow balcony off the bedroom. The sun had set, kissing the horizon. I jumped up onto the white-painted railing, looking out across the property. All was still before me. No breeze, no unusual noises. No magic other than Christopher and Aiden below, and Paisley skulking in the shadows along the garden fence. There was no foreign power that was close enough for me to feel, at least.

I jumped off the railing, dropping straight down onto the brown grass at the base of the kitchen patio stairs.

Aiden, behind me on the patio, muttered some sort of curse at my abrupt appearance. Another arcane word, perhaps. Thankfully, it didn't carry any magic. I hated getting hit with friendly fire.

Assuming the sorcerer actually was friendly.

Assuming I hadn't been royally hoodwinked. Though I'd never yet met anyone who could truly lie to me, foiling my empathy.

But this life was full of firsts, for good and bad.

I turned to look at the sorcerer. The lights of the kitchen behind him cast his face in shadow. He had the baseball bat settled over his right shoulder, the carved runes along its length glowing a soft, deep blue.

A slow grin spread over his face. His teeth were a white flash against the ever-deepening dark. "This was where you wanted me, yes? At your side in a fight?"

If Aiden was going to hurt us, if he had come to hurt us, Christopher would have picked it up by now. I answered his smile with one of my own.

Christopher stepped out from the kitchen, laughing huskily.

"Where are they coming from?" I asked. "These things I'm supposed to be decapitating?"

"Right in front of you, Socks. You won't be able to miss."

I strode forward, barefoot in the dry grass, pausing about five meters out from the house. Paisley slipped out of the shadows along the edge of the garden to my left.

"Come to play, have you?" I asked, lazily warming up my arms and wrists.

I glanced back at Christopher and Aiden. They'd stepped off the patio, following me a few steps onto the grass.

Aiden lifted his baseball bat, holding it by the base with the tip pointed down. He slammed it onto the ground, muttering an arcane word in a language I once again didn't understand. Though it sounded vaguely Arabic, it might well have been a tongue that only his family spoke, commanding their magic with it, passing it down from generation to generation.

The Azar family. Not the Myers. Because the Azars were the sorcerers. Witches didn't carve runes into bats and copper rings.

Magic shot out from Aiden's bat, etching a bright-blue pentagram across the grass. The energy Aiden had collected with the baseball bat drained from about half of the runes carved into it.

He stepped to the side, gesturing Christopher toward the pentagram. The clairvoyant laughed, but he stepped over the fiery blue lines and into the center. He hadn't armed himself.

Then Aiden repeated the process of calling a pentagram forth, completely draining the bat's reserves. He stepped within the second defensive ward.

A prickling sensation ran up my arms. A dark energy slithered up my spine. Magic that was incompatible with the natural power held within the earth itself.

I turned my attention back to the horizon, already knowing what I'd be facing.

Demons.

The vestiges of the red-orange sunset began to fade from the sky.

"Tell me what you see, Knox." The blood tattoo on my T3 vertebra—my connection to Christopher—tingled. Then it triggered at my request.

SIX

"THREE STRIKER DEMONS." CHRISTOPHER'S VOICE rang out clear and strong behind me, filling the early evening with his magic as he fell into a shorthand we'd developed over many years and many fields of battle. Still, I knew that if the other three had been with us, we would have quashed the summoning of the demons before the witch—Magenta, Aiden had named her—had even pulled the first of those creatures through to our dimension.

That was the threat we were facing, assuming I was putting the pieces of the puzzle together correctly.

"Striker?" Aiden asked. "What classification is that?"

"Placement on the field of engagement," I said, glancing back over my shoulder. "Meant to cut through the line of skirmish." In this case, I was that line. Placed in a defensive mode rather than hunting down the summoner, because I had Christopher and a home to protect. "The summoner is far enough off site that I can't sense her magic at all."

"The first wave is backed by enforcer demons." Christopher's eyes were the full-blown white of his magic, not a hint of iris remaining.

"Enforcers for what?"

"A snatcher."

"Teleportation?"

"Yes."

Damn.

"I'm not following," Aiden said. A hint of a frustrated growl threaded through his words.

Christopher laughed. "Keep thee in your pentagram, sorcerer Azar."

"Sorcerer Azar is my father," Aiden said stiffly. His face was shadowed, his expression inscrutable. "Or if he's dead, my eldest half-brother."

My heart grew heavy in my chest—which was an annoying reaction, especially since I'd already known Aiden was connected to one of the members of the Collective. "Kader Azar?"

"Have you met?"

"Once."

"I'm surprised he let you go, with magic like yours. Though perhaps you were a little young, even for him."

"My leaving wasn't his choice."

Aiden frowned. Given his tone and the comment about his half-brother—and his claiming to not know if his father was even alive—it was obvious that he and Kader Azar were estranged. That certainly lined up with the fact that he used his mother's family surname. Unfortunately, tone could be faked even more easily than a passport.

My empathy worked only with skin-to-skin contact, and touching the sorcerer had a way of confusing the situation more than it clarified it. But I simply didn't believe that Aiden was lying. And if the sorcerer, the demons, or the black witch were directly connected to the Collective, Christopher would have seen some hint of that in his visions.

The clairvoyant was casting his gaze over the backyard now, murmuring quietly under his breath. Running the vision through in his mind over and over, and reminding me that I had more immediate concerns.

"Who is the snatcher coming to grab?" I asked Christopher. "You?"

The clairvoyant glanced toward Aiden.

So not the Collective. Not yet, at least. "Apparently, someone has gone to a lot of trouble to collect you, sorcerer," I said wryly. "Would you like to go?"

Aiden shook his head, tension radiating through his shoulders and stiff back. "No."

"Well, then, I shall do my best to foil the attempt to kidnap you."

"I doubt you ever do less than your best, Emma," Aiden said. "But the house should be warded. Even better, the entire property."

Christopher laughed. It was a clear, bright sound, filled with the joy of using his magic unfettered. "Socks is the wards."

Leaving the conversation behind me, I started walking toward the demon horde I could now feel coming through the back field. The cleared section of our property stretched all the way to the forested edge that bordered the north side of Cowichan Lake. So thankfully, none of our neighbors stood between us and the demons about to pay us a visit.

Aiden was about to see me. See who I really was. That idea equally thrilled and terrified me. Because if the sorcerer was stupid enough to not run when faced with me—the real, whole me—then I might have no choice but to invite him to stay. And not just for a quick tumble in his bed. Whether or not he'd been born or even raised as an Azar. After all, there wasn't anything any of us could do about our parentage or DNA.

Yes, we were the sum total of our parts. But I firmly believed it was what we chose to do with our talents that made us who we were. I knew who I wanted to be, and who I avoided being. I was just presently stuck somewhere in the middle of those two, stuck between Amp5 and Emma Johnson.

But both those halves were the same in one fundamental way. They would do whatever was necessary when there was no other way forward.

"First three, coming right down the middle," Christopher called out. "Triangle formation … "

Holding my blades at my sides, I stepped twice to my left, centering myself in the yard.

Just slightly ahead of me and to my left, Paisley snorted, pawing the ground. Her magic bristled over her, writhing pulses of energy. Her head and shoulders expanded, bulking up. As she slammed her front feet into the ground, a set of long sickle claws burst from her flesh, gouging the brown grass. A mane of tentacles crackling with dark energy sprang up all around her head and shoulders. She opened her now-massive maw, displaying her double rows of two-inch-long teeth. Then she roared.

Her challenge faded into the darkness.

"Holy shit," Aiden whispered behind me.

Three inky-scaled monsters tore out of the night in tight formation, barreling straight for me. Sleek, elongated heads. Blood-red eyes—two sets, one facing forward and one to either side. Powerful back legs and slimmer, taloned front legs.

I'd seen this type of demon before. I'd slaughtered their kin by the dozen, also called forth by a black witch. She had wronged the Collective in some fashion and been put down by the Five as punishment. I'd been nineteen or twenty at the time.

"Their claws are wickedly sharp," I said to Paisley. "Don't let them bite you. They deliver a wallop of venom, and—"

Paisley gathered her legs under her. She was the size of a massive lion now, easily two hundred kilos. Leaping into the fray, she took out the lead demon, she and the creature rolling across the yard in a tangle of claws and teeth.

That left two for me.

I lunged forward, my blades aimed for their chests. The demons avoided me, separating, then attempting to strike me from the front with their tails and at the sides with their claws.

I jumped the dual tail strikes, tucking my knees as I flipped and twisted. The demons spun to engage me. I struck downward with my blades while still in the air, landing facing the house. I'd skewered one demon in the shoulder and the other in the back of its head.

"Right," Christopher barked.

I released my hold on my left blade, leaving it embedded in the demon's head. I spun right. Its claws scored my back as it fell forward, shuddering and dying.

My other blade was still stuck in the other demon's shoulder. I swung underneath its claw strikes, using the blade to jump up on its back. I braced my feet on its shoulders, needing leverage to get my weapon out of its black carapace. It leaped upward, flipping forward with the intent of crushing me under it when it landed.

I abandoned the second blade, leaping from the back of the demon and landing next to the creature I'd already taken down. I yanked my first blade out of its head, dropping under a vicious strike just in time to skewer the second demon through its neck and up into its brain.

"Behind you," Christopher shouted. "Three ... "

I wrenched my second blade out of the demon's shoulder, decapitating it along with the one at my feet for good measure. They began to crumble into ash.

"Two ... "

I jogged back to my first position, facing the dark sky again. Off to my left, Paisley was snarling and batting her fallen prey around.

"Stop playing with your food," I said without heat.

"One."

Two beaked, black-scaled enforcer demons dove out of the night on dark wings.

That was unexpected.

The first caught me around one shoulder with a taloned claw, lifting me off my feet as I tried to gut it. Its acidic blood splashed over my arm and up the side of my neck, searing my skin.

It dropped me, crashing to the ground behind me. Not dead, but incapacitated enough that I could leave it for a moment.

I charged back into the fray, both blades in play.

Paisley sank her teeth into the neck of the second winged demon. Together, they spun away, clawing at each other with their back feet.

A third enforcer landed on taloned claws before me, wings spread as if hiding something behind it. I spun, striking at its webbed wings in rapid succession, severing multiple tendons. It slashed at me with its beak, missing my shoulder and then my face by only inches.

Through its shredded wings, I got a look at the demon that lurked in wait just behind the third enforcer—a thick-skinned black creature so smooth and sleek that it blended almost perfectly into the night.

The snatcher.

The winged enforcer clamped onto my shoulder with a taloned front arm that I hadn't seen folded under one wing. I struck at its neck and chest while it held me fast, battering me with its wounded wings and trying to peck out my eyes.

I was too near, too close to my target. My blades couldn't penetrate its flesh deeply enough without being able to put my full body weight behind the strikes. So I brought the blades together, lopping off the taloned claw the demon held me with.

"Right leg," Christopher called.

I slammed a kick to its right leg, throwing it off balance. It clamped my already wounded shoulder in its beak, but struggled to gain leverage with both its right wing and leg compromised. I brought both blades forward, thrusting upward under its beak, then decapitating it.

The demon fell.

Leaving me facing off against the snatcher.

A teleporter. According to Christopher's vision.

It craned its long, sleek head toward me, regarding me with four sets of glowing red eyes, all front facing.

Paisley landed next to me on all fours, hitting the ground so hard that she actually jostled me.

The snatcher whipped its tail forward in a lazy strike, testing the distance between us. Then it raised itself up to its full three-meter height, clicking its long front claws, four on each front leg. It also had two thickly curved talons on each of its back feet, meant for gutting its prey.

"Mine," I murmured to Paisley.

Magic shimmered across the snatcher's chest, drawing my attention. It had a phrase seared across its smooth carapace—*The Last Son of Azar.*

That wasn't overly dramatic at all.

It was an easy guess that that was where Christopher had picked up the sorcerer's lineage in his vision. But I knew that the demon must have been more than simply branded in order to be directed and controlled so specifically. The others had been aimed at a named target, but the snatcher would be under a compulsion to return that target to its summoner. Because when they weren't tightly controlled, demons slaughtered everything in their paths.

In order for the demon to be controlled in such a way, the snatcher would have been called forth and bound with something intimately tied to Aiden. Something that held his magic. But hair, skin, or saliva wouldn't have held enough energy for a binding of this magnitude. This level of summoning would need blood.

Or semen.

The snatcher demon disappeared.

I brought my swords up in a crossed block, scanning the yard.

"Right!" Christopher roared.

I stepped right. But not far or fast enough. The snatcher appeared behind me, clipping me on my already wounded shoulder and sending me flying. I lost hold of my blades.

Paisley attacked the demon.

I hit the ground, tumbling uncontrollably until my back slammed up against one of the fence posts edging the garden.

My shoulder screamed with pain, my arm hanging limp. I stumbled to my feet, feeling Aiden trying to call forth magic, but spell after spell failed to catch. He'd put too much into casting the barrier spells of the pentagrams.

Paisley and the demon tore at each other.

I took a few running steps, then stumbled. I fell to my knees, then made it to my feet again.

The demon disappeared.

I ran, scooping up one blade with my good arm, leaving the second in the dead grass.

The demon appeared and slammed into Paisley's back, riding her down to the ground. Her neck was tight in its maw.

Paisley shrieked. The demon clamped down hard. A killing strike.

"Jump!" Christopher shouted.

I raised my blade, leaping up.

Slow, too slow.

Out of shape, out of practice.

I slammed into the demon instead of landing fully on its back. But I still managed to skewer it near its upper spinal ridge—and to hang on.

It released Paisley.

Then its tail struck me over and over again as its claws tore at any part of me it could reach, trying to rip me from its back. I held on, yanking the blade free. Using my still-wounded arm, I double-fisted the hilt of the weapon and struck at the back of the demon's neck.

It stumbled.

Magic gripped me. A darkness compressed me, squeezing my head, my lungs. The demon was trying to teleport.

I screamed as I stabbed it again. And again.

The darkness shifted around us.

I couldn't breathe, couldn't think.

All I could do was pull my blade out of its flesh and stab it over and over. Its blood seared my thighs, my hands, speckling my face with fiery motes of pain.

I lost hold of my weapon.

I lost hold of myself, falling.

Falling.

Then hitting the ground.

Stars appeared overhead.

I sat up, trembling from a terrible chill. The brightly lit house swam into view. It was much, much farther away than it had been a moment ago.

The snatcher slammed to the ground beside me, my blade sticking out of its head. I rolled over, reclaiming the weapon. My shaking abated as I gripped its hilt.

Paisley limped out of the darkness. She grumbled at me, then proceeded to tear the snatcher demon apart. Each piece that she gouged and spat out crumbled into ash. Apparently, the snatcher wasn't good enough to eat.

I made it to my knees, then my feet, forcing myself to cross the lawn, to return to the house. I didn't know if more demons were coming.

"Socks," Christopher murmured, shocked when he spotted me. He was still in his pentagram, still safe. I could see Aiden standing motionless from the corner of my eye, but didn't look at him.

I retrieved my second blade, taking a moment to glance down at myself. My T-shirt and sundress were ruined, torn and bloody. Both of my arms were burned. My face and neck felt the same.

I turned to scan the yard, carefully rotating my wounded arm, stretching and keeping the tendons loose as my magic caught up to healing my shoulder.

Paisley romped around us, trampling each disintegrating demon corpse in turn.

The burns on my arms, neck, and face faded to a dull ache. Energy flooded through my limbs, healing me with magic I'd stolen and claimed for myself so long ago that I couldn't remember who I'd drained it from anymore. Couldn't remember if any of those Adepts, all forced on me by the Collective, had died under my touch.

"Is that all you've got?!" I cried into the dark night. Then I laughed, loud and clear, reveling in the destruction I had just wrought. My soul forever tainted with all the darkness I'd consumed, whether by command or simply to survive.

Christopher chuckled behind me.

I turned, finally looking back at Aiden.

He swept an inscrutable gaze over me, head to toe, then back up again.

Yes. I was more than simply an amplifier.

"Those blades need sharpening," Christopher said, scrubbing his foot across the edge of the penta-gram seared into the grass and effortlessly breaking the seal.

Aiden frowned.

And yes. Christopher wasn't just a regular clair-voyant either.

"Were you being blocked?" I asked. Even with all the directions he had called out to me, Chris-topher had been unusually quiet during the skirmish.

He shook his head. "Not specifically. Demons are always difficult to read. The snatcher more so."

"It was passing in and out of dimensions," Aiden said, stepping out of his own pentagram, though he didn't power it down. "I thought … it was carrying you with it, Emma?"

"Yes."

He nodded, but then didn't vocalize whatever else he'd wanted to say.

"Socks is difficult to kill," Christopher said.

Aiden grunted.

"We need to figure out a way for you to practice," I said. "If we're up against a summoner. The winged enforcers were particularly nasty. Maybe with Paisley attacking me?"

Christopher shook his head, his tone remote. "I know her too well. And so do you."

"How do you know you aren't simply telling Emma what she's already going to do?" Aiden said, thoughtful. "If you see the immediate future? How do you know you won't distract her at the wrong time?"

Christopher eyed Aiden coolly. "You'd prefer that Emma get hurt? More than she was already?" He walked away, crossing through the crumbling remains of the demons toward the garden.

"He didn't," I said, watching the clairvoyant and speaking without thinking. "Once. As an exercise. He wrote down what he saw instead. I didn't move where he would have moved me. It took me a week to walk again, even with the best healers money and influence can buy."

I was watching Christopher as he inspected his garden fence for damage—specifically at the spot I'd crashed into. But at Aiden's continued silence,

I glanced over to find the sorcerer staring at me intently.

"Under whose supervision?" His tone was rough, and heavy with some emotion I couldn't quite identify.

I had said too much. Exposing the tender parts of my past, along with Christopher's. Something about the sorcerer loosened my tongue. As well as other parts of my anatomy.

I stepped away, climbing up the patio stairs and through the open French-paned doors into the kitchen.

Aiden swore under his breath, then called after me, "Thank you."

I glanced back at him. My heart thumped once, painfully, at the sight of him through the open doorway, bathed in the soft light filtering out from the kitchen.

"You assume all of this is meant just for you." I wrestled with my reaction to his … beauty? Charisma? "And it might be just the witch playing with you. But based on the unfinished business Christopher has seen in his cards … I think maybe you've gotten tangled up with someone who's decided to strike at us, coming through you."

"Never … " Aiden's voice was husky with the same darkly tinted emotion. "I would never bring harm to you if I could help it."

"We'll know either way soon enough."

"I'll reach out tomorrow, make my … position clear. I shouldn't have delayed. I shouldn't have stayed. I just … " He cast his gaze around the kitchen, not finishing his thought.

Giving him space to assess the situation for a moment, I turned to the sink to clean my blades. The ash was easily brushed away, but Christopher was right. I needed them sharpened. I just didn't wield the magic necessary to do so myself.

Maybe the past few days had all been about Aiden rejecting the witch, and I was just paranoid. But no matter how personally beguiling I found the sorcerer, I was having a difficult time believing that any witch would risk the ramifications of such a sum-moning—the power drain, the chances of having the demons turn against her, or drawing the atten-tion of the powers that governed magic in the Adept world—just because he'd spurned her.

But then, I didn't understand people or relation-ships terribly well.

Stepping through the patio doors, Christopher slipped past Aiden and crossed into the kitchen. He pulled a foil-covered casserole dish out of the fridge, placing it on the counter beside the stove and pre-heating the oven. "Put this in for thirty minutes covered, then thirty minutes uncovered."

"Where are you going for an hour?"

"It probably won't be an hour. But I need to feed Paisley."

We kept a supply of raw meat in the fridge in the barn for Paisley. Normally, she fed herself. Eating dinner with us was just a fun game. But Christopher meant she needed live prey. To heal properly.

"I can do it," I said.

He sniffed at me. "You stink of demon. And your clothing is about to fall off you." A grin flashed across his face. "Though the sorcerer would certainly like that show."

"Where are you going to take her?"

"She wants a cow."

Paisley didn't actually talk. But as far as I had deduced over seven years, if she thought about what she wanted long enough, Christopher eventually picked it up in a vision. "Do you have the money?"

He nodded. The Wilsons, our neighbors to the west, owned cows.

"You'll shadow her?" I definitely didn't want the demon dog's evening cow hunt to draw attention. "And double-check that the demons didn't stray off course?"

"They didn't. The witch obviously had them tightly bound. Plus, you would have felt it."

"You would have seen it. But you'll do a circuit anyway?"

He nodded. "And I'll leave money in the mailbox for the cow."

A full-grown cow was expensive. "She earned it," I whispered, fairly certain that the snatcher demon had come close to killing Paisley. We had no real way to train her for such confrontations, not until they happened. Paisley had gone up against demons only once before, when she and Christopher had rescued me from the contract job in San Francisco. The sorcerers attempting to hold me had thrown their entire magical arsenal at us, including a few summoned pets. We had chopped through them all, taking the summoners' heads when the demons were vanquished.

Christopher swiftly crossed through the back patio doors and into the yard.

Aiden crossed paths with the clairvoyant, setting his baseball bat on the kitchen island and staring down at it. Its carved runes were devoid of magic now.

I poured two glasses of water, sliding one across the quartz counter toward Aiden. He reached for it.

I snagged his wrist, holding him tightly enough that he'd know it would be difficult to break my grasp, but not hard enough to hurt him.

He lifted his piercing blue eyes to meet my gaze, a curl of a smile softening his grim expression.

My heart pitter-pattered. I ignored it. The situation had moved way beyond what I could justify simply because I desired him sexually.

His smile faded, but he didn't try to pull away.

"Azar," I said. Magic prickled under my hold, my empathy triggering some reaction from his dim power. "That's something you might have mentioned."

"Myers," he said mildly. He felt tired, drained. As expected. But also frustrated. Confused. "There was no way for me to know that my parentage might be important to you. Or why you think it's even relevant right now." He paused, evidently waiting for me to fill in the blanks for him.

I didn't.

He huffed, his exasperation clear even without my feeling it through our empathic connection. "The witch … Magenta has nothing to do with my father. He made it very clear that I wasn't worthy of being his son, many years ago." He waved his free hand, though his piercing gaze remained glued to me. "The demons, the games, are beneath him. If he wanted me, he'd come himself. He wouldn't lower himself to acting through a witch."

I nodded, trying to align Aiden's version of his father with what little I'd gleaned of Kader Azar myself. "You took your mother's name? At birth?"

"No. I chose to, myself. A few years ago." Nothing felt devious in his answers. Though I wasn't overly skilled at using my empathy—I rarely chose to touch anyone, for obvious reasons—it usually detected lies reliably.

"Emma Johnson."

"Yes."

"Were you so named by your parents?"

"No. My passport."

He nodded, as if he'd already expected that answer. "Christopher calls you Socks. Only using the name Emma when he remembers to do so. So the nickname is older than the passport."

"Yes."

He twisted his hand in my grip gently.

I loosened my hold.

He slipped his forefinger and middle finger across my inner wrist, so that he was holding me as much as I was holding him. Our arms stretched across the kitchen island, hovering above the counter.

"Are you sure the empathy doesn't go both ways?" he murmured, his gaze locked to mine.

A flush of desire curled within me. My own. But I could feel his steady resolve under his weariness, and his ... ease.

"It doesn't," I said.

His lips curled. "Have you practiced? You've obviously trained with the swords. That was masterful dual wielding. A skill it not only takes years to perfect, but you need the magical fortitude to back it."

"Either that or having both swords in hand from a very young age."

"How young, Emma?"

I didn't answer. I wanted to withdraw my hand. But I had questions of my own that still needed to be asked.

"Did your father send you here?"

"No. I haven't seen him in over five years."

"What do you know of the Collective?"

He tilted his head. "Nothing. Not by name." That was the truth as far as I could tell. "Is that what you're researching?"

He meant the grimoire. "No."

The oven pinged, proclaiming itself to be up to temperature. I tugged my hand away from Aiden. He tightened his grip, then let me go. But not before I caught a flush of frustration through the empathic connection.

I put the casserole in the oven.

"When did you meet the mighty sorcerer Kader Azar?" he asked, sarcasm laced through his words.

I turned to look at him, to watch his reaction. "Seven years ago. I rescued him. He'd been kidnapped."

Aiden laughed. "I doubt that anyone would be capable of doing so."

"Yet I pulled him from a building, fought my way through dozens of shapeshifters, and buckled him into a helicopter."

He frowned. "You're a mercenary? For hire? Since your early twenties?"

I wasn't. "Is that difficult to believe?"

"Not at all. You're obviously so much more than an amplifier with a secondary touch of empathy. But … " He waved his hand offishly. "I would have heard of you, of someone of your power."

I didn't know how to respond to that statement, so I didn't.

He dropped his gaze to the baseball bat on the island, running his fingers along it thoughtfully.

A comfortable silence stretched through the kitchen, almost as if it was carried by magic. I wanted to linger within it. Instead, I remembered to set the timer on the oven for thirty minutes, then crossed toward the hall. Christopher was right. I desperately needed a shower. The conversation could be continued over dinner.

"I was useless out there tonight," Aiden said, not looking at me.

I paused in the doorway to the hall. "The pentagrams would have held, had I been overwhelmed."

He laughed harshly. "I doubt it. And it's becoming obvious that the clairvoyant didn't need my protection either. Though I didn't think it possible for someone to see their own future."

"He doesn't. But he sees mine, and…we're tightly bound enough that it allows him to understand his portion of that future. He usually arms himself, if I'm going to have trouble."

Aiden nodded, falling silent.

I turned away.

"Shall I come with you?" he asked archly.

I glanced back at him.

His lips stretched into a tight smile that wasn't reflected in any other part of his expression. "To the shower."

"Payment for services rendered?" I asked mockingly.

His shoulders stiffened, but he tilted his head casually. "If you wish."

"And the witch? The summoner? Magenta. Is that how you paid her?"

He didn't answer.

"The snatcher had to be bound with blood … or semen." I let the statement fall softly between us.

"And there are only a few spells that drain magic as thoroughly as yours has been drained."

"Are you accusing me of being a whore, Emma?"

"No, Aiden Azar Myers." I deliberately combined his chosen name with his father's surname in order to emphasize my point.

He frowned darkly.

"I'm accusing you of being power hungry," I continued. "And willing to do whatever it takes to insinuate yourself with an Adept of power."

"Such as yourself."

"Well, I imagine you would have deemed Christopher more difficult to seduce."

He clenched his hands, then deliberately relaxed them, spreading them across the smooth quartz counter. His voice was low and deadly when he spoke, sending tiny shivers of desire through me. "You were the one who came up to the loft, Emma."

"Yes."

He gave me a look that indicated he required more of an answer than that.

I ignored it. I had no idea why I was accusing him of anything. Or why his sexual connection to the black witch who had used him bothered me.

"Magenta has nothing to do with us, Emma," he said. "And when I've healed, I'll deal with her. Then I'll come back and prove it to you."

"If I invite you back. You did just cause a lot of damage to Christopher's garden. And we're going to owe the neighbor a cow."

He laughed, seemingly surprised that he did so.

I turned away before the conversation took another turn.

"So…" he called after me, teasing now. "Still a no on the shower, then?"

From halfway up the stairs, I laughed. "Take the foil off the casserole if the timer goes off before I'm done. And put it back in for another thirty minutes. Please."

He laughed quietly to himself.

I hustled to my bedroom, grabbing clothing and actually internally debating inviting him into the shower with me. I had no idea what that would be like—not only being intimate with someone enough to stand naked with them, but also being able to simply accept them for who they were in the present moment.

To disregard what had brought Aiden into my life and simply accept that he was now part of that life seemed irrational. But didn't I want to be accepted on the same level? Hadn't I wanted him to see me vanquish the demons, and still want me? Didn't I want him to know all about my past and to not care about any of it because he wanted me in the present?

Me.

Not my magic.

Not Amp5.

Me.

Emma Johnson.

I was more than simply a name on a passport now.

I climbed into the shower alone. Any decision about being intimate with the sorcerer was about more than sharing a bed, sharing a shower. Being intimate with me meant sharing magic. And though he hadn't admitted it outright, Aiden was interested in accumulating power. Maybe even addicted to it.

I didn't want to be anyone's addiction. But I was actually starting to realize that I was becoming open to the concept of building something, building a life with someone of my choosing. A choice in partners.

Except that choice, that intimacy, that trust, would have to go both ways—and I didn't think Aiden Azar Myers was capable of such things. Just as I didn't think I was truly capable of it. So that left us with me in the shower, him in the kitchen, and our pasts firmly wedged between us.

BEFORE I WENT DOWN TO DINNER, WHICH SMELLED incredible wafting up the stairs, I emailed Aiden's full familial connections to Ember Pine. It felt under-handed to do so for some reason, but I didn't doubt that the sorcerer had sought out the same information on me and Christopher when he requested a passport and credit card from his own lawyer.

He, of course, wouldn't have dug up more than our passport information—the same level of detail that Ember's first inquiries had gotten on him. But I already knew that attaching the Azar name to Aiden would garner many more details.

My chest still felt heavy after I hit send, though. Regular people learned about each other in the present, didn't they? That was the natural state of things.

I combed out my wet hair and reminded myself that there was nothing natural about me, and that I had Christopher, Paisley, and even the other three to protect. The regular way of doing things wasn't an option.

SEVEN

A SHAPESHIFTER WAS IN MY HOUSE. I HAD ROLLED off the bed and taken three steps to the door before I recognized the weak tenor of her magic.

Constable Jenni Raymond.

In my kitchen, as far as I could sense.

Paisley let out a teeth-rattling snore, then rolled to take over my side of the bed. I'd slept heavily enough that I hadn't felt her climb onto the bed without an invitation—a liberty I offered her only occasionally. Being near me for long periods of time had magical consequences. My amplification power leaked when I slept. The Collective had tracked my output while sleeping for years, inducing dreams, then nightmares, to see if that increased the volume of energy.

It did.

But I couldn't remember dreaming anything the previous night.

Exchanging bodily fluids with me had simi-lar consequences, though what those consequences might be was more theoretical. The Collective hadn't ordered me to have sex with anyone in order to track the results. Actually, they had actively discouraged fraternization among the Five. And the seven years I'd been out of their reach but still running hadn't been conducive to forming any relationships, with mundanes or Adepts.

I couldn't begrudge Paisley crawling into bed with me, though. It had been years since we'd exerted ourselves as we had the previous night. In fact, taking down those demons was the most vicious skirmish she had ever faced.

Unless she was a secret demon hunter. But I doubted that was the case, or the neighbors would have complained by now about all the missing cows.

I laughed quietly.

Paisley cracked one red-hued eye, huffing at me indignantly.

"We have company," I said. "And since when are you allowed on the bed?"

She snorted, then tucked my abandoned pillow under her head as she burrowed deeper under the sheets and the rose-patterned quilt. The metal bed frame creaked.

I shook my head, pulling a freshly ironed dress out of my closet and pairing it with a green cardigan that Hannah Stewart had said made my eyes glow. It was possible that the thrift-store owner occasion-ally caught glimpses of magic, just as it was possible that Aiden did. And I found, despite all my half-articulated resolutions to the contrary, that I wanted to look nice for the sorcerer.

Seven years into my life as Emma Johnson, and I could still discover new things about myself.

JENNI RAYMOND WAS PERCHED ON A STOOL WITH her elbows on the kitchen island, a steaming mug of coffee in hand, and her gaze on the sorcerer leaning next to the sink.

She wasn't in uniform.

Her dark-brown hair was free from its usual bun, tousled around her neck and just brushing her shoulders. Her feet were bare, pink-painted toes curled around the metal cross brace of the stool. She was wearing an oversized white T-shirt over jeans.

A men's T-shirt.

Aiden, also barefoot and wearing the charcoal henley again, was smiling thinly at something she was saying, sipping from his mug. He had obviously made coffee. Again. But this time, for the shapeshifter as well.

She had spent the night. Some portion of it, at least.

My stomach bottomed out, souring.

Aiden glanced over at me, his smile widening.

I'd been hovering in the doorway like an interloper. In my own house. A slow simmer of anger replaced the hollow in my stomach.

Jenni Raymond followed Aiden's gaze, spotting me and stiffening her spine.

Honestly, I'd never met such a useless Adept. She should have heard me coming down the stairs. I forced myself to be polite. "Good morning."

"Oh, hey, Emma." Jenni's tone was edged with a false cheer. "We were just discussing last night."

I leveled a gaze at the sorcerer.

His smile gave way to a furrow of his brow. Then he glanced over at Jenni and his expression shuttered.

I stepped onto the tile, reclaiming my kitchen for myself as I crossed toward the fridge.

Jenni's expression turned wary. Her shoulders remained stiff.

I grabbed the apple juice, stepping back to close the door after setting the jug on the island.

Aiden reached up over his shoulder, opening the glassed cupboard behind him to reveal my four crystal water glasses. I reached past him, taking a glass.

He leaned almost imperceptibly into my space, and I paused to meet his soul-piercing gaze.

"You look lovely this morning," he murmured.

I narrowed my eyes at him, but found it increasingly difficult to hold on to my anger at having my home invaded.

A smile ghosted over his face as Aiden settled his gaze back on his mug, taking a deliberate sip of coffee—as if he knew how enamored I was by the way the muscles in his neck shifted and moved when he did so.

I carried the glass over to the island, pouring myself some apple juice, then leaning back on the opposite side of the sink from Aiden, sipping.

"What about last night?" I asked calmly.

Jenni Raymond's light-brown gaze flicked between me and Aiden. Both of us remained silent as we sipped our drinks.

"I was on duty last night when the Wilsons heard a roar and then a kerfuffle in their back field."

Paisley.

Jenni Raymond set her mug on the island. "They called it in, thinking it was a cougar snatching one of their calves."

"But none of the calves are missing," I said. Not quite a question.

"No. But the envelope in the mailbox with the cash in it, indicating that a cow had been taken, was a dead giveaway. I presume the Wilsons will find the cash and get a head count of the herd this morning. Then they'll call the station with an update."

"But you think you've already put it together, do you?" I asked coolly. "Did you actually use your nose, shifter?"

Jenni Raymond stood up abruptly, knocking her stool over behind her.

Aiden set his coffee mug down on the counter beside the sink.

I didn't bother freeing my hands up. I could take the shifter without spilling a drop of juice. And I made certain she knew that every time I looked at her. "I hope you haven't chipped my tile or dented my stool. In my home. Into which you were not invited."

Jenni Raymond lifted her chin defiantly. "I was invited. By Christopher. It's his house too."

I glanced over at Aiden. He dipped his chin in a shallow nod.

I laughed harshly. "Caught him in the act, did you? Depositing the cash in the mailbox?"

There was no way she'd snuck up on the clairvoyant. Meaning he must have revealed himself to her for some reason. I'd thought she was wearing Aiden's T-shirt, which was actually Christopher's, of course. My initial assessment of the tableau waiting for me in the kitchen had been emotionally tainted. That slip in perspective was another reason that having the sorcerer around was dangerous.

The shifter had slept over. Just down the hall from me, I presumed. With Christopher, not Aiden. Her already dim magic would have been easily overridden by the clairvoyant's constantly simmering power. And I had slept heavily.

I stalked forward, topping up my glass of juice with slow deliberation. "So not only did you not actually use your nose to solve the supposed crime, you screwed the suspect."

"It's hardly a crime if you pay for it. There was fifteen hundred dollars and an apology in that envelope. I checked."

"Oh, you checked?" I laughed. "As part of your investigation? Or was that the precursor to the sex?"

She snarled. "Why the hell do you hate me so much?"

I shrugged. "You're an unnecessary complication in our lives. A complication that, given your early-morning appearance in our kitchen, has now turned into a liability. Denying your magic doesn't make you strong, Jenni Raymond. It weakens you. And any weakness that can be used against you can now be used against us. Against Christopher. If someone tries to come for us, they'll use you, then roll right over you."

Jenni clenched and unclenched her hands. Then she shook her head defiantly. "That just sounds like a shitload of garbage. If I didn't know better, I'd think you were acting like a jealous bitch. You're Christopher's sister, not his keeper."

"Actually," Christopher drawled, "Emma is my keeper." His voice pulled my attention to the doorway to the hall, where the clairvoyant stood in a navy-blue T-shirt and dark-washed jeans. "The brother-and-sister designations just make our relationship more … relatable for others." He padded across the tile over to me, barefoot as always, stealing my glass and draining the remaining juice.

Jenni Raymond watched him, a confused twist of emotions playing over her face.

Christopher refilled the glass, passing it back to me and crossing around to set the empty pitcher in the sink. "Good morning, Aiden."

"Christopher."

"Scrambled or fried?"

Aiden inclined his head toward me. "Emma? Eggs?"

"Soft boiled," I said. "Lightly salted and peppered, over tomato slices."

"Oh!" Christopher moved toward the fridge. "Maybe I should give that cheese sauce another try, with less flour in the roux."

Jenni Raymond picked up the stool, checking it for damage and setting it down at the island. She glanced toward the front of the house as if thinking of leaving. Then she reached for her mug and took a sip of her coffee.

She was staying.

That was interesting.

"How's Paisley?" Christopher asked, stepping around me as he grabbed ingredients and kitchen implements.

"Snoring."

He laughed. "Yes, I heard." He glanced at me sideways, giving me an opening to mention anything about what I might have also heard last night.

I checked his eyes, finding no magic simmering within them. He looked relaxed, present. Christopher didn't take sexual partners often. And like me, he rarely selected one from the pool of the magically inclined. Still, I was exceedingly surprised that he'd chosen Jenni Raymond. For multiple reasons.

"What can I do to help with breakfast?" Aiden asked.

"Toast," Christopher said. "Melissa left a sourdough of some sort in the stand yesterday. Rye, maybe."

I stepped to the side, clearing the kitchen for Christopher and Aiden. It was none of my business who either of them slept with. Christopher's flings rarely lasted more than a couple of days. But if Jenni Raymond was going to start making regular appearances in my kitchen, I definitely wanted some ground rules in place.

A conversation for later.

I opted to set the table with napkins and cutlery instead. The shifter settled back down on a stool.

Then Christopher's head suddenly snapped up, his magic flaring. The white cheddar he'd been grating tumbled from his hands.

Aiden caught it before it hit the ground.

I took a step back, then to the side, moving away from the magic that felt as though it was questing across the kitchen toward me.

"What the hell?" Jenni Raymond muttered.

His back stiff, Christopher slowly pivoted his head to look at me. The white of his magic ebbed, so that it only ringed his light-gray eyes. He smiled. "Fish."

"What?" Jenni asked.

Aiden held his hand up to silence her, his attention trained on me. She shut her mouth, but she clearly didn't like having been ordered around.

"Do I need my blades?" I asked calmly, though my insides were churning.

Christopher laughed, magic heavy in his voice. "Soon and always, Socks. But not this morning."

The magic of the blood tattoo on my spine shifted, tingling as if waking up. I reached back over my shoulder, pressing my fingers to the tattoo on my T1 vertebra—Nul5's blood, anchoring his magic to me. A tattoo that had been dormant for over seven years.

"It can't be a coincidence," I murmured.

"Of course not." Christopher laughed, his tone still remote, speaking into the future. "Have you been trying to convince yourself of that, Socks? Nothing is a coincidence. We take each step, endlessly moving to where we were always going."

He walked away, heading for the front door.

I rested my gaze on Aiden, suddenly achingly sorry for everything I thought we might have been building between us. Everything that was about to be torn down before it was strong enough to survive the revelations of my past.

"I'm sorry," I whispered.

Aiden frowned questioningly.

"What the hell is going on?" Jenni asked.

"I suggest you use the back door, shifter," I said, not taking my gaze from Aiden.

"Like hell I will," she snarled, standing up and following Christopher. "I'm not here by your leave."

I laughed a little shakily.

The shifter exited into the hall.

"I gather she isn't going to like whoever is about to come through the front door," Aiden said.

"I don't know, actually. I don't know him at all. Not anymore."

"Am I going to need my bat?"

I sighed. "It wouldn't work against him."

"A bat can be a very effective weapon, magic or no magic."

I laughed in spite of myself.

I heard Christopher fling open the front door, banging it hard against the stopper. Footsteps sounded on the patio, then laughter and back slapping.

I glanced over at Aiden. "I need you at the far side of the counter, please."

He stepped back, placing the long length of the island's quartz counter between him and the doorway—and tugging a chef's knife off the cutting board across with him, so that it lay within easy reach.

I stepped around the other side of the counter, situating myself directly in line with the front door. Still laughing, Christopher wandered toward me down the length of the fir-floored corridor with his arm slung across the broad shoulders of a dark-haired man. The newcomer was dressed in dark jeans and a leather jacket that I didn't doubt came with a motorcycle. One he'd most likely parked by the road, so that he could cross onto the property undetected. At least until my blood tattoo had alerted me that he was near, just as his tattoo would have picked up the presence of my magic.

Daniel Jones.

Fish.

A nullifier.

One of the Five.

Daniel laid his light-brown-eyed gaze on me. He'd kept his hair cropped short. And he had bulked up, as men apparently did in their late twenties. The smile faded from his face. His gaze flicked over my shoulder and to the left, taking in Aiden, then settling back on me. His features had broadened as well, leaving only a hint of whatever Asian heritage came with the genetic composition the Collective had used to cook the nullifier up.

My chest tightened at that thought.

Daniel dropped his arm from Christopher, stepping to the side.

Jenni Raymond hovered in the background behind the two reunited men, completely forgotten.

"Are we going to fight, Amp5?" Daniel asked mockingly.

"No," Christopher moaned, pained.

I stalked forward, my anger at having my home invaded by a shifter completely stoked by Daniel's appearance. He wasn't supposed to be anywhere near either me or Christopher. His presence—and specifically, having all three of us in one place—was capable of drawing way too much attention.

I smiled, feeling the false expression taking over my face as I lifted my arms to the sides, offering an embrace.

Daniel fell for it, stepping forward.

I wrapped my hand around the back of his neck, fingers over the blood tattoo that bound him to me. I yanked him against me, pressing my lips to his ear.

He gripped my shoulders harshly.

"Please, no," Christopher whispered.

"You want Amp5?" I snarled, low and fierce, for Daniel's ears only. "You've got her."

He twisted, spinning and slamming me back against the wall. His magic spread down from where he gripped my arms, numbing me.

"Fuck!" Jenni shouted, darting around Christopher. He grabbed her arm and held her back.

I reached for the nullifier's power, gathering it swiftly under the fingers I still held against his tattoo.

Daniel gasped, shuddering. He released my arms, holding his hands out to the sides.

I held his magic at the back of his neck but stopped gathering it. The power that fueled the nullifier was as heavy and thick as it had ever been. Maybe even more so.

I met his fierce gaze. "You shouldn't be here," I said. "You put Christopher in jeopardy by being here. I won't have it."

"Always so cautious," he murmured, his gaze falling to my mouth. "So careful." He grinned deviously. "Until pushed."

He grabbed my face, slamming a harsh kiss against my mouth. I bit him, catching his lower lip.

He snarled, half laughing, half pained.

I released his lip, kneeing him between the legs instead.

He stumbled, groaning.

I stomped on his foot, smashing an open palm across his ear.

Daniel fell, holding his genitals.

I snarled down at him. "You don't have permission to touch me."

Christopher stepped in between us. "Please, please, Socks."

"I'm not the one who attacked first."

Daniel rolled over onto his back and started laughing. "You did, actually."

Christopher glared down at him. "She didn't. We don't use those names in this house, in this life." He stalked off toward Jenni Raymond, who was still hovering in the doorway. Then he escorted her out of the kitchen and through the front door.

Daniel remained sprawled at my feet, gazing up at me. "So you missed me then, Socks?"

I stepped around him, crossing back into the kitchen so that the width of the island was between us. For the nullifier's protection, not my own. I was having a difficult time reining in my anger.

Daniel laughed, rolling into a crouch and eyeing Aiden.

The sorcerer's gaze was inscrutable. He hadn't moved from where I'd asked him to stand.

"And you did give me permission, Socks." Daniel straightened, his gaze still on Aiden, not me. "Many times. Over and over again. To touch you."

"No," I said. "Each time was an individual agreement."

He nodded sagely. "I see. Well, then, I'll wait with bated breath for my next invitation."

Christopher strolled back into the kitchen, grinning at all of us as if Daniel and I hadn't just been tussling. "Eggs?"

"I like mine hard boiled," Daniel said, settling down on the stool Jenni Raymond had just vacated.

Christopher started bustling around the kitchen, making breakfast. But I didn't bother stepping out of his way this time.

"Why are you here?" I asked.

Daniel glanced over at Aiden, sneering. "You've got a witch sniffing around. But I have a feeling you already knew that."

Aiden stretched his hand across the island to-ward Daniel. A move that placed the chef's knife just under his elbow. "Aiden Myers."

Offering to shake the hand of an unknown Adept was a completely ballsy move, even if Aiden's magic wasn't still partially drained. I squashed the smile that rose at the sorcerer's display of daring, tilting my chin into my chest.

Then I noticed that Aiden had inked a rune, in blood, on the blade of the knife. Sneaky.

Daniel gripped Aiden's hand. "Daniel Jones. Your reputation precedes you."

Aiden dropped the handshake. "Yours doesn't."

"Well, we like to keep it that way. Don't we, Emma?" Daniel's use of my name was pointed, deliberate.

"Yes," I said agreeably. "Which is why you're leaving. Now."

"I've invited him to stay," Christopher said quietly, setting a pot of water to boil on the stove.

Completely displeased but uncertain what to do about it, I looked at all three of them, one at a time. Then I turned and left the kitchen.

"She hasn't changed a bit," Daniel murmured behind me as I climbed the stairs to my bedroom.

"Look closer," Christopher said.

CHRISTOPHER FOUND ME WATCHING AN EPISODE OF *Downton Abbey* in my sitting room. He brought soft-boiled eggs smothered in cheese sauce, along with two wedges of sourdough and rye toast, glistening with butter and still warm. We finished the episode together in silence, Christopher on the floor with his back resting against the couch.

Paisley pushed open the door, wandered in, and collapsed over Christopher's feet.

We stayed that way for a while, willfully suspended in that moment as if the large blank spot—Daniel's nullifying magic—that I could feel in the kitchen wasn't a relentless reminder of our past, of everything we'd run from.

Aiden had crossed out of the house only moments after I'd settled down enough to turn the TV on. I couldn't feel his magic from this distance, but if I closed my eyes, I could visualize him in his pentagram in the loft, fueling his baseball bat.

My chest ached when I thought of the sorcerer like that, so close to being within reach. One touch and I could give him back everything he'd lost. Everything that had been taken from him.

But I wasn't going to get the chance to invite him into my bed, to offer him my magic in exchange for mutual pleasure. Or to offer him anything more than that. Because I could also kill him with a single touch.

Daniel's presence only underlined that, forcing me to truly acknowledge the reality of my life. I'd been building some vision of my future, piecing it together in my mind. But there was only the present. There was always only the present. Possibilities, dreams, desires didn't exist for me. For people like me.

I was a killer, not a lover.

I set my cheese-smeared bowl down on the floor with a half-eaten piece of toast within it. A tentacle swept out, gently dragging the bowl along the fir flooring. Paisley, accepting my offering, licked the bowl clean.

Christopher suddenly leaned forward, elbows braced against his bent knees, face in his hands. "I'm sorry."

I paused the show.

"For what?"

He sighed. "For Jenni. I could have ... you were asleep by the time we got back to the house."

"You didn't have sex in the back of the Mustang, did you?"

"No."

Good. "I want to be the first one to do that."

Christopher laughed quietly, then rested his head against my leg. I didn't push him away. We were beyond that now. Daniel's appearance boded nothing but bad tidings, and the clairvoyant would see it all just moments before it collapsed around us, whether or not he sought comfort from me now.

"Even if I hadn't gone back for Aiden ... even if we'd run ... " I didn't finish my question.

Christopher nodded. "Even then, this was coming. The lavender card. The footsteps of fate."

The past coming back to bite us, according to Christopher's oracle cards. "Unfinished business is easier for me to accept."

He snorted. "It's the same thing, Socks."

I sighed, gazing out at the backyard and feeling Daniel's magic shifting around one level below as he slowly prowled through the house.

"You really couldn't distract Jenni Raymond any other way? When she caught you dropping money into the mailbox?"

"She didn't catch me."

"Of course she didn't."

"You got the fight, the demon slaughter. The adrenaline surge, the pain, the victory. I ... I just watched."

"If they'd gotten past me, you were the only thing between the snatcher and Aiden. With his magic drained, he was vulnerable."

"I know. But watching you was ... stirring. Breathtaking. First in my mind, over and over, and then echoed in reality."

I snorted. "So you propositioned the shifter."

"Well, you would have kicked me out of your bed."

His comment hung between us for a moment. I considered not addressing it. We hadn't been raised as siblings. In fact, it wasn't until the Collective recognized that we needed to socialize with each other, to function as the team they wanted to create, that they allowed us to spend time together for more than training and educational sessions.

I was almost fourteen when I first figured out how to break out of my room, exploiting weaknesses in the security system that the Collective quickly plugged, over and over. But it was Fish I'd gone to once freed. Not Bee or Zans or Christopher. Because I could touch Fish without being afraid of hurting him. And because I wanted to touch someone without killing them, so … desperately.

Then they'd given us the blood tattoos, tying us to each other so tightly that I could have taken all of Fish's magic. I could have killed him. Instead, I got to feel his emotions through my empathy for the first time. I got to feel his desire rise under my hands, under my deadly touch. I got to sense the accumulation of the pleasure I gave him. And in those brief moments in the dark, I knew, I hoped, that I was more than just a killer. More than what the Collective had made me, what they'd made me do.

"You aren't just Amp5, Socks," Christopher whispered. Sometimes his glimpses of the future made it seem as though he was reading my mind. "You never were. None of us were. That was the flaw in their plans. They needed us to be able to make intelligent, informed decisions in the moment, but they hoped to play with us like puppets."

I settled my hand on the back of his head. He leaned into my touch. I slid my hand down until it rested over his blood tattoos. Those tattoos were twins to mine, except it was my blood tied to his T1 vertebra, not Fish's.

He sighed. "I love you, Socks. I'm not just here because you were always the strongest."

"I know."

He glanced over at me. The white of his magic ringed his irises. "I don't think you do. I think that deep down, you believe that the only reason anyone wants you, wants to be with you, is your magic."

I didn't answer. But I didn't drop my hand either. "If this is some lead-up to telling me you're leaving with Daniel, it isn't necessary. It was always your choice. Daniel will keep you safe."

He sighed. Again. This time as if I was insufferable. "Daniel isn't going to let me into his bed either. He's obviously grown beyond that."

Fish hadn't turned any of us away when we'd broken out of our rooms and into his. But as far as I knew, he'd never chosen to come to any of us of his own volition either. We'd all used him. He hadn't complained. But none of us would have ever called him brother. And now that I knew a little more about relationships, about the human need to be connected, I felt a little sad for him.

"I'm not leaving with Fish," Christopher said. "But he's staying."

"No."

"Yes."

"It's not going to screw up anything between you and Aiden."

"That's not the point." And it really wasn't. "The reasons we need to stay away from each other still hold."

Daniel appeared in the doorway, leaning against the frame with his arms crossed. I'd felt him move up the stairs and into the bedroom across from Christopher's room at the front of the house. He was the same height as me, but somehow he filled the doorway.

"Exactly." Daniel smirked at me. "And the two of you are about to expose us all."

"Yeah," Christopher said. "That."

"And how do you know?" I asked. "Or am I just to take your word for it?"

Daniel grinned nastily. "No one is asking you to change, Emma. I have a couple of side projects going on right now. One of which brought me in contact with an old buddy of yours. I'm here to broker a meeting."

I didn't have 'old buddies.' "Kader Azar?"

Daniel tilted his head sharply. "The Collective's esteemed sorcerer? What contact have you had with him?"

"None."

He frowned. "Then why the assumption?"

I didn't answer. Daniel would make the connection from Aiden to his father soon enough. "Why would you need to broker a meeting between me and anyone?"

He flashed his teeth at me. "I think your greeting tells the tale of why anyone wouldn't wish to surprise you, darling. And few can survive your touch as well as I can."

"Daniel." Christopher sighed. "Be nice."

"Don't worry, brother. The hugs and kisses will come later." He leered at me, but with more anger than desire. "After midnight, eh, Emma?"

I gave him a withering look. "I doubt you'll survive nightfall, nullifier."

He snorted, then pointed down the hall. "I take it the northwest room is mine? I could use a shower."

"Who is the meeting with, Daniel?" I asked frostily.

"Oh, it's lunch. At that diner you like, 2:00 P.M."

My stomach twisted. Someone had been keeping tabs on my movements, my routine, and I hadn't known it, hadn't sensed it. "With who?"

"Mark Calhoun." Daniel grinned at me nastily.

A flush of shock down my spine chilled me almost as effectively as Daniel's nullifying power could. Mark Calhoun. The commanding officer of my extraction team, without whom none of us would have made it out of the compound alive.

The weapons specialist was the only other Adept I'd ever slept with.

"Yeah." Daniel eyed me darkly. "Your boyfriend's back. And he can't wait to get reacquainted."

"You brought him here?" I asked, my voice low and dark. "With who else?"

"Making a kill list, Socks?"

"If I was, your name would be at the top," I spat.

Christopher brushed his fingers against my bare ankle, calling me away from the rage I was riding.

"And which name would that be?" Daniel asked mockingly. "Who would you be murdering when you drain me, amplifier? Nul5? Fish? Daniel Jones?"

"If you're going to talk nonsense, get out of my sitting room," I said, layering on as much dispassion as I could muster. "When you're feeling more rational, we'll discuss the specifics of your betrayal."

It was an old argument between us—that I was the supremely rational one, better suited to lead. It was nasty for me to use our past as a weapon. Of course, Daniel had started that process the moment he'd laid eyes on me.

He opened his mouth, anger etched across his face.

I tilted my head, eyeing him coolly.

Then he shut down all his anger in a genuinely impressive display of control. "I would never betray us."

"Not knowingly."

He dropped his gaze to Christopher, looking for the clairvoyant to back him.

Christopher didn't speak. Thick ropes of tension stretched between the three of us. Because we would always be bound together, never free of each other. Till death do us part.

Daniel stepped away, striding down the hall. A moment later, I heard the shower turn on in the main bathroom.

"He is such an asshole," I said.

"Yeah," Christopher agreed mildly. "But so are you, Socks."

I couldn't really argue with that. So I unpaused my show and tried to figure out what the hell was going on.

Someone needed to be seriously interrogated—Aiden, Daniel, or Mark Calhoun—but I hated reacting angrily. It increased my body count, and I had too many souls on my hands already.

So instead, I would think over the questions that needed answers, then figure out who could answer them. That way, I'd know where to direct my anger.

And once I quashed whatever unknown forces were shifting into play around us, I could go back to building a life without expecting demons to show up in the backyard every evening.

If I was efficient, I'd be back by teatime.

EIGHT

LANI ZACHARY WAS CHATTING WITH A STRIKINGLY
familiar woman next to a blue convertible Corvette
parked on the opposite side of the street from the
diner. The ex-air force technician, wearing her typical
jeans and a printed T-shirt, was grinning and gesturing toward the vehicle. The unknown woman's black
jeans and figure-hugging black leather jacket were
way too warm for the weather, likely indicating she'd
just arrived in town and had expected it to be cooler
in Canada in mid-September.

I'd considered purchasing a similar model of
Corvette—1965, if I wasn't mistaken—from the
same seller I'd purchased the Mustang from, but the
two-seater would have been too limiting when I had
Christopher and Paisley. Yes, apparently I could be
wooed into doing idiotic things by a bit of eye candy.
Thankfully, that weakness had—thus far—been lim-
ited to a vehicle totally inappropriate for the weather,
and one hell of a sexy sorcerer with a murky past.

I hesitated at the door to the Home Cafe, reaching out for the familiar woman's magic but sensing none. Daniel, who had walked with me into town in silence, brushed his fingers against the back of my hand.

I flinched at the unaccustomed contact.

He frowned, then tipped his chin, indicating he was planning to cross the street. So the woman was familiar to him as well?

He looked both ways, then jogged out between a slow-moving green pickup truck and a white minivan. He had left his motorcycle and jacket at the house, and had changed into blue jeans and a black T-shirt that was too tight across his shoulders.

The dark-blond woman glanced over at Daniel's approach, then she continued turning as she laid eyes on me.

Becca Jackson. Aka X3.

Sorcerer. Demolitions expert, specializing in rune spells. A former member of my extraction team.

She'd let her hair grow since I'd last seen her. It was wavy now, brushing her shoulders.

I remembered her watching me, watching the Five, through the security glass in the foyer of the compound—right before I demolished the entire building, its surrounding fortifications, and the rainforest it was hidden within for kilometers in every direction. Becca, along with Flynn and Calhoun, had helped us escape. She had also been the one who helped Bee source passports and money for us.

A regular person would have been overjoyed to be reunited with someone who'd played such a pivotal role in their lives.

I wasn't.

Maybe I was incapable of such feelings, of building such a connection with anyone whose blood wasn't tattooed under my skin. But it was much more likely a reaction to the fact that Jackson was wearing some sort of warding spell that dampened her magic. So much so that even knowing who she was, I couldn't feel her power. And that was disconcerting not so much because I cared about being able to sense her magic, but because of what it implied about the clandestine nature of her presence.

Why wear such a charm unless she had plans to sneak up on someone who could sense magic? Namely me. Or Christopher.

Jackson smiled, waving at me.

I didn't wave back.

She dropped her hand, speaking to Daniel as he drew near. He glanced back at me, but then pointedly offered his hand to Lani Zachary instead of answering the demolitions expert.

I turned, pushing open the glass door of the diner. The disconcerted feeling stuck with me, along with the echoes of the memory of the day we'd fought for our freedom and won—and had sacrificed so much, so many souls, to do so.

For a moment, standing between the bulletin board and the back of the first red-vinyl booth, tucked into the normally comforting surroundings of the diner, I felt dampened. As if my emotions, my reactions, were trying to swallow me.

I paused, steadying myself. I had forced myself to calm down before I left the house. I'd acknowledged that things might be poised to happen, but was secure in the fact that I could handle anything thrown my way.

I just hadn't expected my own mind, my own memories, to be the biggest hurdle.

I swept my gaze through the diner, taking in the long counter. Over half of its red-topped stools were occupied by locals enjoying their lunches. I caught a glimpse of Brian's balding head in the kitchen through the heated stainless steel serving window. Melissa was making change for someone at the cash register.

And Mark Calhoun was seated in the farthest booth, facing me.

Sorcerer.

Weapons specialist.

Former commanding officer of my extraction unit.

The one time I'd had sex with him was the night before I almost died. We had known each other—as much as I'd known anyone outside the Five—for over two years prior to that evening. Feeling freed from the confines of the compound, I'd knocked on the door to his hotel room. I'd climbed into his bed without more than two or three words exchanged, and he had followed me. I'd never slept with anyone but Fish up to that point. And the sorcerer had been different, so different. His magic warm, inviting. Not chilly like the feeling of touching Fish, nothing like his ever-present nullifying power.

"I'm sorry, dear." Melissa stepped around the counter toward me, holding a menu. Her blond curls tumbled around her face, laugh lines crinkled around the edges of her blue eyes. "I didn't know you were coming in. Your usual spot is occupied. Would you like to sit at the counter? We could have a chat?"

"No." My lips felt weirdly numb. "I … I'm … I'm joining someone."

"Oh? Really? Lani?"

I shook my head, staring at Mark Calhoun. The sandy-haired sorcerer slipped out of the booth, standing to one side. He was wearing a worn light-brown suede jacket over a tight T-shirt and jeans.

I stepped past Melissa, remembering to smile at her so she didn't know that something was wrong with me, that everything was jumbled in my head. Moving forward was the only way to work it all out. It was always the only way. Standing still was practically the same as dying, unless you were lying in ambush for someone. But I was the one being hunted now.

Halfway to the booth, to Mark, I stopped walking. The tile under my sneakered feet suddenly felt as though I had somehow transitioned to walking barefoot on cold concrete. The seven-year-old scars across my stomach flared with pain. My chest constricted.

I wasn't breathing.

In my mind, in my memories, I was somehow back in the corridors of the compound, slowly being gassed to death. And my body was reacting to that re-collection. My mind was somehow overriding years of training, years of threat assessment, of overcoming impossible odds with ease.

How that was even possible, I didn't know. But it was happening, coming in waves, and I couldn't seem to keep it dampened, to keep moving through it.

Mark Calhoun's face swam in front of me, seven years younger in my mind's eye, and filled with a fierce, determined fear. His gun was in his hand. Magic rampaged down long concrete corridors, pressing us back, stopping us up.

I was having a panic attack.

Yes. A panic attack.

And somehow, figuring that out, acknowledging it—no matter that it should have been impossible to rattle me to that extent—loosened my chest. It allowed me to take a full breath, then another.

My past had caught up with me. But I wouldn't go quietly. I was actually incapable of walking away or sacrificing myself. Such action would have gone against everything I knew myself to be on a fundamental level. When faced with an impossible situation, I would fight. And now, even more than the last time I'd laid eyes on Calhoun and Jackson ... now I had so much more to lose.

The sandy-haired sorcerer removed his jacket, draping it over the back of the booth in an exaggerated motion. So that I could see both his sides and back. So I could see he wasn't armed.

He had misunderstood my hesitation.

And somehow, that allowed me to continue to breathe steadily, and for my mind to reboot in a much more rational, useful mode.

I was about to be manipulated somehow. About to be played. Mind games weren't my forte, and human interactions and relationships were often baffling to me. But it took a lot to bring me down. I knew that Jackson and Calhoun wouldn't risk the wrath of those who governed this territory by creating a disturbance—specifically, the coven based out of Vancouver on the mainland.

Rumor had it that the witches wouldn't tolerate anyone or anything operating outside their authority. Ironically, that had been a plus when I'd first chosen Lake Cowichan as a place to try to settle. The witches were far enough away that Christopher, Paisley, and I might go unnoticed, but were close enough to potentially keep others away.

So whatever attack was about to be leveled my way would have to be subtle, localized. Likely specific to me.

And that I could handle.

I stepped forward, finding that my limbs obeyed me once again.

Smiling tentatively, Calhoun reached for me as if he expected some form of physical greeting. I stopped just out of his reach.

"Calhoun."

"Emma." His tone was low, warm, intimate. As was his hazel-eyed gaze. I didn't know whether Daniel or Jackson had told the sorcerer my new name, but

I didn't like hearing it from him. I didn't want 'emma' claimed by any part of my past.

That was a ridiculous thought. So I blamed it on the residual reach of the panic attack and slid into the booth. My back was to the door because Calhoun had claimed the other side.

I glanced out the window, spotting Daniel and Becca Jackson still chatting. Lani had left.

"You look … amazing." Calhoun shook his head. "Your hair. I mean, I knew it was red, but—"

I looked at him.

Brow furrowing, he stopped talking.

"Daniel says you have something to tell me?"

"No. I mean, I have a client in need of your services."

"What services?"

Calhoun glanced around, but no one was paying any attention to us. At least no one within earshot. "We're working on a project for a witch."

"Magenta?"

"Yes." He twisted his lips wryly. "Big pockets. Big goals."

"And she sent you here?"

"No. I've been working with Daniel on and off for the last three years or so. I contacted him about you specifically."

"When?"

"About three months ago."

"And he told you that he wasn't in contact with me."

"Right. But then I got wind … " He frowned as he trailed off, as if forgetting what he'd been saying.

"Got wind of what?"

"I'm … of you. So I contacted Daniel."

"And he brought you here?"

"No … I … " He shook his head.

I leaned toward him, scanning him for any obvious charms. I wasn't sensitive to magic, so he might have been wearing something without me picking it up. But all I could feel was the normal hum of his sorcerer power. "And the witch, is she proficient in memory spells?"

"Memory spells?" he echoed.

A woman laughed from somewhere to my right.

Calhoun and I both glanced over.

There was no one seated at the section of the counter nearest us.

I was about to get blindsided with my eyes wide open. I placed my hands on the table, palms down, fingers spread.

"Emma?" Calhoun whispered.

"Have you got a no-kill clause in your contract, Mark?" I asked casually, needing to know if his employer would sacrifice him to get to me.

"Yes. Of course. Why?"

"What are the ramifications? A curse?"

"Yes."

"And did you see the witch sign it herself? Did you see her draw the blood?"

"Yes. And … no."

As swiftly as I could, I slid out of the booth, stepped across the aisle, and sat on the empty seat to my right. At the same time, I grabbed the arm of the witch hidden under an obfuscation spell on the stool next to me. She'd been raising her hand to cast something.

I clamped down on her rising power, stifling it but not grabbing for it. I had no idea what the spell was, so taking it for myself might have been her intention. Because I had to admit, she'd been one step ahead of me all the way so far.

The still-invisible witch laughed again, her voice sounding like discordant tinkling bells. The noise crawled up my spine and embedded itself into the base of my brain—some sort of magic. I fought back a sudden instinct to run, to flee.

The witch was powerful.

I twisted her invisible wrist in my hand. Not enough to break her arm, but enough to hurt it, enough to break her focus.

The obfuscation spell dropped with a snap. And for a moment, the appearance of the witch was muddled—blond hair over a dark backdrop, clear blue eyes over black orbs, creamy complexion over pale skin.

I blinked rapidly.

A petite, voluptuous blond sat before me. The witch's wrist was still captured in my hand, somewhat hidden beneath the counter.

To our far right, Melissa dropped the mug she'd been about to fill with coffee, pressing her hand to her chest. "Oh, my goodness," she cried. "I didn't see you there before. Everything okay, Emma?"

"Yes, thank you."

"I'll be right over for your order."

"No rush."

The witch smiled at me, power writhing under her skin. "Are you going to drain me, amplifier?" she whispered playfully.

A chill settled deep in my stomach. The list of people who knew what I could do was an exceedingly short one. Though with the reappearance of Jackson and Calhoun, I had to add two more names to that list. Or three, counting the witch in front of me now.

A fissure of betrayal cracked open, situated right around my heart.

"Oh, dear." The witch laughed again.

I had to stop myself from trying to brush the sound away as it tinkled and crashed around me. It held too much power. Way too much power. The witch was on the edge of losing it. She was combustible.

Draining her would have been a service to the world.

"You know men," she said, grinning manically. "Unable to keep a single secret once you've got them in hand." She leaned toward me. "One look at you, darling, tells me you know exactly what I mean." She winked.

I caught another glimpse of the other witch, the face behind the one she was currently presenting to the world. Dark hair, black eyes, pale skin.

I blinked.

The witch leered at me in her blond aspect. "I've been dying to meet you, Emma."

There was something in the way she said my name that caused the hair on the back of my neck to stand up. And I didn't like that she was wearing some sort of additional masking spell, or whatever was going on with the second aspect I kept catching glimpses of. But I loosened my hold on her nonetheless.

I wasn't in a position to judge her, let alone to mete out preemptive justice. I would do what I needed to do in order to move the witch along, to divert her attention. Then she'd be someone else's problem.

"What is going on?" Calhoun hissed tensely. He'd stayed seated in the booth but was turned toward us.

The witch waved a hand at him dismissively without looking away from me. "Get Emma and me some tea. And pie. Pumpkin if they have it. With whipped cream."

Calhoun stood, frowning and glancing between us. He leaned back and grabbed his jacket, then stepped up beside me. "It's good to see you, Emma. I'd like to ... do so again."

I nodded, not taking my gaze off the witch.

"You had Mark, did you? And he wants another taste?" The witch swept her gaze over me, then chuckled huskily. "I can see why. Think of the burst of power you must deliver each time you orgasm." She lowered her voice. "Can't keep it so tightly coiled then, can you? What sorcerer wouldn't want to bed you?"

Mark, who hadn't moved, opened his mouth angrily.

I shook my head, just once, falling into our old mission shorthand.

He hesitated, then stepped away.

The witch eyed him appreciatively as he did. "I wouldn't mind having him on a leash. But I never mix business with pleasure."

But she'd implied that she'd been sleeping with Calhoun earlier, hadn't she? I glanced to my left, looking for Daniel. He and Jackson weren't by the Corvette.

"Ooh, you are smart," the witch whispered. Then she stood up, stepped across the aisle, and slid into the seat Calhoun had occupied. She patted the table. "Join me, Emma."

I moved to sit down across from her. I didn't have much choice. Not yet.

"You apparently know my name," I said.

She tittered that annoying laugh, but its effect on me had eased. Definitely some sort of magic, but perhaps she simply leaked it. Or maybe it was an odd resonance of the image-enhancing spell she used. Either way, my natural immunity was mitigating its effects. Another twenty minutes and I'd probably start seeing through the cloaking spell as well.

"I am Magenta," she said magnanimously. "But I doubt we actually needed to be introduced to each other, Emma. We already know each other, don't we?"

Melissa hustled over, depositing two mugs of tea, a tiny pitcher of milk, and a single piece of pumpkin pie with whipped cream.

"I asked for two pieces of pie," the witch snapped, suddenly on edge. Nasty.

Melissa calmly placed a set of utensils rolled in a paper napkin beside the pie. "Emma doesn't eat pie."

As the witch eyed Melissa, her magic flickered again, like a light bulb shorting out.

I considered reaching across the table and killing her. She carried a lot of magic, but if I took enough and was quick about it, it wouldn't escalate to a fight. It would look like a heart attack.

The witch looked at me.

Her eye twitched.

Melissa patted my shoulder and walked away.

I added milk and a packet of sugar to my tea. I couldn't drink Melissa's regular Earl Grey black.

Magenta unrolled the utensils, lining the fork, teaspoon, and knife up beside her pumpkin pie, making certain the bottoms of each were only an inch away from the edge of the table.

I smiled. She had just provided me with weapons of opportunity and a bit of insight into her psyche. Compulsive tendencies were easy to exploit.

The witch's gaze flicked to me as she carefully selected the fork, then took a bite of the pie. She chewed, frowning, then pushed the plate away. "I don't know why I bother. I never like pumpkin."

I raised my mug to my mouth, sipping tea slowly as I glanced outside. Calhoun crossed by the window, leaning against the streetlight to the right of the diner and pulling out his phone.

Magenta followed my gaze. "Let's trade." She smiled at me with overly straight teeth and empty eyes.

I didn't respond.

She leaned across the table, speaking conspiratorially. "You've collected my wayward sorcerer, amplifier. I want him back."

"He got your message." His name. Carved into the chest of a snatcher demon.

The witch laughed that ridiculous laugh, waving her hand at me. "A love note. You know how it is."

"Why are you here?"

"I'd like to buy a favor."

I waited.

Frustration flitted over her face, but she suppressed it. "You did a job in San Francisco for an ... acquaintance."

And that so-called acquaintance was now dead. By Christopher's hand, moments after he'd broken our contract and tried to hold me against my will.

"An amplifier is one thing," she mused. "But backed by a clairvoyant? So, of course, I knew who you were. One of the Collective's experiments run wild." She eyed me hungrily. "Power like yours shouldn't be hidden away."

She knew too much, or she had access to too much information. And it was idiotic of her to parade that knowledge in front of me. Now I had no choice but to kill her.

Finding I wasn't at all displeased with the notion of ending the witch's life, I settled back against the booth, dropping the pretense of sipping my tea. "Oh, yes? It should be used to boost your own?"

She laughed.

That was getting irksome.

"I sent you the sorcerer," she said. "To see what you'd do with him. To test your ... inclinations." She glanced pointedly at Calhoun out the window. He was standing sideways, still leaning against the lamppost and pretending to be looking at his phone, but obviously keeping an eye on us and the street.

"And I already had an idea what ... who would turn your head."

"You just indicated that you had no idea Mark and I had any kind of previous relationship."

Her face blanked, but she recovered quickly. "Did I? Well, it was a good guess."

"And what's the end game? With you and the sorcerer you deposited on my doorstep?"

"Did you power him up for me, amplifier? My beautiful, passionate, irresistible boy?"

"Why?" My tone had turned dark. I didn't like her claiming any kind of ownership of Aiden. "Are you planning on draining him again?"

"Of course. His magic is … potent. And he is open to suggestions, open to experimentation. As I'm sure you've discovered."

"Make your request, witch. So we can move on."

Another spike of frustrated anger glitched out whatever cloaking spell Magenta was holding around her, and I caught another glimpse of her true face. There was something familiar about her, but I suspected I was still feeling the effects of the panic attack, and muddling the unexpected arrival of Daniel, Jackson, and Calhoun with hers.

I wasn't surprised that a summoner of her power level would go to great extents to hide her true face. Black witches weren't pretty, creamy-skinned blonds with crystal-blue eyes.

Magenta got herself sorted out and her mask firmly back in place. "Would you be amenable to having me join you and the sorcerer? Just the three of us, him fully powered by you, one night. In bed."

My jaw unhinged, dropping before I could snap it closed.

Magenta smiled, magic gleaming from her eyes.

"That's it? That's all?" I asked, covering my initial shock by mocking her. "You want me to boost the sorcerer and then have sex with the two of you? So you can … what? Summon some greater demon, bind it permanently against its will? How … common."

MEGHAN CIANA DOIDGE

She curled her lip in a snarl. Her magic rose up around her, black overwhelming her irises. But I kept pushing, keeping my tone conversational.

"You say you know me, witch. And what I can do. Yet you request magic that any morally flexible amplifier of any power level could cast. Why go to the trouble of tracking me down? Of dumping the sorcerer on my doorstep? Of placing the memory spells on Calhoun? Games within games. And you lead with sex?"

She laughed harshly, the sound carrying magic that scraped over my forearms like steel nails against the bones.

I shook my hands, easily breaking whatever magic she was casting, whether it was intentional or not.

Surprise flitted across her face. "You're right," she said. "I was just testing the waters. I would pay well, of course. And I'm sure you would enjoy yourself. The sorcerer is skilled. Skills I can personally attest to, if you haven't experienced them yourself."

She paused as if waiting for a reaction.

I dropped my gaze to my mug of tea. I'd already known she and Aiden had been having sex, but I wasn't certain why she felt that fact should hold any power over me. So I decided to play along.

She clicked her tongue. "Oh, dear. Perhaps I should give you some time to think about everything. Shall we meet back here? Tomorrow, same time?"

I nodded. If it came down to it, I'd be gone with Christopher and Paisley before sunset. And with Aiden, if he wanted to join us.

I suspected the witch's summoning powers would be most potent at night, though I'd once encountered a witch who could pilot a greater demon in the full sun. But Silver Pine was dead. I had fed her a death curse of her own construction, then brought an entire compound down on her head.

Magenta rose, gathering her magic around her like a dark cloak. Wielding so much darkness carried a toll. She wouldn't be able to pay it for much longer, not without drawing the attention of the Convocation. And I really didn't want the witches' attention drawn to Lake Cowichan. I didn't want to answer the battery of questions they'd rain down on me.

No, as I'd resolved earlier, it was better to take Magenta out now myself. I slid out of the booth, tracking the witch as she sauntered out of the diner. I would follow her, but only after allowing her the impression that she was walking away.

Melissa waved a brown paper bag at me, and I paused as she stepped around the counter with a spray bottle and cloth in her other hand, ready to clear and wipe down our vacated table. I knew without checking that the bag contained pastries for Christopher, so it would have been rude not to accept it. Though I had a black witch to kill before I could deliver it to him.

And in that moment, I understood something. A realization anchored by the sight of the brown paper bag.

I wasn't leaving.

This was my home. The witch was the interloper, not me. And unless they got in my way, I'd leave Calhoun and Jackson alive, because I was certain, given a choice, that they'd do the same for me.

I accepted the bag from Melissa with a smile, tracking the witch as she crossed out of the diner and sauntered over to speak to Calhoun. He tilted his head, listening to her but watching me through the window.

Melissa bussed the plate, utensils, and mugs from the table, then started wiping it down. There was a couple waiting at the door, and all the other booths were full with locals lunching. I hadn't noticed. That was unlike me.

"It's an experiment," Melissa said, nodding toward the bag I was holding. "Strawberry and rhubarb filling. Just let me know if he likes them, dear."

Outside, the witch stepped off the curb, crossing toward the Corvette. Calhoun glanced at me through the window, lifting his hand up to his ear as if to indicate he'd like to call me.

Another conversation with the sorcerer wouldn't hurt, though he wouldn't be able to conduct it by phone. Not with me, at least.

I nodded, agreeing to the concept if not the actual method of communication.

"Oh," Melissa said. "How adorable! Did your friend drop this?"

She stepped over, passing me a fabric doll she'd picked up from the seat Magenta had just vacated, then waving the new customers toward the booth.

I took the doll, my gaze still riveted to the witch through the window. She was climbing into the Corvette—

Something sharp underneath the doll's hair pricked the tip of my ring finger, drawing blood. I gasped, gazing down confused at the stuffed toy in my hand.

I didn't pull away.

I should have dropped the doll.

I needed to drop the doll.

But I was mesmerized by its red yarn hair, its pale fabric skin, its shimmering green eyes.

"Very cute," Melissa said, brushing her shoulder against mine as she collected the dirty dishes she'd set temporarily on the counter behind me. "Those eyes almost look like real raw emeralds, but that would be awfully expensive for a fabric doll. I have my eye on a copper ring with the same kind of stone, but I can't decide between the emerald or the ruby. Actually ... " She laughed as she glanced from me to the doll in my hand. "Actually, it looks like you, Emma. Does your friend make them?"

It was me.

A replica of me.

And those were real raw emeralds. Because gemstones could hold magic. Magic triggered by a drop of blood.

My blood.

I'd been spelled.

I was in the process of being spelled.

I tried to draw away. I tried to drop the doll. But its power reached through the blood it had drawn, binding the spell to me, clamping down on my mind. Dampening my thoughts.

"Emma?"

"Yes?"

Melissa shook her head. "I can see your mind is elsewhere. Go, go then. Just let me know what Christopher thinks of the pastries. I used his strawberries. He's getting such a great crop for this late in the season." She hustled away with the dishes.

"Okay," I mumbled. Then I exited the diner without another word, without another thought.

A sporty, vintage Corvette sped away down the street, followed by a silver SUV.

I hadn't seen the SUV before, but it must have been parked on the street behind the Corvette. A silver SUV.

Silver.

Silver.

There was something… something familiar about… silver.

I glanced down at the doll still in my hand. There was a red stain on the side of its face. I'd ... bled on it? That wasn't good. That was ...

Wait.

I was supposed to be doing something. Something important ... something urgent. I'd come to the diner with someone, hadn't I? And he ... was it a he? He shouldn't have left me all alone. Or maybe I was supposed to be meeting someone? No. There was something urgent I needed to do. I walked down the sidewalk, knowing I was going somewhere.

Just ... where exactly was I going?

MAGIC WAS TRYING TO PUSH ME FORWARD.

Push me.

Push me.

Push, push, push me.

There was something in the river, downriver, deep within the river that needed me, needed my attention.

But it was cold, freezing my feet, ankles, and calves. And I didn't want to move any farther, to go any farther.

So I perched on the river-slick rock, crouched over the raging water. Waiting ... waiting ...

But for what, I didn't know.

The sun slowly set.

I started to shiver.

I clutched the pretty, red-haired doll to my chest, protecting it and all the shimmering magic it held from the hungry river. The hungry, hungry river wanted to gobble me up.

Something urged me to let it do just that. Something begged me to dive into the cool water, to let it drag me away, batter me against the jagged rocks, fill my lungs with water. Drown me. Kill me.

I was supposed to die now.

I didn't really deserve to live.

I had never deserved to live.

But … there was something else I was supposed to be doing. Something holding me in place. I couldn't move forward or back. I'd made it this far, to the edge of the river. And now it was getting dark … and I was cold.

And … and …

"Emma? Emma!" A woman was shouting from the bank of the river behind me. "Emma, what the hell are you doing?"

I looked up. The wind grabbed my hair, whipping it around my head, half free from its ponytail. It was red too. Red like the yarn hair on the doll.

"Emma!" the woman cried again.

I could hear her moving toward me, splashing and cursing.

Then she was standing before me. The breeze that followed the river snatched at her dark-brown hair. Her hazel eyes were scared but determined. "Emma! We've been looking everywhere for you!"

Emma.

Emma.

I was Emma.

The river tried to gobble up the woman, tried to grab her legs, tried to sweep her away.

I reached out—quick, quick—grabbing her back. The river didn't get to have her. She had come for me … was looking for me.

"Jesus Christ!" the woman cried.

I was holding her upright with one arm. She scrambled, trying to get her footing, clinging to the rock I was perched on with her free arm.

"I've got it. I've got it." She straightened, feet planted firmly on either side.

The river surged around her, but she wouldn't get caught again.

I let her go.

She shook her arm as if I'd hurt her.

"Emma. Are you okay?"

I could see her magic. There it was, hovering just between her eyes, buried deep. I lifted my hand. I could reach for it. I could pull it forward, fill it with my own power.

She grabbed my hand. "Do you need help?"

I shook my head. Then I looked downriver again.

There was somewhere I was supposed to be, supposed to go.

"What's that?" the woman murmured.

She tried to take the doll from me.

I cried out, holding it away from her.

She pressed her hands to my face. Her skin was icy cold. "Emma!"

She shouldn't have been touching me. Touching me wasn't a good idea. Because I was dangerous. I was morally compromised. I could hurt, kill her, let the river have her.

I didn't want to hurt her.

Not 'her.' She had a name. Like I had a name.

She was Lani Zachary.

I was Emma Johnson.

Lani was standing in the middle of the raging river, trying to … rescue me?

Keeping her gaze locked to mine, Lani slowly reached down and pried my hand from the doll, one finger at a time.

"Damn, you're strong." She ripped the doll from me, tugging at the magic that bound it to me. "What the hell is this?"

I gasped, trying to grab the doll back.

She threw it into the river.

I cried out for its loss. I was supposed to protect it. I tried to lunge after it.

Lani grabbed me back. "No! There's something wrong with it. It's wrong. It's off, Emma."

She touched my face again, pulling my attention back to her.

"You shouldn't be touching me," I mumbled.

"I know, I'm sorry." She grabbed my hand. "You're bleeding." She tugged my arm down, down.

Down into the river. To wash the blood away from my finger.

"Lani," I murmured. "I'm in the river."

"Yes, you bloody well are. And I'm here too, freezing my ass off. We've been looking for you for hours."

"How did you know…how did you know the doll was…wrong?"

She shrugged, avoiding my gaze. "I knew. I know."

Shivering, I scanned the area.

The swiftly moving river was narrower along this stretch than it was in town, where it was closer to the lake that fed it. Large smooth rocks edged the churning water, with forest spreading beyond to either side. No buildings or homes within sight. I looked upriver, hoping to catch sight of the lake, but seeing only the water winding through thick expanses of trees. I was nowhere near town, which meant I was even farther from the property. It was dark and getting darker.

"The sun has set."

"That it has. How do you feel about getting out of the river? Good idea, yes?" Lani tugged at my arm.

I climbed off the rock, helping her more than she helped me. I'd left my shoes somewhere. My legs were numb, my mind not much better.

"How did you know to look for me, Lani?"

"The big guy, Daniel. Your…boyfriend? He was really clear that you weren't related. He came back into town a couple of hours ago, said he hadn't seen you or the people you'd been having lunch with. But Melissa said you'd left the diner. Alone. She said you'd eaten alone too. Couldn't answer any of Daniel's questions about the people he'd thought you were meeting. Melissa called Jenni. And Jenni called a few of us. Hannah, Daniel, and I split up, looking for you. Melissa started a phone tree."

I had no idea what a phone tree was. "Who's at the house?"

"What do you mean? Your place?"

"Yes."

"Christopher, I think. Daniel said Chris would phone if you turned up there, though he was pissed he had to stay behind. Daniel took Paisley out over by Meadow Lane Farm. Though why they thought you'd go there, I don't know."

"Christopher might have sent him. Peter Grant has been … " I shook my head, not wanting to explain that Grant had been contemplating running me over for a few months now. Not wanting to explain that I hadn't done anything about it because he was a mundane.

"Harassing you guys? For finding Hannah? Asshole. Have you told Jenni?"

We made it to the shore. I was shivering violently now, but there wasn't any time to worry about hypothermia. Or anything else.

"Paisley couldn't find me?"

"Well, I imagine they're still looking." She pulled out her phone, sighing. "It's wet and powered down. Do you think I should try starting it up? Might fry it."

"I've got to go." I stepped away.

"Emma!"

"I'm fine, Lani. Thank you. But I've got to get home."

"At least let me drive you!"

"Where's your car?"

She pointed downriver. "About two or three kilometers? I parked in the Skutz Falls parking lot and doubled back."

"I'm going in the opposite direction." For a sudden brief moment, I fought through an urge to jump back in the river—residual from the spell attached to the doll. It had been trying to get me to commit suicide, but wasn't strong enough to compel me all the way. Very little magic could compel anyone to do anything that went completely against their natural inclinations. I might have hated myself for who I'd been, the person the Collective had made me. But I would never kill myself.

"Don't be insane," Lani said. "What are you going to do? Run?"

I did just that, scrambling up the rocky bank, darting through the undergrowth and the evergreens. I lost Lani behind me almost immediately. If we were anywhere near Skutz Falls, then Cowichan Valley Highway wasn't as far away as I'd thought.

I made it to the road.

And I ran.

Muscles warming, stretching. Feet bare. The pavement was smoother in the middle of the road. My hair and cotton dress quickly drying, I ran.

The black witch had spelled me. Maybe the spell was meant to wear off, or maybe it just wasn't strong enough. But regardless, she had spelled me so she could do something while I was out of the way.

So I ran. Because it was faster than slowly following Lani to her car. I ran because Daniel was looking for me with Paisley. Which left Christopher and Aiden on their own against a witch smart enough to realize I'd accept something handed to me by a friend. A witch strong enough to bind me in the first place. A witch wily enough that she was also somehow preventing Paisley from tracking me, an ability that was embedded in the demon dog's genetic code.

Unless that was Daniel's doing.

My chest constricted. "Please don't let it be Daniel," I whispered. That would hurt Christopher too much, damage him irrevocably.

Because I would have to kill Daniel. Fish. My not-a-brother. Fish, whose blood teemed with magic in the tattoo under my skin. That magic was prickling and shifting as I raced toward the future I was certain had already unfolded. Running toward the relentless, remorseless future that had always awaited my arrival.

I wasn't even certain I could kill Daniel, if he'd betrayed us. Magic might not let me. The attempt might kill me as well.

So I ran.

NINE

THE FRONT GATE WAS CLOSED, AS IT SHOULD HAVE been. No cars were parked in front of the house. No magic rained down on me as I leaped over the gate without pausing and raced along the gravel driveway.

But Christopher hadn't turned on any interior lights. Even if he was in the kitchen obsessing over a new dish for supper, I should have been able to see light spilling out from the east-facing windows. The barn and the loft suite within it were dark as well.

I was gasping for breath, my lungs on fire from running flat out all the way from the river's edge. I leaped up the stairs onto the front patio, wrenching open the door and throwing it back with such force that it slammed into the wall, pulled from its hinges. The front windows cracked.

I paused on the threshold, waiting, panting, feeling for magic.

Nothing stirred within.

Not bothering to turn on the lights, I stepped into the darkness. The fir flooring was smooth under my road-torn feet. I was leaving bloody footprints behind, but that didn't matter. Not yet.

A scent hung in the air, barely there but pulling me toward the kitchen. As if Christopher had tried to light a fire with wet, sap-filled wood and it hadn't caught.

Aiden's rune-carved baseball bat was lying halfway between the base of the stairs to my right and the far doorway leading into the kitchen. It was devoid of magic, drained. Again.

Creeping forward slowly, I scooped up the bat as I stepped past it. The worn wood felt comforting in my hand. Aiden was right. Filled with magic or not, it made a damn fine weapon.

I approached the doorway to the kitchen, pausing a half step away from where the fir-floored hall gave way to broad white porcelain tile. I scanned the room, feeling a cool resolve settle over me as I did.

The double patio doors hung open, wrenched from their upper hinges, glass shattered. Claw marks scored both doorjambs. The kitchen table was partially embedded in the drywall to the right, likely jutting through into the laundry room. It had been thrown with great force.

Blood splattered the lower cabinets and the tile surrounding the island.

A pentagram had been etched onto the tile directly in front of me. Placed in a defensive position with direct line of sight to the front door and the back patio doors. The five-pointed star was marked out precisely with black marker, but the lines had been scorched on either side—likely when its magical protections were breached. It was large enough that two people could have stood within its center.

I didn't need to search the house any further to know that Christopher had been taken, along with Aiden. The pentagram, the baseball bat, the blood, and the absence of the constant hum of the clairvoyant's magic were all the evidence I needed.

What I didn't know was whether either of them was still alive.

They might have been forced into the house defensively. Or they'd been surprised. Christopher wouldn't have chosen to fight in his kitchen.

Wrapped in an emotion-numbing blanket of logic, I stepped onto the chilly tile, crouching by the largest bloodstain. I broke the surface tension of the liquid with my fingertips, feeling the hum of the magic—Aiden's magic. The blood was cool, overflowing the edge of the pentagram. Whatever wound Aiden had sustained had happened after his barrier spell had been compromised.

The sound of something being dragged across the kitchen patio drew my attention to the broken doors and the darkening night beyond.

I straightened, raising the baseball bat defensively. I couldn't feel anything magical approaching. But I was at least vaguely aware that I still wasn't fully functional myself. A residual effect of the spell held in the doll, perhaps, or the shock of finding that

Christopher had been taken. Christopher, who I'd devoted my entire life to protecting.

Paisley's blue-furred snout appeared at the bottom edge of the doorway. Then her dull red eyes, her ears and head. She hooked her claws on the edge of the doorjamb, struggling to pull herself over the threshold.

I lunged across the kitchen.

She was … savagely injured. Massively hurt. The trail of blood behind her was thick, viscous. Her entrails were exposed through an open belly wound, and caked in dirt.

Her magic was dreadfully mute, draining from her.

She was dying.

Dying.

Something broke inside me. A howl of pain tore through my throat. I crashed to my knees beside her, reaching for and gently cradling her head in my lap. She mewed, pained. She brushed a tentacle against my wrist, unable to curl it around and hold on. Her left eye had been clawed out. Her jaw was broken.

I sobbed.

Just once.

Then I screamed.

I screamed, releasing all the terror I'd been holding at bay. I screamed for what had been ripped from me without warning. I shrieked in frustration over everything that I'd allowed to happen.

And then I howled all the vengeance I would rain down on the black witch.

"Magenta…" I turned her name into a magic-laden curse.

Soon she'd be the one with her guts strung across the ground.

Soon she'd be the one mewing in pain.

Soon.

Paisley sighed, drawing in a rattling breath.

Shaking with emotion I had no capacity to contain anymore, I placed my hand on her claw-scored head. Then, betraying every promise I'd ever made to myself, I reached down and dug my fingers into the open wound at her belly.

She screeched, pained.

But I could feel her heart fluttering. It was still trying to beat. It was still trying to pump blood—and her magic—through her wounded body.

And I wasn't about to let it stop.

A long time ago, I had told myself I wouldn't get involved. That I would allow life to unfold the way it was destined to, and without my interference. I would try to take myself out of the equation altogether. Promising to look after Christopher—my Knox—and Paisley, but nothing more.

I had retreated.

I had tried to build a quiet life free from all the death and destruction I was capable of wreaking.

"If you want Amp5," I muttered, "you've got her…"

The black witch wanted an amplifier to play with?

She could choke on me.

I reached for Paisley's power—the magic buried deeply within her, as well as the energy glistening in the blood trail behind her.

I dropped every shield I normally held between me and the world. Power flooded from me, seeking the energy slowly seeping from Paisley. I twined my amplification through her magic, mirroring her energy, then bolstering it. Expanding it, pumping it up.

My magic was a bottomless well that I'd only ever managed to completely drain once before. A power I had once hoped would never return. It had taken a year, but it had come back. Stronger than ever.

The power to boost, to amplify.

And with that power, I could also take.

To have.

To hold.

To wield.

The power to destroy everything and anyone magical in my path with a single touch.

I channeled Paisley's amplified magic back into her damaged body, forcing it to flow through her.

She shrieked. She snarled.

I kept pushing, building, boosting, amplifying. I was no healer, but Paisley had her own healing ability. Even I didn't heal as quickly as she usually did.

Her jaw widened, her head shifting in my lap as her broken bones enlarged, snapping back into place. Her double rows of teeth sprang forth. Thick, sharp, two-inch claws tore through her paws. Her legs lengthened, bulked up. Her muscles rippled, doubling her size.

My hand was pushed from the wound in her belly as it attempted to seal. Her entrails slithered and slid, sucked back into her body.

Then, on paws the size of my head, Paisley staggered to her feet. She stumbled, turning away from me until she was facing out into the dark yard, facing the night. Then she bellowed.

I felt her vicious, snarling anger run down my spine.

The sound faded, swallowed by the darkness that had enclosed the yard, leaving only her ragged, pained breathing. Paisley lowered her muzzle to the floor and began licking up the blood she'd left behind.

I got to my feet.

I was going to need my blades.

MOVING AROUND IN THE DARK—BECAUSE THIS WAS my home, my place, and I knew every corner, every step within it—I stripped my bloody dress off just inside the door to my bedroom, tossing it to the side. I pulled leggings, a fitted exercise top, and a tight T-shirt from the drawers of my bureau.

Walking while I dressed, I stepped into the bathroom. I brushed my hair into two pigtails, braiding each and securing them with doubled elastics pulled as snugly as I could get them without breaking them. I probably looked ridiculous. But I'd never gone into battle with long hair before.

And yes, based on whatever had come for Aiden—whatever had fought its way past Paisley, along with Christopher and the sorcerer himself—I was walking into a battle.

Back in my bedroom, I added a water-resistant nylon jacket to my ensemble. The jacket was intended for jogging in less-than-sunny conditions—tight fitting with stretch panels on each side—but was adaptable to wielding dual swords.

I tugged on socks, then running shoes.

I knelt beside my bed, pulling the wooden box that held my weapons out, then setting it on the quilt with its pattern of speckled roses. I flipped open the lid.

One of the three raw diamonds set in the hilt of the blade nearest to me was glowing softly. Dark blue.

Sorcerer magic.

Aiden's magic.

A terrible pain ripped through my chest, clamping down on my heart and wringing it. I gasped, pressing my hand where there was no physical wound.

Aiden had slipped into my bedroom, found the weapons, and shared his magic with me. Magic he didn't have enough of to safely share.

And now he'd been taken. Likely murdered or badly wounded in the process.

I pressed my forehead to the edge of the bed, trying to get my emotions, my reaction under control. Reaching through the presumptuous grief for a detached rationale.

The sorcerer needed me at my best. Therefore, the blades had needed sharpening. My skirmish with the demons sent to snatch Aiden had made that blindingly obvious. So it was far more likely that he had found a spell that would do just that. It would trigger when I touched the gem. He had probably intended to spell one of the gems in the second blade as well, but had run out of time.

The ache that had settled in my heart refused to believe my mercenary assessment of the sorcerer's gift. My heart had never been so irrational, so easily wooed.

I picked up the blade, covering the softly glowing gem with the palm of my hand. Magic stirred at my touch as I raised the weapon before me. A wash of dark-blue energy flooded up its double edge, leaving a residual glow.

I laughed darkly. Grabbing the second blade in its sheath, I jogged out into the hall and down the stairs. I had a witch to find, and the perfect weapon with which to decapitate her.

PAISLEY HAD CLEARED THE BLOOD FROM EVERY SUR-
face of the kitchen and patio by the time I made it
back downstairs. The pentagram, the shattered
French-paned doors, and the broken kitchen table
remained as they were.

So too did the claw marks on the doorjamb.
Three deep slashes that had bitten deeply into the
white-painted wood.

Aiden and I both bore similar marks on our
abdomens. Matching wounds—his still fresh, mine
seven years old.

I cinched my sheathed blades in place, so that
the weapons were held crossed between my shoulder blades on my back. Then I crossed the kitchen to
place three of my fingers on the gouges in the wooden
doorframe. The marks from where a massive creature
had pulled itself into my home, most likely fighting
against whatever magic Aiden had called forth and
thrown at it.

When I factored in the black witch who'd had
trouble holding onto the magic she was using to
cloak her true face, my past clicked into place with
my present, pointing to my immediate future.

I knew what I was facing.

A greater demon.

A demon called forth by a witch who was
powerful enough to cloak it in so much magic that it
could stand the daylight long enough to incapacitate
me. A demon that had hurt me so badly it had taken
me three months to heal—and even then, I'd barely

been able to get out of bed and walk five steps into the bathroom.

But I had gotten a piece of that demon. I had wounded it enough that its summoner had vanquished it back to its own dimension. And after that, I had suddenly and inexplicably been deemed expendable. An unofficial kill order had been issued for me. Then for the other four.

I had never figured out who I'd been ultimately up against then. I still didn't know whose plans I'd disrupted when I successfully rescued Aiden's father, Kader Azar. I honestly didn't know whether that event was even connected to what was happening now.

All I did know was that I'd failed some sort of test that day, that my empathy had been blamed for that failing, and that the Collective had been convened to discuss my fate. But as far as I knew, that meeting had never had a chance to take place.

There hadn't been time for questions, or an opportunity to beg for answers as to why my life was suddenly worthless. We Five had broken out of the compound, smashing anything and everything in our path, erasing ourselves—and destroying over a century of the Collective's work toward creating the perfect Adept.

I'd faced off against a black witch that day. A black witch more than capable of calling forth a greater demon.

Another black witch had sat across from me in the diner just hours before, strong enough to bind me to a doll made in my likeness with a single drop of my blood.

And now there were signs that a greater demon had broken into my home and snatched people under my protection from my kitchen. The same type of demon that had almost killed me, and that had marked Aiden.

The two witches were one and the same.

Silver Pine.

I laughed harshly.

I wasn't supposed to have rescued Kader Azar. That was suddenly crystal clear, seven years later. Silver Pine must have had a grudge against the sorcerer. The demon summoning had most likely been meant for him. But we had gotten him clear of the roof that day in LA before the demon's arrival, because summoning and binding a greater demon wasn't a precisely timed magical art.

I had stood between Silver Pine and her target—a target she had presumably helped the rogue shapeshifters kidnap in the first place.

Based on her obsession with Aiden, Silver Pine still held a grudge against Kader Azar. And she clearly still held a grudge against me, because I'd inadvertently disrupted her plans. I'd gotten Azar to safety. Then I hadn't died. The kill order had been her way of tidying up her betrayal.

In the end, I had destroyed the Collective. I wasn't certain how they'd run their organization, but it was an easy guess that the sorcerer Azar had stood between Silver Pine and something she wanted. Perhaps control of the Collective itself?

So I had disrupted an internal coup, by way of destroying everything the Collective had created.

That definitely justified a massive amount of animosity.

I felt a little lightheaded.

It was so simple. And I had missed it. Being on the run and fearing for your life could muddle things, apparently. But now I'd been dragged back into the middle of Silver Pine's plans for revenge. Aiden was caught within those plans as well, even though he wasn't aligned with—wasn't even in touch with—his father.

It was all a game.

A power play.

Between Silver Pine and Kader Azar.

And I had killed so … so … many people. I'd destroyed kilometers of land and buildings.

For a grudge.

And when Silver couldn't get her hands on Kader? Was that what had inspired her to take Aiden instead? Apparently, she'd been looking for me for the past seven years as well. And she had picked up a trace of me in San Francisco when Christopher had to reveal himself to save me. Then she found Fish through Mark Calhoun.

And now she had found me.

Her and her pet demon.

Except that demon wouldn't find me so easy to dispatch this time. Not because I was faster or stronger. In fact, I was softer and weaker than I had been then.

But now I had something to fight for, beyond myself and my obligations to the Five.

I had a reason to not just stand aside and let the future play out as it willed.

Paisley climbed onto the patio, dropping what appeared to be the bloody leg of a brown cow at my feet.

I sighed. "Is that the same cow?"

She hunkered down, licking her chops, then nudging the leg toward me. Apparently I was supposed to eat it to recoup my strength. We were going to owe the neighbors another fifteen hundred dollars.

"Thank you," I murmured, kneeling in front of her so I could match her eye level.

She had reverted to her large blue-nosed pit bull form, but her blue fur was crisscrossed with thick white scars. Her left eye had healed, but the flesh around the socket was likewise scored with claw marks. One ear was still missing a chunk of flesh.

"I can't ask you to risk your life for me," I said. "But if you would try to lead me to Christopher, to Knox, I would appreciate it."

She regarded me without blinking.

Magic shifted along my spine, announcing Daniel a moment before he climbed up onto the patio, leaning heavily on the railing. Lani had said that he and Paisley were looking for me at Meadow Lane Farm. Even as badly injured as she was, Paisley had made it back to me first.

"You think she wouldn't follow you into battle?" he said. He'd been beaten badly, though the bruises were already darkening, healing. "You think any of us wouldn't follow you?" He laughed harshly, scrubbing his hand over his head, then stretching his neck. "Hell, we're all waiting to follow, Emma. Desperate to follow."

"This isn't your fight, or Paisley's. It wasn't seven years ago, and it isn't now."

He narrowed his eyes. "You think it's connected?"

I straightened. "Yes."

He shrugged, and I saw pain flash across his face. His ribs were broken or at least badly bruised. "We were bred to be yours, weren't we? Our commander and our warrior?"

"We always had different interpretations of our roles," I said stiffly.

He smirked.

I hardened my tone. "We aren't controlled by our breeding."

Daniel snorted. "Keep telling yourself that, Socks."

"You left Christopher alone. Vulnerable."

"I was running around a pig farm looking for you! We headed back when Christopher texted, but Paisley and I got hit by demons on the way. Plus, how was I supposed to know your sorcerer was useless?"

I ground my teeth, but now wasn't the time for petty fights. "Are you coming with me or not?"

"Yes. You never have to ask."

I leveled my gaze at him. "Did you know the witch was Silver Pine in disguise?"

"What?" Daniel laughed. "She's dead. I watched you kill her."

"You've been in touch with Christopher this entire time?"

"Yes, of course. I wasn't going to leave you all alone."

"I'm not alone."

"You know what I mean."

I didn't. "You led Silver Pine here."

"I did not."

"She spelled me this afternoon."

"How?"

I shook my head. "A look-alike doll. A blood-triggered spell. I'm not certain, but I think I was supposed to kill myself."

"I'm surprised it grabbed hold of you at all. Magenta isn't that powerful. Why do you think she wants the sorcerer to do her bidding?"

So Daniel had known that Aiden was the witch's objective before he'd shown up at my front door. Well, one of her objectives. "She's obviously very skilled at memory charms. She has Mark Calhoun all tied up in one as well."

Daniel laughed again. "Please. I'd know. Plus nothing like that would work on me. I'm not stupid enough to trigger some trap with my blood."

"You're sleeping with her, aren't you?"

His shoulders stiffened. "What does it matter to you? You're sleeping with the sorcerer."

"I'm not," I said quietly. "Not yet." And now Aiden might well be dead. I shoved away the well of grief that tried to choke me at the thought. "But he showed up here five days ago, completely drained of magic and missing any memory of the previous three days."

"Oh, yes? Did he meet you in a back alley? Can you wipe memories when you steal magic now?"

Ignoring his attempts to unsettle me, I plowed ahead, clicking the last pieces of the puzzle together. "Then a snatcher demon showed up with Aiden's familial title carved on its chest."

"Teleportation?"

A rare trait, even for demons. "Yes."

"You're thinking it was blood tied … "

I waited. He was putting it together.

"You think … the witch and the sorcerer were sleeping together."

"I know they were."

"Well, the guy is an idiot to let a witch … " He trailed off, his expression going blank.

"Did you use a condom?"

He shook his head. "You, more than anyone else, know I don't have any reason to…" Then he grimaced. "Semen. Fuck. Fuck me."

Yeah, Daniel had led the black witch to our doorstep. She had played with us all for a while and then snatched Christopher.

"Silver fucking Pine," Daniel snarled.

"Yes."

"I was fucking Silver fucking Pine. Who tried to kill you, kill us. I thought… you destroyed everything in and around the compound. For kilometers! Fucking shit, she's ancient. She's got to be sixty fucking years old."

I laughed, completely inappropriately.

Daniel eyed me darkly. But then he started laughing himself. "Silver Pine. Silver Pine. The fucking Collective."

"Yes."

"Why aren't you losing it? You should be losing your shit as badly as I am."

"I lost it earlier, Daniel. Now I need to move forward. I need to find Christopher."

"Right. Right." He scrubbed his hand over his face harshly.

"When was the last time you slept with her?"

He shook his head. "Over a week ago."

"How long can she keep the semen viable? Three days?"

"Presumably. If it's the same as blood. But…"

"Aiden had been here for four days before she tried to collect him, and he'd likely been knocked out, drained and disoriented for a day or more before."

"So she can hold the semen in stasis, and the magic contained with it. For, say, a week at least."

"Yes. Though the timing might be a clue."

"Maybe only a week."

"Yes."

He looked at me grimly. "She still might be able to manipulate me. If I get within a certain range of her. Line of sight at least."

I grinned. It wasn't a nice smile. "Not as well as I can."

He snorted. "Too true. No one can fuck with me, with any of us, as well as you, Socks."

There might have been a compliment buried deeply within Fish's accusation, but I wasn't interested in figuring it out. I didn't want to figure anything else out. I wanted to be moving, doing. I turned to the demon dog, who'd been listening to the entire conversation. "Paisley? Have you got a bead on Christopher?"

She blinked her red-hued eyes at me.

"I'm going to need Knox's sword," Daniel said. "I didn't want to try to bring mine over the border."

"Under his bed."

He stepped by me, pausing in the doorway. "Wait for me, Emma."

"I will."

He nodded. "She won't have hurt Christopher."

"No," I said wryly. "His semen is too valuable."

He laughed harshly. "Six months, Socks. I waited. I thought after we were free, of the compound, of the others, that you'd finally come to me. And stay. That you'd choose me, freely. Not because I was your only option. But you didn't even reach out. After that, you couldn't have possibly expected me to be a fucking monk."

"I never expected anything of you, Daniel."

"Yeah, right. Because I could never measure up."

I looked out at the dark night, feeling Aiden's magic within the honed edge of the blade slung across my back. I was ready to use it. And not even remotely interested in discussing the past.

Daniel snorted, pausing to wrench the kitchen table out of the wall before walking away through the house and up the stairs.

TEN

A SHAPESHIFTER WAS PROWLING ALONG A SIX-METER length of the property's back fence, where an entire section appeared to have been crushed.

Obviously, it was beneath a greater demon to climb over anything in its way.

Jenni Raymond, out of uniform again, was hunkered down and digging her fingers in the churned and trampled grass.

She didn't even notice as Daniel, Paisley, and I approached. It was full dark now, but that shouldn't have compromised her eyesight or her hearing.

"Some shapeshifter." Fish curled his lip in a sneer at the oblivious RCMP officer. He was carrying Christopher's steel shortsword over his shoulder, the gems that decorated its pommel and cross guard long drained of the magic they'd once held.

I snorted.

Jenni Raymond stilled, reacting like prey, not the predator she was supposed to be. She raised her head, scanning the field before her, but she still didn't see us enveloped in the darkness. Granted, we three were unique predators. And if the shifter refused to use all her senses, then she didn't have a chance against any Adepts who could mask their presence as well as we could.

That was a pathetic excuse, though. No matter how quietly we moved over the dry ground, a shifter should have heard us. And Jenni Raymond had been in my house multiple times. I'd actually touched her bare skin. She should have easily catalogued my scent, should have been able to pick it up meters away, and to track it for kilometers.

Paisley gathered herself and leaped, landing in the churned grass next to the shapeshifter. She lowered her broad head and snarled—a rippling, fierce declaration of might.

Evidently, the demon dog was out of patience.

Raymond scrambled back in the dirt, jaw dropping as she stared at the demon dog. But she didn't transform to face the sudden threat. She didn't utilize any of her magic to defend herself.

I stepped up beside Paisley, gently laying my hand on her head. She snorted and shuffled, then returned to tracking mode. We had followed the demon's tracks from the house, trying to see if and where the path it had taken onto the property diverged from the path taken out. The path it had taken with Christopher and Aiden in tow.

Thankfully, the demon didn't appear to be capable of teleportation.

Jenni Raymond's gaze flicked to me, then Daniel.

Fish scoffed. "So, completely useless then?"

"Yes." I sighed, peeved. Apparently it was time to pause for another chat. "Can we help you, Officer Raymond?"

The shapeshifter scrambled to her feet, jabbing her finger toward Paisley, who was systematically covering the area in short steps, nose to the ground. "That ... that ... " She shook her head, then gestured to the broken fence and the surrounding darkness. "What the hell is going on here?"

"Cows," Daniel said, completely straight-faced.

"Cows. I'm not an idiot." Raymond jabbed her finger toward me. "First you were missing. Lani Zachary texts to say she found you, but won't say where." She jabbed the same finger over my shoulder. "And now the house is dark. The house is never dark this time of night."

"How would you know?" I asked, hearing the threat threaded through my question. I needed to calm down, stay focused.

She ignored me. "Which means Christopher isn't on the property. And Christopher never leaves."

"Knox doesn't leave the property?" Daniel asked quietly.

"He does," I said, not offering any specifics in front of the ranting shapeshifter. "Occasionally."

"Something came through here." Jenni Raymond jabbed her finger toward the crumpled fence and the ruined grass. Her voice was far too loud in the still of the evening, grating. "It smells like ... " But she caught herself before admitting that she could smell something a regular person wouldn't be able to sense.

I laughed. It wasn't a nice sound. But it was better than running her through with my newly sharpened blade to get her out of my way. "Smells? You've been using your nose, shifter."

The demon did smell. Though to my insensitive nose, its reek—a scent like burned wet wood—was already fading, as it had been in the house.

"And now ... now you two." She waved her hand. "With the swords."

"This isn't any of your business, shifter," Daniel sneered.

"I represent the law in this town."

"You represent enforcement of that law, actually," I said coolly. "And we aren't under human jurisdiction. And neither is this situation."

"So there is a situation," Raymond crowed, as if she'd just won some sort of game.

Paisley stopped her snuffling about five meters to my right. She looked back at me over her shoulder, blending into the dark night so much that all I could see were her blazing red eyes. She only paused and looked at me that way when she found blood.

"Time to go," I murmured to Daniel.

He stepped toward Paisley without another word.

I followed.

Jenni Raymond darted forward, grabbing my arm. "You're not going anywhere until you answer—"

I looked at her. "Remove your hand, shifter."

"I ... I ... have a responsibility ... " She gulped.

"You don't want to tangle with me," I said almost gently. As if chiding a toddler to not touch a hot stove.

"Christopher ... "

"You don't want to tangle with him either," I said. "Though it's obviously too late for that. And I'm not his keeper. Remove. Your. Hand."

She loosened her hold, stepping away from me. But then she jutted her chin out stubbornly. "I'm coming with you. You think Paisley will be able to track ... whatever took Christopher, yes?"

She'd put that together quickly. Evidently, her ability to problem solve was more functional than her magic. "Can you even achieve half-form?"

"I ... I ... "

So no. "Can you transform into your animal?"

She sputtered. "The moon is only five days away from full. So yes, if I have to."

The moon was, in fact, drawing close to full. It just wasn't visible yet. It also had nothing to do with the shifter's ability to transform, which she should have been capable of doing anytime, anywhere. "You are useless to me, Jenni Raymond. Untrained. Weak. You don't even pay attention to what should be instinct for you. Like not touching me. I can't be saving your ass when I'm already tasked elsewhere."

"I'm trained. Well trained. In hand-to-hand combat and firearms—"

"Both are useless against what we're facing." I leaned toward her. "You know how a shapeshifter kills? With tooth and claw. With a strength that should be capable of tearing someone's head off. If you could do that, I'd be asking you to come with us."

"That's insane."

I walked away.

She didn't follow.

And that was for the best. Though I was fairly certain I had just made an enemy when I had only wanted to blend in.

I had just wanted to be.

I left those desires in my wake. I had run as far as I could from my past. And now I was standing with blades in hand, ready to confront that past again. For Christopher, who had saved me from myself on more than one occasion. Who kept me grounded and focused. And for Aiden, who I thought I just might be able to love. If I had the capacity. If we both took a chance on each other.

THE FIRST FLOOR OF PETER GRANT'S HOUSE WAS LIT from within. Standing by the open gate at the top of the dirt drive, I could see the soft glow from the fireplace in the living room. The demon had crossed from the main road and through the northern fields of Meadow Lane Farm, crushing the wire fence.

The location couldn't have been a coincidence. But I had no idea how a mundane like Grant or the derelict pig farm could have been connected to Silver Pine. And I didn't like not being in possession of all the facts. Not one bit.

Daniel turned off his flashlight. We had traced the demon along the back edge of the Wilsons' property, where it had run up against the lake and veered north to the main road. Apparently, the demon either didn't like water or couldn't cross over it. Which was an interesting observation, but which didn't seem likely to help us vanquish it in the least.

Daniel had scanned the edges of the road as we'd jogged the fifteen kilometers from our property to the Grants', looking for signs that the demon had veered off or dropped its human cargo along the way. It hadn't. Paisley hadn't paused at all, so her read on Christopher was steady. Whatever spell Silver Pine had used to block the demon dog from tracking me—likely something built into the replica doll and strengthened with my own blood—she wasn't using it to mask the clairvoyant.

She wanted us to follow the demon's path. She was using Christopher to lure Daniel and me. And she wanted whatever confrontation she had planned to take place away from town. But why?

I didn't know yet. But it was all fine by me. I preferred not to play games or piece together puzzles. I was much more skilled at taking down what lay immediately in front of me than I was in figuring out rules or collecting clues.

I could see in the dark to a certain extent—another ability that had been stolen on the path to the Collective making me their ultimate tool. But I wouldn't have minded keeping the flashlight on or having the moon make an appearance. Paisley could see in the dark perfectly well, though, so we left the road without discussing it. Daniel fell in behind me, ghosting my footsteps and following my magic through the deep gloom of the evening.

He had once told me, after we'd shared an intimate moment, that I glowed. That we all glowed to him, each of us a slightly different shade of white. Christopher was the purest. I was the brightest, kissed with light gray, like a fallen star.

I had left his bed then and hadn't returned for three months. Six months after that, I'd slept with Mark Calhoun, had almost been killed by a black witch and her pet demon, and had destroyed the Collective. Daniel ... Fish had never murmured anything intimate, anything suggesting that what we shared was more than physical, to me again. As I'd intended.

Paisley led us on a diagonal across the property—the same path we'd taken seven months earlier when tracking Hannah Stewart. The further confirmation that our present location wasn't a coincidence put me on edge, enough that I caught myself clenching my teeth and holding my blades too tightly.

The pigpen that had been empty the last time was empty again. But for a very different reason. A swath of blood and body parts indicated that the pen had recently held pigs. But the fencing had been shattered at either end as the demon swept through, most likely consuming those pigs without even stopping. The remains didn't smell yet, so the carnage had been relatively recent.

I paused, glancing back at the house. "They must have squealed. Loudly, if briefly."

Daniel shrugged. "Drunk."

I glanced at him. "I've been here before, tracking a woman... Hannah, who the owner's son had beaten and chased into the forest."

He nodded. "Christopher told me about it. And that the old guy carries a grudge. Which is why we came through here earlier, Paisley and I. Grant was already tying one on when he ran us off." He laughed darkly, likely at the idea of him running from Peter Grant. "He'll have passed out by now. I didn't bother with him because I knew you hadn't been on the property recently. It's devoid of magic, even naturally occurring. Which is actually odd."

"And Paisley couldn't track me. Did you figure out why? Was she spelled directly?"

He shook his head. "She seemed confused. But we've never worked together, so I'm not certain. Knox said that this idiot had given you some trouble." He grinned at me, his teeth just a flash of white in the dark. "It's awful when you can't just scare everyone into submission, isn't it Socks?"

"Oh, he's scared." I stepped around the pigpen. Paisley had already moved on, and I didn't want to lose her in the dark. "We're lucky the demon can't teleport. Paisley might not be tracking Christopher so easily right now either." Though I honestly wasn't sure how true that was. When I'd rescued Paisley from the compound in the middle of destroying it, Zans had indicated that the demon dog was genetically programed to track the Five. But we had never tested that ability or her range—which was idiotically shortsighted of me.

"We're lucky no one noticed a fucking demon racing down the road."

"It has to be cloaked. Even Silver Pine isn't stupid enough to draw attention to herself that way. At least, not more attention than what she wants to draw."

"Because there's a reason Paisley can track Christopher but couldn't track you."

It wasn't a question, but I answered it anyway. "Yes. The witch is playing with us."

"Drawing us in now, but not before she was ready for us."

"Maybe. Or maybe the spell on the doll was just to distract me long enough for her pet demon to grab Christopher. And Aiden. Maybe this was her endgame all along."

"Or she's insane and simply reacting in the moment."

That was a disconcerting option. A crazy black witch would be far too unpredictable. "Yes."

I strode across the field with Daniel at my heels, not at all pleased but trying to keep my uncertainty in check as Paisley led us to the same section of fence where I'd found evidence of Hannah Stewart's attempt to flee her abusive boyfriend. Another un-justifiable layer of coincidence. But again, I could see no reason for Silver Pine to get involved in the lives of mundanes. Or why she would have masterminded a plan to draw Christopher and me off the property seven months ago, but not follow through until now.

"How long ago?" I asked, looking over the broken fence at the dark forest stretched out before us. "How long have you been working with Mark Calhoun and Silver Pine?"

"Mark, off and on for about three years. Silver for about three months."

"And how long have you known where we were? Christopher, Paisley, and me?"

He hesitated, surprised. "Always, Socks. Knox checked in every three months or so at the start. Then more frequently after he figured out how to keep the texts and emails from being traced." A wind picked up, rustling the looming evergreens. "He didn't tell you?"

"I knew. But I thought it might have been Bee he was keeping in touch with."

"Her too."

"And Zans?"

He didn't answer. Which meant that Zans—Samantha—was doing something I wasn't supposed to know about. Like tracking down the rest of the Collective, as I'd long suspected.

I turned, eyeing Daniel in the dark. "It wasn't San Francisco, then. When Christopher had to reveal himself to rescue me. It wasn't that botched contract that called Silver's attention to us." That had happened in October 2017, almost a year earlier. But Silver had only hooked up with Daniel at the beginning of the summer.

"An amplifier and a clairvoyant working together? That was pretty stupid."

"Who would have known outside the Collective, outside of the Five? No one." I leaned toward him. "If you and Zans have done something ... if this is part of some mission you two are working on to take down the members of the Collective that's gone wrong, and if Christopher is dead because of that, I'm coming after you both."

"I won't be hard to find. I'm standing right next to you. Where I'd always be, if you gave me the choice. Where you should always be, with us."

"Did you hear me?"

"Yeah, I heard you."

I vaulted over the fence, following Paisley into the dark woods. Daniel followed and clicked on the flashlight, keeping the beam low and just ahead of my feet so as to not compromise Paisley's vision. It would call attention to us. But the demons I had no doubt we were about to face lived in the dark, so they could easily track us either way.

THE FIRST TRAP WAS SET ABOUT TEN PACES INTO THE forest. It ghosted over Paisley's back and targeted the most magical thing in the vicinity—me. Energy exploded around me, malicious strands of magic that wrapped around my torso, pinning my arms to my sides and instantly rendering my blades useless. Not that they would have been able to cut through the magic anyway. The tentacles of the spell cinched tighter, intending to crush me.

I didn't struggle or attempt to free myself. I simply paused, allowing the spell to slide and slip across my arms as if it were unable to maintain its hold. It didn't find my magic terribly tasty. And with nothing to fuel it further, it shriveled.

I brushed the remnants of the spell from my arms, already continuing onward through the forest.

"Is that a new ability?" Daniel asked, as if what magic I might have stolen in the last seven years was a topic for casual conversation.

"No." I glanced back at him. "Apparently, I was only raised to be a sociopath. It doesn't come naturally."

His face was simply a lighter point among the dark trees, but I thought he might have frowned. "I'm not judging you."

"I am."

"You didn't kill as many people as you think," he said. "Once you got the ... draining under control."

"Did their magic come back?" I asked, already knowing the answer but making the point just so he knew where I drew the line these days.

"I don't know."

"And for an Adept, having their magic stolen is like murder, isn't it?"

He didn't answer.

I didn't expect him to. We'd never seen eye to eye about walking the line between being light and dark. I couldn't live in the light—my soul had been stained from the moment of my birth. But I could try to not be fully dark.

Which was why I'd tried to save my team seven years ago from the greater demon I was fairly certain Paisley was currently tracking through the woods. Because sacrificing them—including Mark and Becca—hadn't even been an option, not even a thought. That choice was still the linchpin moment of my life. The transition between being Amp5 and becoming Emma Johnson.

In rescuing my team instead of draining them or dying myself, I'd unwittingly drawn the ire of a black witch. And her vengeance now had me tromping through the forest, partnered with a man who wasn't my sibling, my lover, or my friend. But still, his magic thrummed lightly against my spinal cord, binding us in life and undoubtedly in death.

The forest slid sideways and tried to swallow me.

More dark, dark magic shifted through the branches and roots of the evergreens surrounding us, causing them to reach, grabbing, tugging at my ankles, legs, arms, and neck.

Ahead of me, Paisley snarled and snapped.

Daniel grunted, straining against the spell we'd triggered. The magic was trying to compress my lungs.

Another trap.

I squeezed the words out, breathless. "It's an illusion."

Fish's nullifying magic welled up, rolling out from him, pushing back the spell attempting to suffocate us with our own minds. His magic crashed over me, chilling me through. His fingers brushed the back of my neck.

Without further prompting, I grabbed the power already emanating from him intensely. Then I doubled it. Tripled it.

He grunted, gathering the magic I'd amplified. Collecting the energy into a huge invisible cloud of power, he cast it out in an arcing wave before us. It stormed through the dark forest, subsuming the active spell as well as absorbing what felt like two more traps set ahead of us before it faded.

Paisley glanced back at us, snarling and completely disgruntled.

I understood her perfectly even without words. Daniel's magic was numbing, dampening.

"All right, all right," Daniel said to the demon dog, laughing breathlessly. "You're the one triggering all the spells."

He moved to take the lead. But he hesitated as he passed me, leaning in to murmur, low and intimate, "I'd forgotten ... what it feels like to be touched by you, Socks. How could I forget?"

"It's my magic, Daniel. Not me."

He laughed again, his own fully primed magic prickling coolly against my neck and face. "After this is done, you'll admit you had fun. You'll admit you missed me. And you'll admit you want to do it over and over again."

"You are an arrogant asshole."

"So are you. We were made for each other. Literally."

"No." I locked my gaze to his, trying to force him to see and acknowledge my seriousness, my certainty. "It's our magic that was made to match, along with the magic of three others."

"Well," he drawled, not at all put off, "I never had a problem having all four of you. When you're tired of running from yourself, let me know."

I wasn't running from myself. I was done running. I knew that with utter certainty, because when I'd laid eyes on Aiden I knew he didn't come without consequences. And I had chosen to stay anyway.

I smiled.

Daniel frowned. Then he stepped away, crossing over to Paisley. I automatically closed the space between us, close enough that I could touch him if necessary. Our training still ingrained after seven years.

Fish's nullifying magic snapped forward, then wrapped around us in a tight dome. "Stay close," he said to Paisley. "Or I'll accidentally nullify you."

She snorted, informing him that he was the idiot, not her.

Tightly grouped, we moved forward more slowly. Our footsteps in the dark underbrush broadcast our every move, though on her own, Paisley wouldn't have made a sound.

It didn't matter either way. The witch already knew we were coming. She'd known the moment she sent a demon that couldn't teleport, the moment she'd taken Christopher. But she'd had to play her best card to foil a clairvoyant and a sorcerer—the greater demon. She had no idea I hadn't amplified Aiden's magic. She assumed I had, actually.

So she'd wanted to get me and Daniel out of the way momentarily, and ...

Wait ...

"What came for you?" I asked. "You and Paisley? You came to the Grants' looking for me. Then you said Christopher texted?" Because of course he would have. "With a vision of the demon in the house?"

"Yes. But we encountered resistance on our return." He cleared his throat. "My vulnerability to the assault makes a bit more sense now."

"She used demons rather than magic."

"Yes." Daniel's tone turned wry. "Most likely targeted to me specifically, because apparently I should have used a condom."

I didn't bother reconfirming what he already knew. What any male Adept sleeping with a morally questionable witch should have known.

"Paisley saved my ass," Daniel said, lightly petting the demon dog's head, which currently came up to his waist. "But I was still knocked out for long enough that she got back to the house before me."

She had, despite being badly wounded. Dying. I rested my gaze on what little I could see of Paisley in the dark, shoving away the remembrance of her magic dying under my hands. Her blue-furred skin was still crisscrossed with scars that appeared white, making me realize they were catching the moonlight. I glanced overhead. The forest was still dark, but a shimmering of light had appeared, filtering through the thick boughs.

"Silver Pine is flinging a lot of magic around," I mused.

"You wondering how she's fueling it?"

"I am."

"I always forget you can't feel magic like I can."

Daniel had to feel magic in order to nullify it. I usually only picked up magical beings easily. Though I could feel magic used against me, obviously, and potent magical objects.

Fish swept his hand forward. "I've been feeling it since we entered the forest. First the absence of magic at the Grant farm, and then ... " He shook his head. "It's localized ahead. Something ridiculously horrendous happened near here, a long time ago. A mass slaughter, if I was going to take a guess. And it saturated the earth, the area, with untapped malignant energy. A necromancer without proper shielding would go nuts out here."

Even nonmagical blood, nonmagical deaths, could leave an imprint on the land—and on the souls of their murderers. Tyler Grant had chased Hannah Stewart into these woods, and she'd run through the clearing I knew was just up ahead. If what Daniel was surmising was true, I wasn't surprised that Hannah had been drawn to this place. And I also wasn't surprised that she'd fought Tyler off and fled farther into the forest. Hannah carried a glimmer of magic, enough that she might have been able to tap into some latent power in the forest. Something that made her fight for her life and win.

The problem was that a black witch could tap into that same energy. And as far as I could theorize without actual evidence, a mass slaughter even far back in the past could and would provide Silver Pine with practically endless fuel.

I was no longer surprised that she'd held me at bay with the doll. Or sent the demons for Aiden, or almost murdered Paisley. The black witch was powerful. Too powerful. Perhaps even impossible to defeat when backed by her pet demon.

But I didn't believe in the impossible. And I most definitely loathed having to acknowledge that I might be wrong.

"We're going to have to kill her," I murmured. "To vanquish the demon."

Daniel grunted in agreement.

There was just one problem. Together or apart, and even backed by Paisley, neither of us was a match for the demon I'd confronted on the roof in LA seven years before. A demon that had already trounced me once—so badly that it had taken me three months to walk again.

WE STEPPED INTO A MOONLIT CLEARING THAT I RECognized even in the dark, including the makeshift firepit set by a decrepit hunting shed. Seven months before, Christopher, Paisley, and I had tracked Hannah Stewart through the clearing, finding evidence that she had hurt her abuser—specifically, his blood on a rock. Then we'd followed her trail deeper into the woods.

The woman currently spread-eagled on the ground by the firepit was a surprise, though. For more than one reason.

Becca Jackson.

Unconscious. Maybe even dead, because I couldn't feel any magic—not from her or from any spell or artifact she would have been carrying as a sorcerer who specialized in demolition magic. Specifically, runed spells.

I stumbled forward, pressing against Fish's nullifying shield. He dropped the magic barring my advancement, but yanked me back harshly enough that he wrenched my shoulder.

"Watch your feet," he hissed.

I glanced down. A circle of smooth stones ringed Becca, barely discernible in the moonlit darkness.

"A spell," I whispered.

"A curse, more like it." Daniel knelt down beside the stone-denoted circle, gazing at whatever magic he could see that I couldn't.

Paisley paced to the far edge of the clearing, then glanced back over her shoulder and snarled at us, impatient.

"We're coming," I said to her. Then I asked Daniel, "Is Becca still alive?"

The nullifier held up one finger, his eyes glued to her.

She drew in a shallow breath, her chest rising almost imperceptibly.

He nodded.

"Unconscious? Or placed in some sort of stasis?" I asked. "Is she fueling the spell?"

"Maybe. Or she's the trigger," Daniel murmured, training his flashlight on the stone nearest to him. "Unmarked."

"Witch magic." Witches rarely used runes, and sorcerers rarely used circles to contain a casting. "So it isn't a barrier spell erected by Becca."

Daniel grunted, agreeing with my assessment.

"We leave her then?" I'd intended that to be a statement, not a question, but I couldn't take it back once I'd voiced it.

Daniel eyed me. "Whatever it is could still kill her. If it's a timed release."

Spells with delayed triggers—meant to release on their own, rather than be triggered like the traps we'd encountered earlier—were a very specific branch of magic. Normally they were delicate. Precise. But that seemed out of sync with who we were dealing with.

"I doubt Silver Pine is capable of such casting. Her magic is … on the edge of imploding."

Daniel snorted. "Not soon enough. But I agree. I would have said the same for the doll likeness you said drove you all the way to the river, though. And it ensnared you easily enough."

I ignored his attempt to needle me—again. "She could have another witch working for her."

"No. Silver Pine isn't the coven sort."

Paisley started pacing and grumbling.

"We have to go," I said.

"You'd leave Becca here, then?"

"She might be so deeply tied to whatever spell is set here that she's already dead. Or maybe we're supposed to try to save her, and whatever lies dormant here is meant to hurt us. Not enough to kill us, but enough that we won't be able to help Christopher."

"You've changed." Daniel slowly stepped around the stone ring encasing Becca, tracing it with his flashlight as if looking for a weak entry point. "You once risked all our lives to save your team."

"I didn't know that's what I was doing at the time," I said stiffly. "And Christopher is my sole responsibility now."

"Your sole mission?" he asked mockingly.

"I'm not going to stand around taking insult after insult from you," I said coolly. "I've always understood my responsibilities."

"While I haven't?"

"You're here, aren't you? You've put both me and Christopher in danger because you had to mix business with pleasure."

"Well, I learned that from you, didn't I?"

"I never mixed. I knew the difference between you in your bed, and you on mission with me."

"Yeah, that was always clear to you." He gestured toward Becca. "What if I can neutralize the spell?"

I stalked forward. "Think for one minute, Daniel. This is Silver Pine. Not only does she know every aspect of our training, she also understands our magic. And maybe even how we'd react to seeing a team member in jeopardy." I glanced at Becca, seeing her take another shallow breath. "At least she knows how I'll react, because she saw it on the roof in LA."

Daniel let out a harsh sigh. "We'll come back for her. Ironically, she might be safer here than where we're going."

I nodded, already stepping away toward Paisley.

"What!?" A woman shouted from the dark woods behind us.

It took me a moment to recognize her voice.

Jenni Raymond.

The shapeshifter charged out from between a tight grouping of evergreens at the edge of the clearing, where she'd obviously been listening to our conversation. I didn't pick up the tenor of her magic until she was only steps away. It was even more muted than usual.

I glanced at Daniel.

He was watching Jenni Raymond with narrowed eyes. "Witch charm," he muttered, indicating that the shapeshifter was wearing magic that helped shield her from our senses.

I nodded. But even so, I knew such a charm shouldn't have shielded the sound of her passage through the forest. Raymond wasn't that kind of shifter. I glanced over at Paisley. The demon dog was sitting with her back to us.

"Some heads-up would have been nice," I said.

Paisley snorted derisively.

Apparently, we were simply idiots to not have noticed the shifter following us. Either that or the demon dog's opinion of the shifter in question was so low that Paisley didn't think she bore mentioning.

I sighed, shaking my head.

"I don't think this is a laughing matter," Jenni Raymond snarled, jutting her chin out at me. "This woman is obviously in trouble. And you're just going to leave her here?"

Daniel started laughing.

I ignored him. "When you had the witch make the charm you're using to sneak around, did you use DNA samples collected from my home, shifter?"

"What?" Jenni Raymond's false bravado slipped slightly. She glanced back and forth between Daniel and me.

Fish wiped his eyes. "It's like…" He started laughing again. "She has no idea…no concept…how dangerous you are."

"She doesn't," I snapped. Then I leveled my gaze on the shifter. "I'll take the charm."

She stiffened her shoulders. "No."

I leaned toward her. "Think carefully, shifter. You're in the middle of the woods with three killers. If you've stolen our DNA and given it to the witch that made that charm for you, we will kill you. We don't even have to hide your body."

"Yeah." Daniel chuckled. "Paisley will just eat you. Yum."

"You are both certifiable."

I was so done with being screwed around with. So, so done. I grabbed the shifter by the throat, yanking her toward me.

Her eyes rounded, then she started to twist, fighting my grasp.

"The charm," I said to Daniel.

He reached into the pocket of her jeans, pulling out an old-fashioned pocket watch.

Jenni Raymond started gasping, clawing at my hand and arm, but her wholly human fingernails couldn't even begin to scratch my skin.

Daniel opened the watch, and the charm held within it immediately dispersed. "Amateur," he murmured, examining the watch further. "Tied to the shifter, not to any of us."

I let go of Jenni Raymond. She fell to her knees, clutching her neck and gasping.

"You ..." She struggled to speak. "You are a terrible person."

I crouched next to her, just so she could meet my gaze. "If your foolishness ever brings harm to anyone under my protection, I won't even need permission from a pack to deal with you. That's how large of a transgression stealing any Adept's DNA is."

"An offense that comes with a death sentence," Daniel said coolly. Then he tossed the pocket watch into the dirt next to Raymond.

She snatched it up, immediately tucking it in her pocket.

I glanced at him questioningly.

He shrugged. "It's engraved. A family heirloom, I assumed. And the shifter might be useful after all."

"How so?"

He nodded toward Becca. "You said Silver Pine knows us."

I looked at Jenni. She stared back at me with a mixture of fear and defiance. "But the shifter would have been beneath her notice," I said.

"Yes."

"The spell wouldn't be set up to thwart her."

Daniel chuckled. "It wouldn't."

I laughed. "Well, Officer Raymond, I guess you're going to get your wish to serve and protect."

She glanced between us. "You are both fucking assholes. I can't believe you're related to Christopher at all."

Daniel started laughing again.

I'd never known him to be the jovial sort, but obviously the shifter's false bravado tickled him.

"If we're going to do something, let's do it quickly," I said.

Still chuckling, Daniel waved Officer Raymond to her feet. She complied, brushing the dirt from her jeans and staring at me balefully.

Fish crouched down next to the stone-marked ring that encased Becca. "I'll need you to be ready, Emma."

"I always am."

He snorted, then looked surprised when I flashed him a smile. He tucked his chin to his chest, pointing at the two rocks nearest to him. "It's easy, shifter. All you need to do is move these two stones out of alignment."

Jenni Raymond hunkered down next to Fish. "And that will do what? Disrupt the spell? I can smell magic."

Daniel grunted. "Residual, probably from the casting. The genius of this spell is that it's dormant. So you wouldn't be able to pick up a scent yet."

Jenni nodded, reaching for the rocks.

I was going to have to revisit my previous assessment of the shifter's bravado. Maybe it wasn't all false. Maybe it just got shaky around me.

"Wait," Daniel murmured, glancing over at me.

I stepped up behind Jenni. She flinched, then remained tense.

"Steady," I said. "The spell might try to grab you. But shapeshifters are naturally resistant to magic, and this casting wouldn't be keyed to you."

"If the spell transfers to you, Emma and I can neutralize it easier. And you should be harder to kill than a sorcerer."

"Should be," Jenni muttered, but her still-outstretched hand was steady.

"Now." Daniel hovered his hand over the shifter's, at the ready but not touching her in case the spell sensed him. In case Silver Pine had tied any of his DNA to the magic she'd set for us to trigger.

Jenni touched her forefinger and middle finger to the stone closest to her.

Nothing happened.

She applied pressure.

Still nothing.

"It's stuck," she muttered.

"Leave it," I said. "We'll come back."

"No." She grunted. Then her magic welled, as if finally waking, rolling down her arm. The stone shifted. Jenni grunted again, wrapping her fingers around the rock. Then she slowly pulled it out of the ring.

Nothing more happened. "That's a strong spell," I murmured.

Daniel nodded, then shifted to his right. "Now this one."

Jenni shuffled over, closing the space between her and the nullifier. She touched the second stone, then shifted it out of alignment with more ease than the first.

Becca arched up, screaming.

The spell embedded in the circle spiraled through the stones, reaching the weak point—the opening Jenni had created—and slamming into the shifter's chest. She flew backward.

Daniel darted back, grabbing Jenni, who was writhing and convulsing.

I lunged forward to Becca, who had collapsed in silence. Magic lashed around my arms, biting and scratching as I grabbed the sorcerer and dragged her out of the circle.

Once her feet cleared the stones, she gasped, then started coughing. She was conscious, for now at least.

"Emma," Daniel snarled, kneeling with the convulsing shifter in his arms. She was foaming at the mouth, eyes rolled up in her head.

I knelt beside her. "Jenni. I need to—"

"Just do it!" Daniel snarled.

"That's invasive—"

"Emma, goddamn it. You know she doesn't want to die."

I sighed, placing my hand around Jenni Raymond's neck for a very different reason now. I reached down deep within the shifter, coaxing forward what felt like almost-dormant magic from her. Then I amplified it, filling it with my magic, boosting it.

She stilled.

I forced more magic into her, stirring up her natural healing abilities, pumping up her strength, her natural resistance to magic.

"Shit," Daniel muttered. "She really is suppressed."

"Wait for it," I whispered.

Jenni Raymond's eyes opened. They blazed green with her shifter magic. She threw back her head and howled—a high, quavering cry, accompanied by a wave of magic that flowed over her.

She convulsed again.

Daniel gently set her on the ground.

A gray-brown furred canine form tore through Jenni Raymond's human visage. Her magic rose up, forcing the transformation to mitigate the spell's effect.

A panting coyote pushed itself up on shaking legs.

"Coyote," Daniel said. "Not wolf. Unusual."

I stepped away, crossing to Becca, but she waved me off when I reached for her. "Save it, Socks. I'm not dying. But even amplified, I'd only slow you down when you face the witch. She's Silver Pine, in case you didn't know."

"We know."

Becca swore under her breath. "She went for Christopher. I didn't see what she was before ... but she couldn't hold the masking spell and command the demon at the same time."

"Is everyone still alive?" I asked.

"Best as I know." She looked up at the sky. "But it wasn't fully dark when Mark and I attacked her. We didn't know, Emma. You know we would never ... "

"I know, Becca. Try to stay out of it now, okay?" I glanced over at Daniel as I straightened up. "We have to go."

Becca nodded wearily. "I'll look after the coyote. What's her name?"

"Jenni Raymond."

The sorcerer laughed quietly, reaching out for the shifter. "Thanks for rescuing me, Jenni Raymond."

The coyote hunkered down, ears flat against its head.

"She won't be so useless now," Daniel said.

He was most likely right. But I had no doubt that Jenni Raymond was going to regret following us into the woods, regret needing to be powered up by me. I hoped she wouldn't be stuck in her animal form for too long. I didn't want the responsibility for that, but I also didn't want to have to call in the West Coast pack to deal with her. And I certainly didn't want to hear her whine about amplifying her without her permission.

I pushed those thoughts away. Taking Becca at her word that she was okay and could watch over the shifter, I crossed toward Paisley. Daniel followed.

We had already delayed too long. I knew Christopher was valuable, but the witch was too erratic to be trusted. She could lose hold of herself and her magic at any moment. Then she'd lose her hold on the demon.

A demon that ate magic, or at least that was my best sense of its power at the time. And having gone up against that creature myself, I wasn't certain that Christopher, Daniel, and I could take it down. Not even backed by all three sorcerers and a coyote—even assuming that Aiden and Mark Calhoun were still alive.

ELEVEN

SILVER PINE HAD SET UP A MACABRE TABLEAU FOR me to stumble upon in the middle of the forest. So I did just that, feigning disorientation from the bright witch lights she'd placed in the upper branches of the massive fir trees ringing the clearing.

Blinking, I gasped as if I hadn't already seen the steel cages glistening with magic, or Christopher and Aiden trapped within them. As if I hadn't noted the churned dirt between the witch and me, or Mark Calhoun lying unconscious and bleeding at the black witch's feet from the wound slashed across his bare chest. A wound that might actually have been a sigil of some sort. A symbol that undoubtedly tied Mark's magic, his life force, to the summoning of a greater demon.

That same demon was currently hulking among the deeply shadowed trees behind the witch, at the back edge of the clearing.

I stared at the massive creature—red eyed, black scaled, double horned—pretending to be struck dumb by its appearance. Though being overwhelmed wasn't particularly difficult to feign. My previously steady heart rate spiked upon actually laying eyes on the creature that had almost killed me.

The witch cackled. As Becca had mentioned, she had dropped the illusion spell, presenting herself in her natural state—black veins webbed prominently across her pale skin, black-orbed eyes, dark hair hanging limply around her robed shoulders. She was barefoot, her fingers crackling with dark magic. Blood magic. The perfect image of a black witch on the edge of madness, driven insane by the deeds she did in order to gain near-limitless power.

All as expected.

It was still disconcerting, though, that Silver Pine would go to such trouble to set a scene at all. She could have killed me much, much easier with the demon fighting me one on one. As such, it was clear that she wanted something beyond simply being the agent of my death. And that was more troubling than anything else, because I couldn't fight whatever madness was in her head.

The black witch had torn up a stand of large evergreens to create the clearing, then had discarded the trees around the edges of that clearing like trash, their tangled roots creating an intermittent barrier. I made certain to keep the roots of the fallen tree to my right in my peripheral vision, as I didn't want to step into and inadvertently activate any barrier circle the witch might have set in place.

I thought about making a crack about the black witch using her demon pet as a gardener, but some of the fallen trees had likely stood for forty or fifty years. Maybe even longer. And the needless, wanton destruction incensed me so much that I couldn't be flippant about it. Silver Pine had once forced me to destroy a huge swath of a South American rainforest in a similar fashion. I had traded that ruthless annihilation for my life, for the lives of the Five. I would do it again, and again if necessary. But that still didn't make it the moral choice.

To my right, behind and to the side of the black witch, Christopher sat cross-legged in the center of his magic-coated cage. He appeared to be meditating, pale but otherwise unharmed.

In the second cage to my left, Aiden was a different story. As I had first stepped up to the edge of the clearing, he'd propped himself up on one hand, pinning his intensely blue eyes on me. He bore signs of a fierce struggle—crusted blood and bruises welling on his face, claw marks across his chest and upper arms.

Inexplicably, he grinned at me.

So I grinned back.

Silver Pine scoffed. "So predictable. I knew that if you didn't kill the sorcerer, which would have played into my plans just as well, that you'd fall for him. Poor predictable, broken Amp5."

Behind me, still in the cover of the forest, Daniel and Paisley split off to either side, circling the clearing. For anyone but me or one of the others, Daniel's nullifying magic made him almost impossible to track, even by the most magically sensitive Adept. He had clipped a charm to Paisley's ear to mask her for a short time as well. But the magic embedded into my spinal cord allowed me to sense the nullifier's magic and track the demon dog's progress.

I intended to let the witch talk while the other two assessed the terrain. Information was always good to collect, whether as ammunition or for gaining an understanding of your opponent's weaknesses. And right now, I'd accumulated only a pile of guesses when it came to Silver Pine.

The witch strolled toward Aiden's cage. The demon watched her. Hungrily, I thought. Now that was useful information.

"I never did get the story out of you, Aiden," she purred, her chaotic magic laced through every one of her words. "What could you possibly have done to get disowned by a bastard as black as your father? Did you try to kill him?"

"No." Aiden's voice was raspy. His neck was raw but not clawed. As if he'd been strangled.

A fierce wave of anger almost had me leaping over the traps that I knew were waiting between me and the witch, though I still couldn't feel any magic in the clearing. I adjusted my grip on my blades, allowing my resolve to calm me—my understanding that the scene the witch had presented had a beginning, middle, and end.

I had every intention of disrupting whatever ending she'd planned—and every ability to see that disruption through.

Silver Pine glanced back at me, grinning. Then she placed her hand on an intricate rune embossed on the top right corner of Aiden's cage.

The sorcerer shifted in response, holding his ribs and abruptly standing.

Magic writhed through the bars of the cage, then across its solid metal base. It gathered under Aiden's bare feet. He convulsed, grimacing.

He'd been attempting to minimize his contact with the floor.

Silver released the trigger, keeping her hand hovering just over it. "Ingenious, isn't it? It not only nullifies the sorcerer's magic, but collects it so I can use it against him. Not enough to kill him, of course. But enough to loosen his tongue. It's a pity you didn't amplify him a bit more, Amp5."

I visualized the five steps between me and the witch, and the one downward stroke that was all I would need to take her head. A terrible smile spread over my face. Instead of dampening my anger, I held it close—and I fed it all sorts of dark promises.

Magic prickled along my spine. Christopher's power. I kept my attention on the witch, who was watching me with a slight smile, as if she expected me to lunge for her. She expected me to react emotionally, irrationally.

She didn't know me at all.

Whatever spells were built into the cages, they apparently didn't dampen Knox's connection with me. And having a clairvoyant on the field would minimize any wrong steps I might take out of anger or fear.

That thought settled me further.

Aiden slumped, hitting his knees hard. His piercing blue eyes sought out and found me. He laughed at something. It might have been the promise of the black witch's murder in my own expression.

Silver Pine continued, seemingly unaware that she was being stalked by death from every direction. "I only had plans to play with you myself, Aiden. As soon as it became apparent that I wouldn't be able to get to your father through you. Bare your soul and I'll give you the amplifier. That would make things even, wouldn't it?"

Aiden threw his head back, still chuckling to himself. "I tried and failed to kill my eldest brother. My father's chosen heir."

Silver giggled delightedly. "Brilliant. Well, we'll just persuade the amplifier to join our cause. With her power in your veins, your father and brother will both fall."

Aiden sat back on his knees, his laughter easing to a quiet, husky chuckle. His gaze was still pinned to me. "And how do you plan on doing that, Silver?"

"Shall I tell him, Amp5? Of what you risked when you went back for the others instead of simply breaking out yourself? I didn't catch all of it myself at the time, but the footage was all backed up off site, of course." She waved her hand dismissively.

The magic on my spine shifted again—Fish's tattoo this time—telling me that the nullifier was crossing back around to my position.

Soon. Soon, I wouldn't have to listen to another word out of the witch's mouth. She'd pay for trying to own my past. There was no way back from killing her now. She'd be just another stain on my already sullied soul in a few minutes.

"You knew, didn't you, Aiden? That the amplifier and her clairvoyant were grown in vats? Trained killers. The uber-Adept. Created by your father, for the Collective."

Aiden closed his eyes, pained. But when he reopened them, his face was stony, blanked of expression.

"We're all killers in this clearing," I said.

"But you were a bad girl, Amp5. You didn't follow orders. And certain things didn't go according to plan."

"Your plans," I said mildly.

"Yes. You ruined my plans. And I haven't been able to get near Azar since. But now you'll come back into the fold. I already have the clairvoyant and the nullifier. And with you, the telepath and the telekinetic will follow." She turned to grin at Aiden. "And your father and every Azar sorcerer who stands with him will fall."

"You haven't gotten to your point, Silver." Aiden's tone was smooth, inviting. A conspirator in a cage. "How do you plan to tame the amplifier?"

"Oh." She giggled. "I skipped over that part. You see, Amp5 has met my demon before. She knows she's no match for it. And after that bloody interlude, she escaped my attempts to do away with her ... " She glanced at Aiden, conspiratorially. "She'd caught your father's eye. You know how that is."

"I do."

"Then you understand why I couldn't have that. Anyway, she beguiled Mark Calhoun ... " Silver Pine wheeled around as if she might have previously forgotten about the sorcerer sprawled on the ground just behind her. Taking quick little steps, she crossed to him and placed her bare, dirt-crusted foot on his shoulder.

He didn't react.

Without being able to feel his magic, I wasn't certain Mark wasn't already dead. Dread deepened into a yawning pit in my stomach.

"Him and his team ... well, Amp5's team, really." The witch peered down at the sorcerer, blinking. Magic churned around her, then sank down into her skin.

Relief flashed through me, just enough to ease the dread before it overwhelmed me and forced me to react irrationally. I could feel the witch's magic over and above the presence of some sort of dampening field in the clearing. But that field didn't quite mask her power, perhaps because she was the caster.

And any magic I could feel was magic I could use.

"I wouldn't have sent them against her when she decided to be naughty, except I didn't have many others in the compound at the time," the witch continued, still seemingly oblivious to all the players settling into place around her. "And I needed a force, you understand."

"Of course. The amplifier is formidable."

Aiden's casually delivered compliment further soothed the anxious anger setting an itching sensation in my palms and feet. Itching for me to move. All this talk, talk, talk wasn't for me.

Silver snorted. "To a point, I agree. Anyway, she should have, could have exited the building. But she went back for the others." She nodded toward Christopher. "So that's my leverage. The clairvoyant will never leave that cage unless the amplifier agrees to lay down her weapons and join my cause."

The demon shifted, tugged forward by the invisible strings that bound it to the witch. It unfolded its massive three-clawed hands over Christopher's cage. Its talons were more than long enough to torture—and to eventually kill—Knox through the bars.

Silver looked at me smugly. "You were never meant to function in the world on your own. None of you. Each day must be filled with an endless dread. An understanding that you will never be fulfilled because you walked away from the only place you belonged."

I sighed, rotating my wrists and shoulders to keep them loose, giving my blades a spin. "I'm not big on the blathering, witch. But since we're all stalling for time, shall I list some of the mistakes you've already made? Would you like to see how your death is coming? Or shall I just surprise you with it?"

She snorted. And as if in response to her derision, the demon wrapped its tail around Christopher's cage and lowered its head, red eyes glued to me.

"Illuminate me," she said. "If you're capable."

Daniel stepped out from the forest behind me.

Though still looking at the witch, I spoke to the nullifier. "Are the cages yours? Your construction? Imbued with your magic?"

"Yes."

"Did you build in a back door?"

"A back…" He exhaled harshly. "No. But that would have been a good idea."

"No matter," I said, sheathing my right blade across my back to free up one hand.

"You were illuminating me," Silver Pine snapped testily. With her black gaze on Daniel, she started gathering power from the clearing. The churned earth between us began to writhe and roll. That magic I could most definitely feel.

"Actually, I'd rather show you."

"Really?" Daniel asked, stepping in front of me. "I'd rather you made a list, because it gets me off the hook for fucking the witch, doesn't it? I'd rather leave that here."

Silver sneered at the nullifier.

I sighed, settling my hand at the base of his neck. "Fine. Mistake number one, thinking that any of the Five could ever be turned against each other."

She laughed, filling the clearing with the sound of her bone-grating amusement. "How childish of you. Your bonds, forged with a shared childhood that has scarred you irrevocably, are unbreakable?"

"Actually, Emma's talking about the blood bond." Daniel sucked in a breath as I let my magic flow into him through the tattoo on his T1 vertebra. My blood tattooed under his skin, forever bound. "You know the one, don't you? Enforced by the Collective in our early teens?"

Silver Pine's eye twitched.

Daniel laughed. "Seems the witch was too low level to get that memo."

"Mistake number two," I said, ignoring Daniel's commentary. "This one goes way, way back, and you are so utterly arrogant not to have learned this lesson seven years ago. I've already proven I'd rather die than be controlled by you, witch."

She opened her mouth to counter.

But I was done with the talking.

I stepped around Fish, the nullifier now teeming with magic as I pulled my second blade again. He settled his left hand on my back, and a shield snapped up into place around me, a cool barrier of intense magic. "Mistake number three, putting Christopher in a cage constructed by his blood-bonded brother."

Silver spun back to look at Christopher.

The clairvoyant opened his blazing white eyes, fixing them on me. "Wait. Wait. Step left, duck, left again, roll right."

I saw the moment the witch realized her miscalculation. She shouldn't have lured me by kidnapping Christopher along with Aiden. She shouldn't have kept Knox conscious so she could taunt me with him—perhaps having planned to torture him in front of me as she'd done with Aiden. And she should have known that cages of Daniel's construction wouldn't completely nullify Christopher's clairvoyance.

The same would have been true if she'd tried to cage me or Bee or Zans. Because the blood bonds the Five shared worked both ways. We could access each other's magic, pull strength from each other—but we also couldn't completely block that same power if it was used against us.

But none of that mattered, because I was already moving forward, already ready for anything the witch could throw at me.

Magic poured forth from the witch as she attempted to snap a barrier into place around the clearing—the preset spell I'd assumed existed but hadn't been able to feel earlier.

That barrier fizzled, but not before the magic lashed back at the witch, stealing a chunk of her power. Enough that she swayed under the brief assault.

Daniel chuckled. Apparently, he'd booby-trapped the witch's own trap on his circuit around the clearing.

The earth churned before us, demons swarming from the ground as if they'd been hidden beneath it. Teeth and claws splintered and shattered against Daniel's shield.

I continued moving, taking one step at a time, patiently closing the space between me and the witch.

Paisley leaped out from the forest—a snarling beast the size of a large lion. She landed on top of the cage that held Christopher, bellowing an undulating challenge to the hulking demon above her.

The demon shrieked as it rose. Its dreadful voice cut through Daniel's shield and rampaged through my mind. I stumbled, but found my footing again.

The demon began tearing at the bond that held it tethered to the witch, trying to answer Paisley's challenge.

"No!" Silver screamed. Streams of black energy flowed from her fingers to the ground. "To me! To me!"

I pressed forward.

Daniel's shield cracked under the sheer volume of demons the witch was throwing at us. If Mark Calhoun's life force was helping her fuel this overwhelming assault, he might not survive it.

I pushed that thought away, though. I couldn't do anything about Mark right now. I could only deal with what was in front of me. Bringing my blades forward, I pressed the tips against Daniel's shield.

The black witch managed to get the greater demon under control, pulling its attention from Paisley and directing it toward me.

Finally.

"Ready?" I asked Daniel.

He nodded, dropping his hand from my back. I would stand against the demon on my own. He would rescue Christopher.

"Wait," I murmured, feeling Daniel's shield tightening around me as he withdrew it. "Wait."

The demon was almost within striking range, actually knocking its smaller kin out of the way as it crossed to me.

But it was the black witch the demon really wanted. Really craved.

No greater demon wanted to be controlled, and eventually, each and every one turned against its summoner. Frankly, I was surprised that Silver Pine was strong enough to have held this creature for so many years.

Paisley grabbed the side of Christopher's cage in her massive jaw and started dragging it toward the treeline.

I ran the clairvoyant's instructions in my mind—Wait. Wait. Step left, duck, left again, roll right.

The demon was before me, appearing even more formidable swathed in moonlight than it had seemed on the rooftop in LA.

But I hadn't had Christopher or Paisley or Daniel with me on the roof that day.

And the demon wasn't the objective anyway.

"Now!" I cried.

Daniel and I darted left at the same time, ducking under the demon's first attempt to maul us. We both lunged forward under its arm, slashing at its ribs with our blades.

It bellowed, spinning to swipe at me again. I jumped to the left, decapitating the lesser demons in my way. Daniel went right, doing the same. The dual movement confused the greater demon just long enough that I was able to cut the tendons on the back of its wrist and elbow.

Daniel got clear.

The demon homed in on me.

I slaughtered two more lesser demons, then rolled right to avoid a third, making it to my feet and coming up face to face with Silver Pine.

She released a torrent of black magic that hit me directly in the chest. At the same time, I slammed a kick to her gut.

We each flew backward. I tumbled directly into the greater demon's path. Silver fell against Aiden's cage.

The demon was waiting for me.

Aiden was waiting for Silver.

The greater demon knocked aside the swarm of lesser creatures reaching for me, raising a massively clawed foot to stomp me, just as it had done on the rooftop. I rolled across churned dirt covered in the ashes of the demons we'd already vanquished. Multiple sets of claws raked my back as I tried to crawl toward the witch.

Aiden thrust his hands between the bars of the cage, snagging Silver's long black hair and yanking her backward. He banged her head against the bars, twice. She hit him with a massive pulse of magic.

He went down without any attempt to break his fall.

Silver stumbled forward, holding her head and trying to get her bearings.

All the lesser demons stilled. The greater demon hesitated, shifting its attention to the black witch.

Exactly as I had expected it would if her hold on it slipped.

My back was on fire as I made it to my feet, barreling toward my goal. I'd lost my blades but it didn't matter. Death was still waiting for me to make my move.

Seeing me coming for her, Silver hit me with a spell that crushed my lungs.

But I didn't have to breathe to hurt her.

Suffocating, I latched my fingers around her wrist as she raised her hand to finish me.

I dragged her against me, mouthing the words more than speaking them. "I don't die that easily."

Spinning, I held the black witch as a shield between me and the greater demon. Then I took her magic, ripping it from her relentlessly. The lesser demons slunk back into the darkness, but they didn't try to flee the clearing.

Silver screamed and screamed.

The greater demon lowered its head, waiting, regarding me with blazing red eyes.

Christopher and Paisley shifted forward out of the forest on my left. Knox bent down, retrieving my blades.

Daniel moved around behind me, opening Aiden's cage, then dragging the sorcerer from it.

I took all the power the witch had at her disposal, feeling the shift in magic as the bond that tethered her to the demon transferred to me.

Then I dropped her at my feet.

She was panting and shrieking, but I only had enough attention for the greater demon. I'd never done what I was planning on doing—but I had no choice now. With all of us together, we might have been able to vanquish Silver's servant. But there would be casualties.

"Oh, demon lord," I cried, throwing my hands out to the sides and making a production of it. Greater beings liked a show. "Take your captor and the bond she forced on you. Depart this land with your kin, never to return. I free you willingly and will never call you forth."

The demon opened its maw wide. Then it chuckled, the sound rasping against my soul, deadening my heart.

It reached one clawed hand forward and scooped up Silver Pine. It tore her head off. Then, raising her over its thrown-back head, it gulped down her still-spurting blood.

"Holy fuck," Daniel muttered, stepping up beside me.

I didn't take my attention from the demon. Even with the stolen magic and the stolen bonds, I wasn't completely certain I had the ability to cement the bargain I'd just made.

The demon tore Silver Pine apart, eating her in pieces and enjoying every bite.

Paisley threw her head back, howling in victory.

The tether I'd collected from Silver along with her magic thinned, as if the demon was gobbling up that magical connection along with the witch.

Then the tether and Silver were both gone.

The demon looked at me, flattening and slightly tilting its head. I wondered if it remembered me.

Daniel raised his sword, nullifying magic flowing out from him to gather around our feet. Christopher stepped beside us, holding my blades at the ready.

Paisley let out a rippling snarl, then howled again.

The demon straightened, turned, and took a step toward the forest. The earth opened up into a churning black hole of magic underneath the creature. Then it disappeared, pulling all the magic and all the other demons that the witch had called forth from the clearing with it.

I spun back, looking for Aiden and finding him propped up against the cage that had once contained him. He'd been watching me. Every moment. He saw me for who I really was. The idea was intoxicating, when it should have been terrifying.

Daniel dropped to his knees beside Mark Calhoun, already pulling rune-marked bandages from the sorcerer's pockets.

"Alive?" I asked, stepping up and leaning over the nullifier. Mark hadn't moved, but the sigil carved into his chest appeared to be slowly crusting over. The spelled wound would have been tied to Silver's magic and would disperse with her death, despite how much of that magic I still held.

"Give me a moment." Daniel slapped a series of bandages onto secondary wounds on Mark's forehead, neck, and arms. Then he hovered his hands over the sigil. "His magic is all torn up. See to the sorcerer."

I pivoted, kneeling beside Aiden without further prompting. His magic was dim. The spell that Silver had hit him with was chewing on what remained of his power.

I held out my hand, laden with Silver's magic. "This belongs to you, I believe."

Aiden sighed, closing his eyes. "If I take your magic, you'll think that's all I want of you."

Christopher hunkered down beside me. "Emma isn't offering her power, sorcerer. She's simply gifting you the witch's magic."

Aiden opened his eyes with a snap. He had missed the part where I'd drained Silver, or perhaps it hadn't been obvious. It wasn't an ability that many amplifiers wielded. Maybe none aside from me.

Aiden took my hand. I gave him the power I'd stolen from Silver as gently as possible, but he still sucked in a breath and pressed his head back against the cage. I let the witch's magic flow from me, careful to not add my own into the mix.

Christopher straightened, crossing away and speaking with Daniel in low tones. I didn't hear what words they exchanged. The sorcerer had me locked to him with his gaze, almost mesmerized.

As had been the case since the moment I'd set eyes on him.

Aiden's grip on my hand tightened. When I didn't pull away, he slowly tugged me closer.

I allowed him to do so, settling across his lap. He placed his free hand on the back of my neck, brushing a soft kiss to my lips.

A sliver of desire slipped through me, blooming at my lips and curling down, deeply down, to awaken in my stomach. I relaxed into it, sighing. Releasing his hand so I could wrap both of my hands around his face, I kissed him back. Deeply. Thoroughly. Drinking him in without reservation. Just this once, unfettered, with the witch's power flowing from me to him instead of my own.

A wave of desire crashed over me. His need, picked up by my empathy. And my need. It wiped away all reason, leaving only a gathering warmth in my chest, filtering down through my stomach, pooling between my legs.

"Well, that sucks." Daniel sighed behind me.

Christopher laughed.

Aiden broke the kiss, pressing his forehead to mine and smiling. "Perhaps somewhere a little more private?"

I returned his smile, willing to play along and believe for just a moment that it could be that easy between us. That we could slaughter a couple of dozen demons, feed a black witch to a greater demon, then share a world-ending kiss.

But I knew, even deeper down than the desire warming my loins, that by the time we made it out of the forest, the rest of the world would come crashing down on our heads. His father's connection to the Collective. The revelations of my past. My inability to actually form any sort of functional relationship outside the Five.

So I kissed Aiden a second time, giving him the last drops of Silver Pine's power. A gift from my heart, even if I couldn't give him myself.

DANIEL HAD PATCHED MARK CALHOUN WITH EVERY runed bandage the sorcerer had on him, but he didn't actually regain consciousness until we'd arrived back at the clearing where we'd left Becca and Jenni in coyote form. The weapons specialist's magic was slowly knitting itself back together, but Daniel was concerned that I would shred it further if I amplified him too quickly or too intensely.

The moon was high in the sky, casting the derelict hunting shed in deep shadow. Becca had obviously been contemplating starting a fire. She'd stacked up a small pile of dead wood in the pit but hadn't lit it yet.

"Oh thank fucking God," she groaned as we crossed into the clearing. "I thought I was going to freeze to death out here."

Daniel set Calhoun down beside her. Aiden and Paisley paced the perimeter of the clearing in opposite directions, as if neither one trusted the other to make certain the area was secure. Still, knowing that Daniel had knocked out all the magical traps on our way in, I wasn't concerned that anything was lying in wait for us.

"I'm going to need a scotch," Becca said. "On the rocks if all you have is crap, but neat if you have any of the good stuff."

I crouched down next to her, holding my hand out. "No alcohol at the house. But I can give you another sort of boost, sorcerer."

"I thought you'd never ask." She laughed snarkily, cringing as she did so. She was obviously still hurt, hopefully not from internal bleeding. But she wrapped her hand around mine readily enough.

I reached out for her magic, picking up her frustration and a hint of fear through our empathic connection. Then I slowly bolstered that magic. Just enough to help get the sorcerer on her feet, though I could carry her if needed, with Calhoun in Daniel's charge.

"Where's Jenni?" I asked.

Becca nodded over my shoulder with a twist of her lips. "Hiding."

I glanced back to see Christopher slowly advancing on the derelict hut with his hands raised.

"Some complex," Becca muttered. "I've never met a closeted shifter."

I didn't respond, though I hadn't either.

"Socks," Mark murmured, raising his hand to brush my arm but then falling short.

"Jesus Christ!" Becca cried, as if she'd only just noticed how wounded Mark was. She started systematically checking every bandage that Daniel had slapped on her former commanding officer. "Why haven't you … " She trailed off, dropping her gaze to the sigil carved into Mark's chest. "Well, that's going to scar." She glanced over at me questioningly.

"Mark?" I asked obligingly, though I didn't like the idea of being bullied by Becca into offering to amplify anyone. "Daniel's concerned I might hurt you, that your magic is still struggling to reassert itself. But now that you're awake, do you want—"

"Yes, please." He sighed, closing his eyes and resting his head back against one of the stones edging the firepit.

I reached for his hand, watching Aiden make another circle around the clearing as I sought out Mark's magic, then amplified it as gently as possible with my own.

Paisley bumped her head against Aiden's hip as they passed. He smiled, running a hand across her head and down her back. She snorted offishly, but then turned around behind him, pacing alongside him now.

"Socks?" Mark asked. "I'm sorry. You know we'd never…" He trailed off.

I nodded, but I didn't respond to whatever he thought he could leave unsaid.

"We need to keep moving," Daniel said, speaking to Christopher. "We need to get Becca and Mark back to the house and get a better look at their wounds."

"I know," the clairvoyant murmured. He was hunkered outside the door to the shed now, reaching one hand into the dark.

"So if you don't have any scotch at home, Socks," Becca asked, resting her hand possessively on Mark's arm the moment I released him. "What do you have to soothe us?"

The sorcerer had fallen asleep, which was unusual after being amplified. But his chest rose and fell as he breathed deeply, so he appeared to be healing.

"Tea," I said. "All kinds of tea."

Becca twisted her lips. "Tea!"

"I don't need to share, Becca."

She snorted. "Have you got anything tasty to go with it?"

I eyed her for a moment, not certain I was ready to forgive her for unwittingly helping Silver Pine get her hands on Christopher, and on Daniel. "Ginger snaps," I said.

"Yum." Becca smiled at me tentatively.

Though I wasn't petty enough to withhold comfort food, I wasn't quite ready to smile back. So I didn't.

A coyote finally slipped out of the shadows of the derelict hut. Jenni Raymond.

She bumped her head under Christopher's open palm, but then sidled away when he attempted to pet her. She pinned me with a baleful stare.

Yeah, I got it. I was an awful person.

"You want Becca or Mark?" Daniel asked, stepping up beside me.

I glanced over at Aiden. He was watching me, his expression hooded. "Becca," I said, already reaching to help the sorcerer to her feet.

"I think I can walk," she said, sliding her arm across my shoulder.

"Not fast enough." Daniel gathered Mark in his arms, lifting the taller man with some effort.

Christopher stepped up, reaching for Becca wordlessly. Jenni was still in coyote form, tucked up at his heels. I took Mark from Daniel. I would move faster with him.

We exited the clearing, Daniel and his flashlight in the lead.

TWELVE

I GAZED OUT THE WINDOW OF MY SITTING ROOM, seeking out and finding Christopher in the garden, harvesting the last of the beefsteak tomatoes. I let my gaze wander out across the property toward the back fence. Aiden had been working on repairing the damage inflicted by the demon for a few days now. Daniel had fixed the front door and hung new doors in the kitchen, and had finished patching the damaged kitchen wall the day before. The kitchen and hallway now just needed another coat of paint.

"He's out front," Fish said from the doorway behind me.

I'd gotten so accustomed to having the nullifier in the house, and the constant muted hum from my blood tattoo, that he'd managed to sneak up on me.

"The sorcerer," he added, leaning on the doorframe casually though his arms were crossed. "Strengthening the northwest corner. Mark is helping him. For the cows."

"Excuse me?"

"Christopher has bought cows. From the neighbors. An adult female and some calves. Apparently, the Wilsons were happy to have the opportunity to expand their breeding pool without having to enlarge their own herd, and Christopher paid too much."

"Cows."

"Yes, cows. For Paisley. He said you wouldn't let him get pigs. Something about them being intelligent."

I looked out the window again, watching Christopher. I was growing concerned about the clairvoyant. He'd been slipping in and out of the present again since the events of that night in the forest. Just momentary blips, but they were becoming more frequent. "I assumed he'd get goats next."

"The fence would need to be taller."

Silence fell between us. It wasn't uncomfortable. But it wasn't as comfortable as being in the house with just Christopher and Paisley.

"So, the sorcerer. Is he staying?"

I had no idea. I had barely been in the same room as Aiden for days—at least not without also being surrounded by three or four other people.

After getting Mark and Becca home, we had decided they could heal on their own with a bit of help from me, and without the need to involve witches or other healers. Though I hadn't been present for the transformation, Jenni Raymond had shifted into her human form and left the property before dawn. She hadn't returned.

Which was a relief, frankly. I wasn't interested in whatever conversation she would try to force on me next. Presumably she'd be livid that I'd amplified her magic. Or she'd want another boost.

Except for the Five, who had already had everything I had to give without question, other Adepts always seemed to want more power.

I was thankful that Silver Pine hadn't sacrificed Becca and Mark in order to quell me. I didn't need any more blood on my hands. But every room in the house had been full for four days while everyone healed and dealt with repairs.

"I'll take your silence to mean you don't know if he's staying. But … "

I turned to face Daniel. "But what?"

He raised his hands. "You don't need to bite my head off. You already know everything I'm going to say. It's been running in your head for days."

It had been. A long list of all the reasons Aiden couldn't stay, all the reasons I couldn't ask him to stay.

"You'll never know for certain," Daniel said softly. "If he wants you for you. You already know where you belong, Emma."

"With you?"

He shrugged. "With me. But mostly with us. We could bring Bee and Zans here—"

"No. And you are leaving. There are too many people in the house triggering Christopher."

"I saw. I see. But his magic will settle. It'll adapt, grow."

I clenched my hands into fists. "You never fucking cared, Daniel. Never cared who you hurt, who you used. You'd have him burn up. You'd have his magic consume him."

"You're wrong, Emma. I do give a shit. About you and Knox, and even the fucking demon dog. Lots of clairvoyants develop an immunity—"

"He's not lots of clairvoyants. Just like I'm not other amplifiers and you aren't like other nullifiers! Those are just … labels. Easy labels they put on us."

He stepped forward, reaching for me.

"No," I said, steely. "I don't give you permission."

He hesitated, chest heaving from some emotion, something more complicated than simple anger or frustration.

It would have been so easy to close the space between us. To reach for him as I'd done when we were younger, slipping into his bed. Cold comfort in the dark.

"I want … I want to be in the light," I whispered. More for myself than him.

"And hiding away here with Knox, keeping your distance from the sorcerer, is living in the light?"

"It's … home. It's mine."

Daniel exhaled, the tension easing from his shoulders. "I see. Well, as always, I'll be at your beck and call when you need me."

"I didn't call you this time, Fish."

"No. You didn't. But you needed me."

"Only because you brought Silver Pine to my doorstep."

He stared at me, every edge of his face hard. "I already apologized for that."

"Don't do it again. Don't bring your shit here."

"Fine."

"Fine."

"Mark, Becca, and I will leave this afternoon."

I nodded.

He turned back to the door, lightly kicking a black bag I hadn't seen him drop. "For your trouble. And so you don't need to be rescued by Knox again." He walked away.

The bag was filled with cash, of course. Guilt money. Presumably part or all of the fee Silver Pine had paid the nullifier to find me. Not that he'd known that was what he was doing for her. After Daniel had packed and gone downstairs, I dropped the bag on Christopher's bed. I wanted nothing to do with it, but I wasn't going to make decisions for the clairvoyant.

I CURLED UP ON A DECK CHAIR ON THE BACK PATIO with a pitcher of iced tea, a plate of ginger snaps, and the grimoire I was still trying to translate. I'd put three crystal glasses on the tray just in case Christopher and Aiden decided to join me. It was slightly chilly in the shade, but the deck was still warm in the late afternoon sun. And yes, I was hoping that the book might trigger a conversation with Aiden if he came by.

Paisley, in stalker mode, prowled around the corner of the house, keeping to the shadows at the edges. She paused by the stairs, gazing out at the garden, ears flicking.

"Gone, are they?" I asked her.

"Yes." Aiden strode around the corner after the demon dog, wiping sweat from his face and neck with a towel. I'd felt the hum of his magic a moment before, still full and robust, amplified by Silver Pine's stolen power.

I tried to not watch his hands, or the way his T-shirt tightened across his biceps. He looked healthier, having gained back some muscle mass along with his magic.

He paused at the base of the stairs, stepping forward just enough to shade his eyes under the patio roof. "Christopher's magic will settle with just you and Paisley in the house."

So he had noticed.

Of course he'd noticed. It was unlikely that there was much he missed. And that ability, that shrewd sense of calculation, weighed heavily on everything that Aiden said and did. The black witch and Daniel were right. How was I to ever know? As stunted as I was when it came to relationships, even my empathy could possibly be fooled.

The sorcerer desired me sexually, yes. That was obvious even to me. But it might have been the power in my veins that he desired most of all. And how was I to know, to feel, the difference?

"May I join you?"

"Yes."

He jogged up the stairs, leaning back against the railing instead of taking the chair beside me. Maintaining distance between us, as we'd both been doing for the last four days.

Paisley shouldered past him, deliberately giving him a shove as she crossed toward me. Well, specifically toward the plate of ginger snaps.

Aiden dipped his chin to his chest, smiling to himself.

My heart squelched. I topped up my iced tea, then poured a second glass for Aiden to cover my reaction to his easy smile.

"Yes," I said to Paisley, who was staring at me so intensely with her red-hued eyes that she appeared to be trying to communicate telepathically. "One."

A tentacle curled out from her otherwise dog-like neck and gently plucked up a ginger snap. She then trundled over to the far corner of the patio, sprawled out in the sun, and licked the cookie reverently. Her tongue was blue. And forked.

Aiden opened his mouth to ask something.

I tensed, steeling myself for the barrage of questions he must have had after everything Silver had revealed about me, everything she'd taunted me with in the forest.

But he closed his mouth. Then he leaned forward, reaching toward me. I curled my fingers in, stopping myself from responding in kind.

He snagged the half-full pitcher of rosy iced tea, brought it to his mouth, tilted back his head, and slowly drained it.

I watched him unabashedly. Heart fluttering and everything else, utterly and idiotically infatuated with the sorcerer. Even with all the stolen magic running through my veins, embedded into my skin and soul, I hadn't gained any immunity to him at all. The feeling might actually have become more acute since I'd almost dragged him to his bed in the loft, since I'd kissed him without reservation in the forest.

Paisley snarled at her cookie, slamming her paw over it, then tossing it into the air.

"Don't play with your food," I said mildly, by rote.

Aiden finished drinking, then leveled a hooded gaze at me. "I can never tell what you're thinking."

That I want you with every fiber of my being? That I'm an idiot for not reaching out and just touching you, touching you everywhere all at once? "That you owe me a pitcher of iced tea."

He laughed quietly. "That I can fix." He stole a ginger snap, eating it as he wandered back into the kitchen with the pitcher.

I followed, bringing the tray with me and setting it on the island. I leaned against the counter, watching as Aiden washed and rinsed the glass pitcher.

"Cold brew? Or hot?" he asked, opening the tea drawer and pulling out the fruit tea blend I preferred iced.

"Cold, please."

He carefully measured the correct amount of loose tea into the pitcher, then turned to the sink and filled it with cold water. He moved as if he belonged in the kitchen, in the house. "It's amazing that you can just drink the water straight from the tap here."

I nodded, weaving the fabric of my dress between my fingers. It was too much, all this tension between us, all this overwhelming emotion. It made me feel desperate.

I'd been desperate only once before, and I hadn't liked it then either. Of course, then I had just wanted to feel the sun on my face before I died.

I hadn't died, though. I'd walked away. And when my magic came back, marking me as different, as valuable, I had struggled to fit into the world. But I didn't fit, so I'd made my own place.

And now Aiden.

Aiden.

I had to get out of the room before I reached for him. I forced myself to move, to just walk away.

I made it to the doorway to the front hall before Aiden's soft-spoken words begged me to pause, to reconsider.

"Emma. I'm so sorry."

I glanced back at him. He was leaning against the counter next to the sink, hands curled over the edge. He was looking at me, and holding himself in a way that might have been meant to look relaxed but didn't.

"I'm sorry for any part of this that was my fault. I'm sorry that Silver said all those things, taunted you with me, with your past. Things I know you don't want anyone to know about you."

"None of that is anything for you to be sorry about."

"And yet ... you're angry. So angry at me."

I almost laughed in relief. He thought I was mad at him. When the exact opposite was true. I should have let the misconception lie between us. I should have shored it up by keeping my distance from him.

And eventually he would leave and never come back.

My chest hurt. I forced the words out. "I don't know how to do this."

"Do what?"

I shook my head, unable to further explain myself.

"Emma ... I need you to elaborate. I know you don't like to ... just ... please."

I exhaled harshly, forcing myself to look at him steadily, to look at him as if he was just an obstacle for me to overcome.

He grimaced. "I see."

He really didn't. "I ... Christopher and I ... " No. It wasn't right to drag Christopher into this ...

"Christopher? I thought…Daniel. And I was pretty sure Mark, but—"

I laughed, frustrated by my inability to even carry on a conversation. "Daniel and Mark, yes. You've now met the sum total of every Adept I've ever had sex with."

Aiden went still, his face blanking in the way it did when he was trying to process a situation.

I had said something wrong. I made an effort to figure out what it was. "But Christopher and I aren't together like that."

He nodded. "So when you said you don't know how to do this…you meant…" He paused to consider his words. "You mean being intimate with someone who isn't a brother or…a friend."

"Yes."

A slow smile spread across his face. "And what I've been taking as you being angry with me?"

"Isn't."

He laughed, low and husky. Satisfied. "I understand."

"What do you understand?"

He tilted his head, looking at me with a grin on his face that made me want to lunge across the kitchen and wrap my legs around him. "I understand where to start."

"Start what?"

"Us."

"I liked our beginning."

He threw his head back and laughed. "Of course you did. I'm surprised you didn't throw me through the window of the diner."

"I considered it."

"Too much collateral damage, though."

"Exactly."

"Fine. Not a start, then. But we skipped a few steps. And normally, as I understand it, that's an okay base for some people. But you need more."

"And you can give more?"

He nodded. "I understand the process. I haven't done it before."

"Because you haven't needed to. Because all the other people you've been intimate with haven't been … emotionally stunted."

Anger etched across his face, running down his shoulders and through his arms. It eased, but not wholly. It also wasn't directed at me. "You aren't stunted, Emma. I haven't done it before because I haven't felt the need."

He turned and put the pitcher of iced tea in the fridge. As if the conversation was done, as if he'd sorted it all out. And maybe he had, and I was just a step behind.

"Like the spell?" I asked. "The spell you put in the gem on my blade? Steps like that?"

He grinned, easy, confident. "Yeah, like that."

"I liked the spell very much."

"Did you?"

"It sharpened the blade well."

He laughed. But the tenor of that laughter let me know—once again—that I'd missed something hidden in our conversation. Flirting, maybe?

The sorcerer stole the last cookie off the plate, winked at me, and sauntered back out into the yard.

AIDEN APPEARED IN THE DOORWAY TO MY SITTING room just after breakfast. He was carrying a bag, and wearing his now pristinely pressed suit. My heart squeezed. Then it didn't let go. I paused the TV and closed the grimoire that occupied my entire lap. But I kept the book between us, between my heart and whatever the sorcerer had come to say.

I'd been compiling a list of questions, trying to copy the runes I couldn't find a translation for. But just by looking at the sorcerer's inscrutable expression, I knew I wasn't going to get a chance to hand him that piece of paper or to share my research.

Aiden glanced at the TV screen, seemingly unwilling to start the conversation. I was deep into viewing the first season of *Downton Abbey* for the fourth or fifth time.

"You're leaving," I said.

"Yes." He set the bag down, pressing his hands together. He was wearing all of his runed copper rings. The bag was big enough to hold the bat.

He was leaving for good.

I didn't understand the conversation we'd had in the kitchen, not even twenty-four hours before.

I didn't understand the perfect dinner the previous night. Aiden and Christopher cooking, laughing. All of us around the table, including Paisley. The sweet 'good night' the sorcerer had whispered in my ear before he'd headed back to the suite.

"I finished the fence this morning," he said. "I'm not... I lay awake all last night. Wanting to come to you."

I gripped the edges of the grimoire instead of leaping up and dragging him across the hallway and into my bedroom. If he had come to me last night, I would never have turned him away.

And then when he'd regretted it the next morning? As he was already regretting even the suggestion that we could try to build something between us? That... that would have been...

My heart turned to lead in my chest.

He cleared his throat. "I can't stay here as I am. Will you... " He sighed, finally looking up at me. "I'm guessing you know, I'm addicted to... the accumulation of magic."

"Yes," I said. And, because of that addiction, being around me had to be excruciating.

"The top-up of Silver's magic was brilliant, amazing. But... eventually... I lay in bed last night and I thought... I thought you'd never know. If I came to your bed as I am. My addiction would always be wedged between us." He paused, giving me space to comment.

I didn't.

"I had thought...with the suite over the barn and the fence to work on, I could detox. And maybe we could ease into whatever we...whatever was happening between us. Whatever happened the moment I laid eyes on you in the diner."

My heart warmed, melting around the edges.

"But then..." He trailed off.

"Silver Pine showed up. And I gave you her magic."

"I'd like to stay in touch while I'm gone, Emma. I don't want to go. But I think I have to, for now. Are you open to that idea?"

"All right."

"Will you walk me to the gate?"

"Yes." I uncurled my legs, moving automatically but not really feeling the steps. Numb as I watched him pick up the bag and step down the hall.

We moved silently like that, me slightly behind him, down the stairs, out the front door, and all the way up the driveway.

I probably should have offered to drive him somewhere, anywhere. But he had asked me to go only as far as the gate, and I figured there was a reason behind that. And maybe it would be easier to say goodbye with my feet firmly planted on my own property.

Aiden waved to Christopher in the garden. Paisley skulked on the other side of the rose bushes, walking alongside us.

My heart still felt like a piece of lead in my chest. But it was molten now, churning, unable to settle into a definitive form.

Aiden stopped at the front gate, resting his hand on the side post. He ran his thumb over something carved into the wood, gazing out at the road. Then he unlatched the gate, set his bag down, and turned back to look at me.

"A rune?" I asked softly, nodding toward the gatepost.

He smiled tightly. "Yes."

"To ward the property?"

"Yes. I'd thought ... I thought I would trigger it when I was at full strength."

Warding two hectares would take a huge amount of power. "Thank you."

Silence fell between us, and we stood like that, staring at each other. With the late-morning sun gently touching our shoulders, and the sound of the chickens, the neighbors' cows, and the wild birds around us. The lead eased out of my chest, drip by drip, replaced with a soft touch of warmth that had nothing to do with the weather and everything to do with the sorcerer.

Aiden smiled, his clear blue eyes crinkling around the edges. He opened his mouth to speak, but I beat him to it.

"I was born to be an assassin. Bred to be a sociopath. Trained to be a ruthless, vicious killer. Conceived in a test tube. Born to be an instrument of death and destruction."

"I could say the same, Emma. Born to a megalomaniac who coveted my mother's magic so much that he enslaved her, forced himself on her ... to breed me." He laughed scornfully. Then he quieted, his gaze resting on me. "What a disappointment we both are to our makers," he whispered.

I didn't mind disappointing the Collective, or the sorcerer Azar specifically. Not one bit. I smiled.

Pinning me in place with his soul-piercing gaze, Aiden reached over and smoothed two fingers through the length of my hair. "I'm ready..." He glanced down, away. Then he rolled the thick lock of hair he'd captured around his hand, two, three times, holding it across his knuckles as if it were a weapon he was preparing to wield. "I'm ready to shed all of that. I'm ready to simply say, to simply believe ... that I was born for you. Born to be here for you. Born to be with you."

My breath caught in my throat. My mind blanked of all the words, all the possible things I wanted to say, to do.

He smiled softly. "Don't worry. I'll prove myself. Prove that it's you I want, not your magic. Then you can decide if you want to give me a chance." He kissed the hair he'd wrapped around his hand. Stepping away, he allowed the thick lock to slowly slip through his fingers. "I left you a present. On your bureau." He scooped up his bag, taking a few steps backward through the gate, all the while grinning at me. Then he turned away, crossing to the edge of the road and setting off toward town.

I wanted to call him back. I wanted to beg him to stay. The words didn't come. But even if I couldn't speak, I could have run after him. I could have flung my arms around his neck. I could have kissed him.

Except ... I would never know. I'd never know for certain that he wanted me. Wanted to build a life here with me, and Christopher, and Paisley. We were a package deal.

And I wanted Aiden to want me, not just my magic.

Pulling my attention away from sorting out my churning thoughts, a green truck with a Home Cafe logo decal on the door pulled to a stop by the farm stand. Leaving the engine running, Brian Martin hopped out, shading his eyes to look at me. "Hey, Emma. Chris texted that he'd put eggs aside for me."

"In the cooler, I think."

Brian sauntered over to the red cooler tucked into the middle shelf of the stand, stuffing money in the cashbox as he opened the lid. "Yep!" He lifted out three egg cartons, then looked back at me. "See you for lunch at the diner?"

"Sure. I'll ask Christopher if he'd like to come with me."

"Good, good." He turned back to the truck.

I raised my voice so he could hear me over the engine. "Brian?"

"Yep?"

"You'll pass Aiden on the road up ahead. Would you give him a ride into town? Then hook him up with a ride to the airport? Nanaimo or Victoria?"

"I can do that." He winked at me, climbed into the truck, and pulled away.

I forced myself to step away from the gate, to latch it, to wander back to the house. Instead of stepping forward to watch Brian drive Aiden out of my life.

A RUNE I DIDN'T RECOGNIZE HAD BEEN CARVED INTO the top corner of my oak bureau. I placed my fingers over it, triggering the spell waiting for me.

A mote of magic spiraled up, hovering just above the rune. That speck of power expanded, unfolding into a velvet-petaled flower.

A translucent black rose.

Identical to the rose on the teacup I coveted at Hannah Stewart's secondhand store.

But ... there was absolutely no way Aiden could know that.

It was delicate, precise magic. The kind of magic that took time and a lot of energy, much like fixing the bowl I'd broken. I cupped my hand around the rose, mesmerized.

Paisley wandered into the room, stretching up on her hind legs to see what my attention was focused on. Then she flicked out her forked tongue and ate the rose.

I sighed. "That was mine. Made just for me."

Made just for me.

I smiled, remembering the warmth that settled in my chest when I had simply looked at Aiden, when I'd allowed myself to just look at him like all I wanted was him.

I rubbed my thumb over the carved rune. "Thank you."

Grabbing a cardigan, I wandered downstairs to drag Christopher out of the garden and into town for lunch.

Acknowledgements

With thanks to:

MY STORY & LINE EDITOR
Scott Fitzgerald Gray

MY PROOFREADER
Pauline Nolet

MY BETA READERS
Anteia Consorto, Terry Daigle, Angela Flannery,
Beth Patterson, and Megan Gayeski Pirajno.

**FOR THEIR CONTINUAL ENCOURAGEMENT,
FEEDBACK, & GENERAL ADVICE**
Venetia Roy – for the 1965 Corvette
Louise Croall – for the typo
SFWA
The Office
The Retreat

About the Author

MEGHAN CIANA DOIDGE IS AN AWARD-WINNING WRITER based out of Salt Spring Island, British Columbia, Canada. She has a penchant for bloody love stories, superheroes, and the supernatural. She also has a thing for chocolate, potatoes, and cashmere.

For recipes, giveaways, news, and glimpses of upcoming stories, please connect with Meghan on her:

New release mailing list, http://eepurl.com/AfFzz
Personal blog, www.madebymeghan.ca
Twitter, @mcdoidge
Facebook, Meghan Ciana Doidge
Email, info@madebymeghan.ca

Please also consider leaving an honest review at your point of sale outlet.

Also by Meghan Ciana Doidge

Please also consider leaving an honest
review at your point of sale outlet.

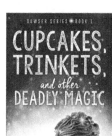

DOWSER SERIES ● BOOK 1

CUPCAKES, TRINKETS, and other DEADLY MAGIC

MEGHAN CIANA DOIDGE

DOWSER SERIES ● BOOK 2

TRINKETS, TREASURES, and other BLOODY MAGIC

MEGHAN CIANA DOIDGE

DOWSER SERIES ● BOOK 3

TREASURES, DEMONS, and other BLACK MAGIC

MEGHAN CIANA DOIDGE

DOWSER SERIES ● BOOK 4

SHADOWS, MAPS, and other ANCIENT MAGIC

MEGHAN CIANA DOIDGE

DOWSER SERIES ● BOOK 5

MAPS, ARTIFACTS, and other ARCANE MAGIC

MEGHAN CIANA DOIDGE

DOWSER SERIES ● BOOK 6

ARTIFACTS, DRAGONS, and other LETHAL MAGIC

MEGHAN CIANA DOIDGE

ORACLE SERIES ● BOOK 1

I SEE ME

"Doidge merges romance, mortality, and supernatural fantasy to wild effect."
— Kirkus Reviews

MEGHAN CIANA DOIDGE

ORACLE SERIES ● BOOK 2

I SEE YOU

MEGHAN CIANA DOIDGE

ORACLE SERIES ● BOOK 3

I SEE US

MEGHAN CIANA DOIDGE

RECONSTRUCTIONIST SERIES ● BOOK 1

Catching Echoes

MEGHAN CIANA DOIDGE

RECONSTRUCTIONIST SERIES ● BOOK 2

Tangled Echoes

MEGHAN CIANA DOIDGE

RECONSTRUCTIONIST SERIES ● BOOK 3

Unleashing Echoes

MEGHAN CIANA DOIDGE

Made in the USA
Monee, IL
04 September 2022

13259391R00203